PRAISE FOR *WALK THE DARK*

"In this exquisitely tender novel, Ollie Curtin is a felon justly convicted, yet a man so otherworldly he's almost a holy innocent. If, as one critic remarked, Don Delillo's characters don't seem to live their lives so much as rent them, Paul Cody's characters can't even manage that: long ago evicted for nonpayment, they stand in the arctic night, gazing in through a bright window at the human comedy, their hearts filled—heartbreakingly—not with resentment, but wonder."

—Brian Hall, author of *The Saskiad*

"Paul Cody's *Walk the Dark* is creepily beautiful, full of stillness and darkness. Cody takes us into places we don't know and shows us strange states of mind that feel absolutely true. It's both soothing and terrifying being in Oliver's mind, because he sees such beauty but also feels forever separated from it.

"For decades now I've seen Paul Cody's work as the ultimate cross between horror and literary fiction, taking us deeper into the weird American night than anyone in either camp. *Walk the Dark* is a continuation of that same world we know from Cody's *The Stolen Child* and *So Far Gone*, both of which are great, terrifying novels."

— Stewart O'Nan, author of *Ocean State*

"*Walk the Dark* is harrowing and vivid, taut as a wire. Paul Cody intertwines terror and hope; he knows how to hook his readers from the start—and on every page. Keep the lights burning when you open this spell-binding book."

— Julie Schumacher, author of *The Shakespeare Requirement*

"This book marks the return of a formidable novelist, whose big heart and golden ear have given us a powerful tale of corrupted lives, tragic happenstance, and, ultimately, the stirrings of hope. Part gritty bildungsroman, part prison picaresque, *Walk the Dark* delivers brutality, bleakness, and dark humor with disarming tenderness and grace."

— J. Robert Lennon, author of *Hard Girls*

WALK THE DARK

Paul Cody

Regal House Publishing

Copyright © 2024 Paul Cody. All rights reserved.

Published by
Regal House Publishing, LLC
Raleigh, NC 27605
All rights reserved

ISBN -13 (paperback): 9781646034482
ISBN -13 (epub): 9781646034499
Library of Congress Control Number: 2023943401

All efforts were made to determine the copyright holders and obtain their
permissions in any circumstance where copyrighted material was used.
The publisher apologizes if any errors were made during this process, or
if any omissions occurred. If noted, please contact the publisher and all
efforts will be made to incorporate permissions in future editions.

Cover images and design by © C. B. Royal

Regal House Publishing, LLC
https://regalhousepublishing.com

The following is a work of fiction created by the author. All names,
individuals, characters, places, items, brands, events, etc. were either the
product of the author or were used fictitiously. Any name, place, event,
person, brand, or item, current or past, is entirely coincidental.

All rights reserved. No part of this publication may be reproduced,
stored in a retrieval system, or transmitted, in any form or by any means,
electronic, mechanical, photocopying, recording, or otherwise, without the
prior permission of Regal House Publishing.

Printed in the United States of America

For Jaynie Royal and
for John Lauricella

"Most of our longings go unfulfilled. This is the word's wistful implication—a desire for something lost or fled or otherwise out of reach."

Don DeLillo, *Underworld*

1

She had so many names that I was never sure what to call her. Mother, Mom or Mommy. Peg or Peggy, Marge, Margie, Mag or Maggie. Margaret too. Margaret was the name on her driver's license, where she was five-foot-six and weighed one-hundred-ten pounds. Where she had brown hair and brown eyes. Where she had to wear corrective lenses in order to see. Where she was Margaret Curtin, all the time.

There were so many boyfriends too, and they each had at least one name, sometimes two or three. Bob, Ben, and Bill could be Bobby, Benny, and Billy. There was a Chad, a Brad, and a Gus. There was a Bert, which was short for Elbert, and a Norb, which was short for Norbert. A Speed, an Ace, a Doc. Elroy was also Roy. There was a Ned, but I didn't know what that was short for.

There was a Bud, and there was a Dub. Honest to God.

There were so many guys over the years, and Mom liked all of them, at least for a while. She said they were fun. She said they were nice. She said they'd give you the shirt off their backs. Tons of guys were giving the shirts off their backs, but none of them were walking around naked from the waist up.

She said that Doc and Billy were real gentlemen. Class acts, Mom said.

Wayne had tattoos all up and down his arms. He had a tattoo of dark blue words on his neck. Words I couldn't read. The tattoos on his arms were called sleeves.

Mom called him Wayne, but once in a while she called him Bug, a name his friends called him. Aside from the sleeves and the tat on his neck, Wayne was short and lean as a blade of grass. He was nervous and twitchy. His hair was getting thin on top, but he gathered the hair from the sides, and had a stump of a ponytail on top of his head. Mom called it a topknot.

She said samurai, these warriors in Japan—she said they wore topknots, and topknots made you strong.

Wayne had eyes that looked black and were glittery, and flickered around, looking at everything, including me. I didn't like when he looked at me. I didn't like when anybody noticed me, except Mom. And maybe Mabel.

Most of the guys were okay to me most of the time. I was Maggie's kid, or Peg's brat, and I hardly made any noise at all. I sat in corners, or sat on a small wooden chair almost behind the couch, and I didn't move. They might notice me for half a minute, and they might say, Hey, or they might say, Oliver or Ollie, because those were my names.

I'd nod or smile a little, or lift my hand an inch or two to wave, and then they'd follow Marge into the bedroom, and I wouldn't see them for a while. The door closed. I'd hear noises. Low laughter and slight groans, and the words, Yes and Oh, again and again.

I almost always wanted to kill them.

Bug was thirty-five or forty years old, as far as I could tell, and that was about the average age of the guys. One guy in a suit and tie was over sixty, I bet. He was Mr. Gleason, and Peg said he had more money than God. His hair was dyed black and was combed straight back like Elvis, and he always left a hundred dollar bill on the box we used as a coffee table.

One night Gus was there, and I heard him ask Mom if I was a retard, or if I had autism or something, because I was always staring at the floor or ceiling. I never made eye contact, Gus said.

Mother said she wasn't sure, that I was always like that. She said, Ollie's always been that way. Always quiet and always shy.

Gus said, Maybe you should get him some special help.

Gus was missing a tooth on top on one side and a tooth on the bottom on the other side, and I wondered if he could fit a straw or a cigarette or joint in the two gaps in his teeth.

Fuck special, Peggy said, then she asked Gus for his lighter, and I heard the scrape of the wheel on the lighter.

I liked the smell of smoke. I breathed deep, and started to feel real calm and almost happy.

Gus was a car mechanic, and his hands were always shades of black and gray, especially under his fingernails. He smiled at me with the gaps in his teeth, and I always wondered what you could fit in the dark gaps.

Gus was one of the nicest men. Once in a while he brought me a candy bar, a Hershey with Almonds or an Almond Joy. Here you go, Oliver, Gus said. He was the only one, aside from Mother, who called me Oliver.

A few others called me Ollie, or Oll, which sounded like All. Bug called me All, then All or Nothing, then just plain Nothing.

Mom said, Bug's a dick.

Sometimes things happened so fast that I couldn't keep up. I couldn't keep track or understand or follow.

What did a person mean when he said I was called Nothing? What was a dick? A pussy? And if a person said one thing but seemed to be saying something else—then, what did it mean?

We lived in rooms and apartments and trailers. In so many rooms and apartments and trailers over the years. They all had brown rust stains in the toilets, and dripping faucets.

From three or four years old, when I began to remember, to almost eighteen, when it was more or less over, there had to have been twenty or twenty-five different homes. On the second or third floors of big old houses, in the basements of others, with small windows high in the walls, to the single-wide trailers where the walls were so thin you could feel the ice wind in February.

Sometimes, but only for a little while, we lived in Margie's car, parked overnight under a highway bridge. We stayed under a striped blanket in the back seat, waiting for our bodies to give off heat.

Mag worried about the cold, I worried about cops, and the men who stood in shadows outside the windows of the car, looking in.

Peg said there were crazy people out there, especially in the dark. People who were like diseased dogs, and might do any lunatic thing. Light the car on fire, kick a window in, stand with a knife or gun or a piece of heavy wood, a log, and start swinging or stabbing or firing.

You never knew, she said, what was moving around in the dark.

That was the thing. That was the thing about night. How there was almost no light. Just a streetlight or traffic light, the squares of yellow or white light in the windows of houses and buildings, a porch light burning all night. But almost everything else was shadow. Dark bushes, hovering trees, black spaces and shapes everywhere.

Even the creeks with the moving water were black. Shiny black on the surface of the water, and the bubbling, burbling noise, soft as night itself. If we concentrated on the sound of water, we could feel almost happy.

We never knew where Maggie's friends were when we were staying in the car. I wanted to ask, but I never did, especially when Mom fished a few pills out of the inside pocket of her coat and swallowed them without water.

She'd get sleepy a little bit after that, and I'd listen as her breathing got lower and slower, and she'd make slight snoring sounds in her nose and mouth. By then, late in the night, her body and my body were like small furnaces, and just outside our bodies, just past our coats and hats and the blanket, the air was freezing, was turning most of the water out there to ice.

Much later, before I came in here, and before Margaret had left, I'd think back and say to myself, Some time in there, in the car or down in a basement apartment, or in the two rooms on a third floor, under the slanting eaves, everything changed completely.

I'd hear somebody yell, or make Yip Yip Yip sounds, maybe in sleep, because there were nearly three hundred guys here on this one block, and they made noise. At noon. At three-thirty in the morning.

Everything was stone and concrete, unbreakable glass, steel, and everything echoed.

Then I'd think that before the block, before all the guys here, I was six or seven or eight. I was dressed in dark clothes. The apartment or trailer was close and hot and smelled of dirty dishes and old laundry. Boiled broccoli. Fried Spam. Mag and Gus or Richard, Bug or Brad, were sleeping heavily in the bedroom. I'd go over stairs, down a hallway, through a door, and outside the air was so beautiful and fresh that I almost cried. The night sounds, a distant car or barking dog, seemed so far away. If there was a light on near the house or trailer, I'd move quickly and quietly out of the light and into shadow. I'd move gratefully into darkness. I'd creep into a world that, even back then, was leading me somewhere that was very different.

No one anywhere could see me.

2

When I was four or five years old, and could notice and remember, Margaret was tall and beautiful, not just to me, but to all the men who were drawn to her, like flying bugs high up on a streetlight on a July night. They couldn't stay away.

Her skin was very pale like Ivory soap, and her hair and eyes were dark and deep and warm. Her hands, I remember, were large, her fingers long, and her legs were even longer. She had gorgeous teeth in those days and a big smile, and when I was sitting on her lap in the early years, and she smiled and put her arms around me—that was the very best place in the world to be.

She smelled like lemon and strawberries and vanilla.

She was fifteen when I was born, so when I was four, she was still only nineteen. She said sometimes that I was more like her friend than her son. More like a brother.

She said she'd never had a brother before, so that might be why she loved me so much.

Marge never had a father either. He was some guy Mag's mother went home with, one night in Boston, where Peg's mother used to live before moving to this city in upstate New York. He might have been Neil or Buzz, Skip or Mike. He might have been tall or short. He probably had dark hair.

Mom loved to go out at night. She wore earrings, a white band in her hair, old cowboy boots someone had bought for her, and a dark purple shirt and leather jacket. She had a thin silvery chain around her neck.

She asked if I minded staying home alone, and I said I didn't mind, even though I did.

She kissed me on the forehead. She said I was her big brave boy, but I wasn't brave at all. I just knew that she wanted to go out, and that she wanted me to act like I was big and brave, even when I was four or five.

Just before she left, she said, I'm locking the door. Don't let anyone in, no matter what. Don't answer a knock or a voice. Pretend you're not here. Nobody's home.

After she closed the door behind her and I heard her cowboy boots going down the hall, then down the stairs, I'd hear the front door open and close.

It was just me in the tiny apartment, on the second floor. I shut off the lights, and looked out the window in front, and there were big houses all up and down the street. There were parked cars and dark trees and bushes, chain-link fences, and people—in ones and twos and threes—moving along the sidewalks.

There were telephone poles and power lines, and there were some streetlights too.

The whole world was dark out there, away from the streetlights, and the dark seemed like velvet, seemed poured from some beautiful inky bottle.

Inside, in the apartment, the dark was different.

It hadn't been poured from a beautiful bottle. It didn't seem like velvet.

I wore pajamas that were too small. The arms and legs were way short. They came halfway up the lower part of my legs and arms, but they had clocks on them, and even though they'd been washed many, many times, you could still see the clocks. If you closed your eyes, very late, you could almost hear them ticking.

The night got darker outside, and in here the only light came from squares and angles of light that came through the window from the streetlight. The squares and angles sat on the floor and walls.

I didn't put any lights on. If a man came to the door, he had to think that nobody was home. If he knocked, I had to be as quiet as an empty shoe. A shoe left in a closet or under the bed.

The couch and bed came with the apartment, and there

was only one bedroom. The couch had rips in the arms where someone might have slashed the leather with a knife, and the mattress of the bed had a gulley down the middle. Peggy and I slept on opposite sides of the gulley, unless one of her boyfriends was spending the night. Mother said that I could never tell anybody that she and I slept in the same bed. We only slept that way because there was just one bed, but nobody would understand. She said that if anyone ever asked about our sleeping arrangements, I had to say that I slept on the living room floor or on the couch, the way I did when one of her boyfriends was there.

There was a dog barking somewhere, and there were voices down on the street. Laughing voices, talking voices, voices that were strong and piercing.

Tom, a woman said, and her voice was high and loud. Then there was a man's voice that was much lower, and I couldn't make out any words.

A little while later, there was a siren, and you could hear the siren move, closer and closer to our house. Then it stopped a few streets over from our street.

The siren came from a police car or ambulance, not a fire engine. Fire engines had the usual siren, but they also had this deep honking sound to tell cars to watch out.

And right then, there was knocking on the door. Soft knocking at first, then a man's voice saying, Marge. Marge. For fuck's sake, Marge.

The knocking got heavy and loud, and the door vibrated. The door was made of hollow wood, and I thought the man could put a hole in the door with his hands.

Then the knocking stopped, and there were footsteps going away, then steps going down the stairs to the front of the house.

I let out a bunch of air, and realized I had stopped breathing. I wondered if the man knew somehow that I was in there. In the apartment, and refusing to answer the door.

Maybe the man was someone who was running from the siren. Maybe he had shot or stabbed or strangled somebody.

That was how killers murdered a person, almost all the time. Mommy had told me, and some of the boyfriends had said that too.

There were footsteps from the apartment upstairs, moving across the ceiling down here. Heavy footsteps, then light footsteps. There were two voices. A low one, and a high one. At first they were yelling—him, her, him, her. But the voices got lower and softer, and after a while they almost whispered. They could have been birds. Up in the branch of a tree.

The apartment was very dark, except for the streetlights falling in the windows. My eyes were used to the dark, and to the black shapes of the chair, the box coffee table, the couch with rips in the fabric. There was a single unlit lamp on the floor at the end of the couch.

Then taps started up on the door, and they turned to soft bangs. Bang, and then ten seconds, and then bang again. They went on for a while. For two or three minutes.

I began to think that it could be Mommy, because sometimes when she drank or did drugs, she left her keys somewhere. One or two times she had slept in the hall, right outside the door. She said she hadn't minded because she wasn't feeling much pain. Maybe she hadn't felt any pain at all. She wasn't sure. She could hardly remember.

The taps and soft bangs kept going on the door. They didn't get louder. The door didn't shake. But they were steady and they were clear.

This was really late, I'm pretty sure. This was past midnight. It could have been one or two or even three in the morning.

I had been alone in the apartment a long time. I wasn't sure how long exactly, because I was four or five at the time. I don't even know if I could tell time back then. But Margaret was out, in some bar or in some room. She was drinking booze, and smoking cigarettes, and taking pills and maybe putting some powder in her nose or arm. Mommy did a little of everything.

All at once, there was a loud kick, low on the door. People all over the building would hear that, even if they were asleep.

There was another kick, just as loud, and this wasn't Mag's cowboy boots with the pointed toes. This was somebody's tan shit-kicker boots, with the laces and the thick soles and steel in the toes.

I went to the door and said, Mom? even though I knew it wasn't her.

This was someone else, someone who would never go away.

All? a man's voice asked.

I nodded, then I thought that he couldn't see me.

I said, Yeah, out loud.

Lemme in, he said. He was whispering loud.

My clock pajamas in the pale light were way small on me. I could feel cool air on my arms and legs. My arms and legs were very skinny and looked like milk in the light. They looked like sticks. They looked like tiny hands on a clock.

Who are you? I said.

He said, Fuck. You little shit.

Who? I asked.

Wayne.

Bug?

Yeah, Bug.

I unlocked the door, and Bug was standing in the hall, he was filling up the frame of the door. He put one boot forward so I wouldn't be able to close the door.

What's up, Nothing, he said. He smiled this thin mean smile, and I could tell from his smile, from his eyes, that he was drunk, or high on something.

He had a brown pint bottle in his left hand. He had the top-knot, the greasy jean jacket, and he was missing a tooth or two.

You gonna ask me in? he said, and then he walked in, right past me, bumping me out of his way.

Bug, I said, then I knew I shouldn't have used that name.

I knew that using that name, saying it out loud, was a mistake.

This was two or three in the morning, and this was only him, and it was only me.

3

My room, my cell, my house, as we call it here, is six feet wide and ten feet deep. If I stand in the middle of the room and reach my arms out, side to side, I can just about touch both walls. Tips of fingers to steel plates. No problem.

On the tier, I'm on the third level. Two tiers above me, two below. On the catwalk, I'm about halfway down. I'm at the center of everything.

The bed's a metal slab, and a thin pad covered in rubber. There's a metal toilet that only flushes some of the time, so for much of the days and nights we live with the smell of our own shit, our own piss, and that reminds us of who we are and where we are. We're basic. We're like air and light and mold. We're here.

I have my own house because I've been in almost thirty years, and I don't cause trouble. So I don't have a cellie. I work in the laundry five days, four hours a day, and I could get a board, I could go before the parole board, in six months. That's not a long time for me. That's no time.

But I did weird, twisted things, and if I was on the board, I wouldn't let me out.

I'm in my late forties, so I could be gone before I hit fifty.

There are about twelve hundred guys in here, and most of them are young. They're full of vinegar. Most of them are looking at long bids, at twenty or thirty, or even fifty years. Some have life without parole. Trapped animals, rats or cats in a cage.

They walk on their toes. These rapists and killers. These armed robbers and pedophiles and drug dealers. It's always surprising how normal these people seem. They nod and smile. They shake your hand, they bump fists. They look you deeply in the eye.

This is D-block, and D-Block is as good as it gets in this place. This is an honor block. Just about everyone on this block has been in at least ten or fifteen years, and some have been in forty or fifty years. Gates, an old man, has been in fifty-three years, and he'll die here. He burned down his girlfriend's house, and ended up killing three people, including an eight-year-old boy.

The girlfriend's name was Sharon, and sometimes you hear Gates, at odd moments, whisper, Sharon, Sharon, Sharon. She would be seventy-four now if it were not for Gates.

When Gates whispers Sharon's name through his ruined teeth, it's like a cave speaking. It's like the earth opened up.

He was drunk and fucked-up on diet pills and Seconal when he lit the house. He did this in a September, when it was late summer and warm. He stunk of gasoline. Then he fell asleep in a back yard, two houses down. He had been up for two or three days before this.

Gates was finally tired. Gates came in here.

Mellor is here too, just one cell over. Sometimes we talk in the vent. Mellor's a Black dude, Mellor's a brother. He's in sixteen, seventeen years, for selling crack, and he's one of the few people here who was never violent. He got fifteen to thirty because he had all these priors.

Mellor's only in his late thirties, and he's got two sons and a daughter, from three different women. The daughter has two kids of her own, but Mellor doesn't know how old they are. He's not sure how old his daughter is. Maybe twenty, he thinks.

The rest of this place is strictly divided by race. The guys enforce this themselves. You don't hang out with the brothers if you're white, and you don't hang out with whites if you're a brother.

But D-block's different, at least when we're on D-block. You hang out with whoever you want. But on the yard, in the shops and chow hall, it's different. You roll with your own.

This whole place is concrete and steel and heavy glass. We

don't ever see grass or trees, and we see the sky mostly when we're out in the yard. Everything's loud, almost all the time, until it's one or two in the morning. Then you hear late-night sounds. You hear snores, and other kinds of breathing, and sometimes you hear a few words from a person who's sleeping. You hear what sounds like crying. You might hear, Nancy, or, Please. You hear, Fuck, or, Shit. You hear, Motherfucker.

Sometimes, somebody yelps like a dog in their sleep. What do these guys dream about? Are they all far away? Some other place, some other time? With people they'll never see again? A mother or grandmother, a girlfriend or wife, a brother or son or daughter?

Maybe they're on a beach, possibly a beach on an island. Maybe they're on a city street, at dusk, and the snow is falling and the sounds everywhere are muffled. They're with a young woman. A young woman he just met, and both he and the woman are shy, are tentative, which is a rare feeling for him. He doesn't know what to do, and then she takes his hand.

Another man is standing on the back lawn of a white house. It's July and very warm, and there are two picnic tables with loads of food. There are three oak trees, sixty or eighty feet high, and maybe twenty-five people talking and laughing. The closer he looks, the more he realizes that this is his family. His brothers and sisters, aunts, nieces and nephews.

There's an uncle who's grown old.

Then he sees that everyone has grown old. That people he thought were aunts and uncles are really his cousins. That twenty-five or thirty years have passed, and a niece who was just wearing pigtails is now a grandmother. It has all slipped away from him, and he didn't even notice, he didn't know.

There's chicken and ham on the table. Cornbread, potato salad, coleslaw, sliced tomatoes with basil, a cold string bean salad. There's beer and wine, lemonade, bright red bug juice.

There's a vase of yellow and purple and orange flowers on each table. The color is so sharp it almost hurts his eyes.

The hum of voices gets louder. A small child screeches. Another voice says, There.

High up, way above the top of the oak trees, there's a single puffy cloud moving across the sky. First one cloud, then another. Solitary and slow as a sailboat. Then a bird, a raptor, I think, riding thermals.

Everywhere else, the sky is blue, a deep blue he didn't think existed anymore. A blue he hasn't seen since he was almost a kid. A blue that he thought had left the world.

It's somewhere between two and three in the morning. I heard two bongs of the church tower about a half hour ago, maybe a mile away. The bells bong every hour, around the day and night, but you can only hear them very early in the morning—from midnight to five a.m.

I'm lying on my back on the cot, the door locked, of course, my eyes open and staring at the ceiling. It's almost totally black in here, and this is as quiet as it ever gets.

Mellor's snoring lightly, and has been asleep since nine or ten. Mellor's told me that he can sleep anywhere, and that that saves him. Nothing gets between him and his sleep.

I close my eyes, and I'm ten or twelve years old. Mom is still alive, and she still entertains her boyfriends, and some days she's away from our apartment for two or three days at a time. Once, she was gone six straight days.

Somewhere around those years, I began to go out at night, when she was gone. If you walked three or four streets over, you were in a nice neighborhood, with bigger houses and lawns, and the feeling was amazing.

All the lit windows in the darkness, and me dressed in black, even a dark watch cap. And people inside, in the lighted rooms.

They didn't know I was outside, but I knew where they were. I crouched in shadows. I could see, and I felt like God.

4

Her name was Mabel, and she was Margie's best friend. Even though they had known each other a long time, for four or five years, at least, Mabel was five or ten years older than Mommy. And it was hard to tell how they had met and become friends.

Mag told different stories at different times about their meeting, and Mabel had two or three stories about their friendship.

They had both worked together for a few weeks at a diner on Madison Street, or they met in the waiting room of the welfare office downtown, on the second floor, on Winthrop Road. There was a nasty customer or manager or a mean welfare worker, and Mabel or Marge came to the defense of the other.

Or they were downtown, on the Commons, this big pedestrian mall, and some homeless man or women, some drunk or crack-head or cop, began to give Peg or Mabel a hard time about something. One of them—Peg or Mabel—starting yelling at the cop or crack-head or drunk, at the customer or manager, at the mean welfare worker.

Pretty soon, both of them were yelling at the guy, and it was always a guy. Then they quit their jobs at the diner, told the welfare worker they would report him to the district welfare office, and they both walked out in triumph.

We told him! they said.

He wouldn't be so quick to fuck with people anymore!

Their job was to tell everyone what was what.

Mother was tall, but Mabel was a lot taller. She was five-nine or ten, and she had shoulders and arms. She wasn't fat, she was meaty and solid, forty or fifty pounds heavier than Mom. She had two or three rings on each hand, and a smeared tattoo of a wasp on the back of her left hand. Mabel said that nobody wanted to get stung by her left. When they did, when someone was at the business end of her left, they'd feel the ground rushing up to their face, so help her God.

Mabel drank almost all the time, from morning till late at night. She sipped and sipped. Beer, wine, gin, vodka, peppermint schnapps, apricot brandy, vanilla extract. She drank whatever was there, as long as it had alcohol in it. But she never tried lighter fluid or gasoline, even though she knew people who had.

Mabel also never did drugs, or almost never. She might do a line of coke, from time to time, or take a hit of the crack pipe, but on principal, she did not do drugs, except for medicine the doctor gave her. Drugs were expensive and dangerous. They were also illegal, and she didn't want to get popped unless she had to.

So even though she sipped things from wakeup to bedtime, she didn't ever get drunk, except once in a while.

Mabel had blond hair that was dark at the roots, and the color varied. It was white blond on top and in the front, and darker blond at the back. And there were streaks that were faintly pink or pale blue on the sides, above her ears.

By early afternoon, after sipping for a while, Mabel's face would get red, and she'd look happy. If she was sitting on the couch, she might pat the place next to her and say, Ollie, c'mere. Here, honey, she'd say, and pat the cushion again.

Marge said, Go ahead. She won't bite.

So I sat down next to Mabel, and she put her big arm around my shoulders, and pulled me close to her soft side and her pillowy front. She smelled like beer and talcum powder, like apple shampoo, like spicy deodorant.

I could hear her voice rumble through her ribs. Vibrating from her lungs and throat and mouth.

Ollie, she said. Such a nice Ollie.

Mother was always telling me that people would not bite, as though some people would bite, but she was there to tell me who would not bite, the people who would be safe.

Some other things were not the end of the world. If she was going out and leaving me alone, that was not the end of the world. And if we were both asleep in her bed at three in the morning, and some boyfriend knocked on the door, it was not the end of the world to get up, answer the door, and for me to move to the couch.

That day, the day Mabel patted the couch and got me to sit next to her, Mag went out around five, wearing a dress and her cowboy boots, and her coat with the fake fur. She kissed me on top of my head, and told Mabel she didn't know what time she'd be back.

She told me in a soft, whispery voice that I was to be a good boy and I was to do everything Mabel asked me to do.

Mabel was sitting on one end of the couch, smoking cigarettes and sipping from a brown bottle of beer. She was staring straight ahead, through billows of smoke, and for a while, she didn't say anything.

She sucked smoke in, and the end of the cigarette was bright red for a moment. Then she sucked beer from the bottle, swallowed, and let the smoke out.

There were clouds and clouds of smoke around her head, as though it might rain. I sometimes expected thunder and lightning.

I'd seen both her and Maggie do this together, at each end of the couch, sometimes not saying anything for a long time. I wondered what they were thinking, and what they might say if they did say anything.

They might say angry, mean things about men, about all the boyfriends, or they might say things about their mothers or fathers, who weren't worth a damn. They hardly knew their fathers, who always moved to some other state, and never sent money for the kids, and their mothers tried, they guessed, but they were never around very much either.

Peggy thought she might have a half brother, who was at least two or three years older than her. She seemed to remember that he looked after her once in a while. He was very skinny, had black hair, and his name was Tom or Tad, Tim or Ted. He fed her dry Cheerios from a yellow box.

Then Margaret was a little older, she was five or six, and this was long before Ollie came into the world. Weeks and months went by, and there was no stepbrother around, ever, anymore.

Where was he? Marge wanted to know, and her mother looked at her as though she didn't know what Marge was talking about.

What stepbrother?

Who?

I looked over and Mabel was still smoking and sitting and sipping. I wondered if Mabel would be as nice as my mother. If she would love me the way Margaret loved me. As big as the world, as warm and bright as the sun.

Mabel wouldn't bite. It would never be the end of the world.

5

For a long time, Mabel lived in a trailer park that was on a road behind the big home-improvement and grocery stores. There were only ten or twenty trailers at the park, and they were almost all single-wides. Three were double-wides, and the double-wides had nicer cars parked in front of them.

A big canal, to prevent floods, ran behind the park, and people threw a couch or a refrigerator or black bags of trash into the canal. They threw bicycles in, including a kid's three-wheeler that had red and blue and yellow wheels. There were old diapers in there. There were empty bottles and cans of beer, there was soggy cardboard, broken dolls and blocks, there were cigarette butts, there were plastic picture frames.

Mabel said that people were pigs, let's face it. She said that plastic would never go away, would never rot into the water or ground, not in a thousand years. It would be here long after the Martians invaded and took over. Even Martians, smart as they'd be, wouldn't know what to do with plastic.

The trailer park was called Sylvan Homes, and Mabel lived there off and on for years. Once in a while she moved the mile or two back in town, but after a few months, after a year at most, she'd move back out to the country, as she called it, to a single-wide.

The manager of the trailer park, a man named Gump, was a friend of hers, and could always get her back in to Sylvan Homes within a month or two.

People, Mabel said, were always coming or going. And it was nice for her to have a place of her own.

Mom left me with Mabel a ton. Sometimes for a night or two, one time for over a month, another time for more than two months, when Maggie met a guy with a black beard whose name was Glenn, and she moved with him to Buffalo or Rochester, where he had construction work. Mabel said that Glenn might be a keeper, and that Peg liked him a lot. Glenn worked very hard, and he was good to Mother, unless he was depressed. Then he would stay in bed and ignore her.

Glenn was in the Program, Mabel said. He worked the Twelve Steps, he went to meetings almost every day. Well, every day he wasn't working. The meetings were in church basements, or in meeting rooms at community centers. There were signs on the walls. Keep It Simple. One Day At A Time. It Works If You Work It.

Marge said that if someone had a problem, and they went to meetings, and asked for help from their Higher Power, and got a sponsor, then their life could get better. People who came out of jail, people who had been homeless, people who had done terrible things—like kill somebody in a car accident—even those people could get better. Not forever, but they could stay clean and sober for one day.

Just For Today, they said.

But if they got through the day, with the help of the Program and a Higher Power, they would try to do the same the next day. One Day At A Time. Sometimes, on really tough days, a minute or an hour at a time.

Mommy and Mabel knew so many people who tried the Program, or should have tried the Program, and they knew or heard about people who had stayed with it. Who had been clean and sober more than a few weeks or months. Even for a year.

Mag had pills that made her feel better, pills that she got from her boyfriends and from people who hung out by the bars. The pills came in strips of aluminum, and had plastic blisters on the other side of the strip that held the pills. There were ten pills to each strip.

Marge said the pills came from all over the world. From Afghanistan, India, from Romania and Mexico and Brazil. Maybe from Nigeria too.

The pills were called diazepam, lorazepam, clonazepam.

They were hydrocodone and oxycodone. Take just one, Maggie said, and the world didn't hurt so much. All the jagged stuff just melted away, got smooth and warm as a stone in the sun. You could lie like a lizard in the sun, and you could sleep any time you wanted. You could feel the heat from high above you, she said.

A half hour earlier, you were ready to jump out of your skin, and now you could settle into your skin all the way to your toes. Your skin was the best place in the world to be.

I didn't know what Mommy meant sometimes. I didn't understand what she said, at first. Jumping out of your skin, and the world being full of jagged things, and a lizard on a rock and a stone in the sun.

Even things in the Program. What Program? A Program for what? People sat in rooms in the basements of churches. They sat and sat, and how was that good for anything? Why couldn't they sit in their own rooms at home?

Mabel had rooms in her single-wide, and they were stacked almost one behind the other like a train car. The door from outside led into the kitchen. Then there was a bathroom, a little hallway, a living room and two bedrooms. They were all small, but they were still bigger than the places where Margaret and me lived. And right outside the windows, in the back, there was the canal, and weeds and skinny trees.

Kids from Sylvan Homes played near the canal. A kid named Shane, and his little brother named Buster, were always throwing things into the canal. Rocks and branches, deck chairs, somebody's dirty white sneakers.

There was a Randy kid, a Jason kid.

Once, they tried to throw a dog in the water, but the dog ran away, and they couldn't catch it. The dog was small and brown, and it was very fast.

Mabel said that I should go out and play with them. But I didn't want to. I never wanted to be around anyone, except Mother and Mabel.

Mabel had a towel wrapped around the top of her head. She had been in the shower, and she was wearing a robe that had big purple and red flowers on it.

She said, Don't you want to play with those boys?

I had seen them, and I knew they were sort of like me. They were very skinny, and there were bald patches on their heads, where someone had given them a haircut with an electric trimmer. They sat in a chair in the middle of the kitchen, a towel draped across their shoulders. They listened to the buzz of the trimmer.

They smelled a little sour, and their teeth were yellow. They had big ears, and their white T-shirts were gray.

They were like me, and I was like them. I didn't want to be anywhere near them.

Try this, Mabel said.

She put half a yellow tablet on my palm, gave me a cup of water, and I swallowed.

That was six or seven years old. Or eight, or even five.

I waited, wondering about jagged and being in your skin.

6

Concrete, steel, bullet-proof glass. Long corridors, tall, tall windows behind mesh on the sides of the cell block. A and B-blocks on the north side, C and D-blocks on the south side. The big yard, maybe half the size of a football field, but not as wide, is in the middle.

I'm in the center tier of five, as I think I've said, and I'd guess that there are fifty, maybe sixty cells per tier. That's a lot of angry guys, with a ton of energy, packed into a very small space.

And D-block, as I've also said, is Honor Block, where almost all of us are fairly calm. Most of the time.

And the noise. Jesus, the noise. All the time, the noise. Except for a few hours in the very dead of night. Though even then, at two, three, four in the morning, a guy or two or three, will bark or scream or shriek in all the silence and darkness.

Heavy steel doors crashing, a radio blasting, someone yelling, Bend over! Hoo-eeee! Motherfucker! Not once in a while, but all the time.

It's halfway through January now, and this is upstate New York, not far from Canada. I've been in Dannemora, which is only thirty or so miles from the Canadian border, and for a while, I was in Attica. You go north or west from Attica, and you hit Lake Ontario or Lake Erie.

After intake, and that was somewhere near Buffalo, I remember, I went to Dannemora, in some tiny podunk town way far north of anything, past forests of maple and ash and pine trees. There were huge stands of forest and hills, lakes and rivers. I had no idea something like that existed.

We sat on the bus, hands cuffed, wrists linked to the waist chain, ankles shackled. The world outside the windows of the Department of Corrections bus looked as near and strange as a movie on a big screen. A boy on a bicycle, two girls walking, houses, a dog then a cat, regular people driving cars and pickup trucks. A yellow house on the side of a small mountain, in a clearing, among tens of thousands of trees.

Who would live in their own yellow house, away from anywhere, among an ocean of trees? Who was that? And why? What kind of life would you live there?

Dannemora used to be the place where they sent many of the new, young inmates. I don't know if they still do.

We called it Gladiator School. There were fights and stabbings. A few guys were killed in my three and a half years there. You get fights and stabbings everywhere on the inside, but you get more where there are the young guys, just settling in.

After that, they put me in Attica, way the hell out there, in the country of upstate New York. Then five, six years later, they put me here. Auburn. The grandfather of New York State prisons. First built in 1816.

I've been growing old here. And I can feel in the walls, in the stone and steel, all the men who have walked these hallways, who have looked out the tall windows on to the yard. All the guys who have died here.

Still, it's mid-January, it's scary cold outside.

Somewhere on a radio, a voice said, It's four degrees at six a.m. Getting up into the teens by mid-day, a woman's voice said. A loud, chirping voice. Then there were ads for things. A car place, Dunkin' Donuts, house insurance, hair color kits. Bright, loud voices. Louder even than the woman with the weather.

Then a song about love, and the voices not so loud. Love you forever, love you still. Love you, baby, on the highest hill.

Oh, honey, I will.

Oh, baby, I will.

I used to love that shit, my ear pressed to the speaker on the transistor radio. It's one thing I had as a kid. A little radio and lots of batteries.

There's not much heat in here. There never is. Cement and bricks, steel and plastic glass—they hold the cold. The warden must think that hundreds of bodies in C and D-blocks, hundreds on each side, would generate heat. But there's only heat in the summer, and then it's way too much. The lowest tier can stay cool the longest, being far away from the roof. And the lowest tier stays almost warm, at least for a while, in the cold.

We can hear the wind outside, and see the sky spitting a little snow. The wind presses the sides of the building, and presses especially hard against the windows.

Everything inside feels still and cold and a little sore. Like we have arthritis, and only sunlight, a lot of sunlight, could thaw us out.

The CO, a white guy named Henlon, walks by and looks in. I nod to him, but he ignores me. I'm awake and breathing, and that's enough for him.

If you were out in the woods, and you stepped on a stick, you'd hear the crack, sharp as a scalpel, and the crack would travel a long way. Animals, I imagine, would huddle in burrows underground, under leaves, in the crevices of trees. Everything would hunker down today.

Gates is moving slow next door. I hear slight grunts and soft groans as he tries to get dressed. Gates is over seventy, I'm pretty sure, and he has arthritis all over. Knees, ankles, hips, shoulders, hands. He doesn't say anything about it, but every move is hard for him. It's aches, and sharp stabbing pains sometimes.

I go to the vent and ask Mellor if he's up and dressed. He says, Sure am.

I say, Mellor, it's fucking freezing.

No shit, he says, and chuckles.

A few nights ago, around ten or eleven, Mellor told me about a cat he had when he was a kid. A big orange cat. Fifteen, sixteen pounds. His name was Crispin, and Mellor didn't know where that name came from or what it meant.

Crispin was around from when Mellor was four or five years old. And he was always there.

Crispin slept on Mellor's bed with him. He curled up on Mellor's back or front or side, and he'd start to purr, really loud. Like his greatest joy in life was being next to Mellor.

Even if it was freezing and there was no heat on, Crispin was warm, and he purred as if this was all the pleasure in the world.

I thought about Mellor and Crispin for a while.

What happened to him? I asked.

Then I waited and waited, but Mellor didn't say anything.

Whatever had happened to Crispin, it hadn't been good.

7

After half a yellow pill, I knew all about jagged and staying in your skin. Because everything got smooth and it was warm as a bath inside my skin. The whole world got soft and waves of warmth licked and lapped at me, inside and outside.

I stayed on the couch, and the knot in my stomach got loose. I didn't feel like I might, any second, throw up. I didn't think or worry about much of anything, at all. My body, the room, the trailer, outside in the world, got softer and softer, and just a little fuzzy. I sat and I think I must have smiled, and kept smiling, for a long time.

Maybe I had never felt this way in my short and puny life. Like the world was sweet, the world was generous and kind. Nobody was going to hurt me, nobody would leave me. Or if they did leave me, that would be fine. That would be easy because I'd find someone else who would be with me.

Abide with me. That's what someone had said somewhere. I don't know who said it or where, but abide, I learned, meant to wait patiently.

Abide was a strong and quiet word. It meant to have faith. To believe. To wait with someone was to know that they were confident in the other person, and they had every hope that the other person was worth waiting with, that the other person mattered.

That's what Margaret did. Sometimes. When she wasn't out with her boyfriends, or in the bedroom with one or two of them. When she wasn't away for the weekend or week or month or two or three. She bought cereal and milk and beer. She found a new apartment or trailer for us to live in.

When a boyfriend was staying the night, Mother made sure I had enough blankets and a pillow on the couch.

Mom hugged me and said I was her beautiful boy. Her favorite boy. The boy she loved most of all.

I was special beyond special.

I didn't know what it meant to be special beyond special, but sometimes on a Friday or Saturday night, we ordered pizza, and a man knocked on our door and brought a warm pizza. The man smiled when he saw Mommy, and you could tell that he liked her. He saw how beautiful she was.

He wanted to be her friend, and she gave him a five or ten-dollar tip.

Back on the couch at Mabel's trailer, I was getting a little sleepy. Sweet and sleepy and smiling.

Mabel was in the shower, the bathroom door open an inch or two. The fan in the bathroom was busted, and if you didn't leave the bathroom door open even a little, the fog got so thick you couldn't see your own hand.

The shower stopped, and Mabel called to me, You okay, Ollie? And it was like a voice from the other side of the world. From the waking world or the dream world or the regular world.

I don't know if it was from any of those worlds. Maybe there was just one world. But we thought there were many.

Mabel had a cigarettes and whiskey voice. Kind of low and raspy. Sometimes Maggie said that a voice was like a thousand miles of bad road. Bumps and cracks, potholes, rocks, rusting mufflers.

Going past empty fields, dying houses, past barbed wire strung between crooked fence posts.

You could drive almost forever. There was tumbleweed, and more wire fences. There were abandoned cars, some of them without doors or windshields. There were very few trees in some places, and now and then there was a billboard with a smiling woman holding a cup of coffee or a beer, and there were bullet holes in her face.

Every forty or fifty miles, there would be a tiny town with a single traffic light or stop sign, and half a block of store fronts, almost all of them empty. A bar with a Miller beer sign in the front window, with a Budweiser sign, with a Ladies Invited sign in red and blue neon, and an eye winking. The eye had eyelashes on top, like a lady.

The bar was open, and the lights were bright in the late evening.

In upstate New York, where we lived, there were always trees. Thousands of trees, millions of trees. Pine trees and maple and ash and oak, some so tall they seemed to touch the sky. The trees covered the small hills and mountains, and there were lakes nearly everywhere.

Lakes in valleys, and some of the lakes were huge. They went for ten or twenty or thirty miles, even more. Enormous glassy lakes. Even in the deep dark, the surface of the lakes reflected the sky, reflected the moon and the stars—and all around them, the black trees which seemed to hold the dark.

Once in a while, during all the years, Marge or Mabel, or sometimes both of them, would take me on drives. Long, dark, and quiet drives, on a Sunday or Monday night, sometimes on a Wednesday.

Never on a Friday or Saturday night, because that's when all the drunks and crazies and cops were out. Stirring trouble. Carrying guns, looking for adventure.

Peggy said we never wanted guns or adventure around us. We wanted to stay as quiet and black as the night. Fly under the radar.

We didn't want to be stopped by anyone, for any reason, she said. We didn't want some character on meth, some fellow who was drunk and who had a knife and a ball peen hammer, some guy who'd had a miserable, abused, and loveless childhood, who was working out his anger issues, his borderline personality disorder, on us, just because we happened to be out, driving and looking at the midnight sights.

One time, it was one or two in the morning, and it was Mabel, Peg, and me. Mom was driving, and Mabel was sitting by the passenger door, and I was in the middle, sandwiched by these ladies who were warm and funny, and who loved me.

Maybe I was seven or eight, five or six, nine or ten. I didn't know exactly, but at the time I would have known. These things blended and swirled, echoed, went past in mist and fog and curtains of dark. The car smelled like beer, and it had that musky smell of Mabel and Mommy. Shampoo and makeup, sweat, deodorant, everything that was good in the world.

The road was rushing at us. The white lines and curves and straightaways, and huge trees on both sides. We could drive a long time, I thought. We could drive off the edge of the known world.

Mom was sipping coffee, and Mabel had a bottle of beer. Mabel started fishing in her coat pocket, and she took out a small plastic bag. In the dark, I couldn't see what was in the bag. The lights of the dashboard were not bright.

Then I saw her take a white oblong pill from the bag. She broke the pill in half, put half in her mouth, and sipped beer.

She gave me the other half, and I did what she had done. Put it in my mouth, and swallowed it with a sip of beer.

You're driving, Mags, Mabel said. Nothing for you.

Margie laughed. She said, You fucking dope fiends.

She laughed some more.

Ten minutes later, twenty minutes—I don't know—the warmth and calm were spreading all through me. In my toes, my left arm, my ears and eyes, everywhere, just everywhere.

Mother seemed to drive faster and faster, and sitting in the front seat, between them, at two or three in the morning, driving through the holy land of dark trees, of northern New York, I wished that I could die. Right then. Right there.

Because I would never be happier anywhere in the world.

8

I went to school only a little. Sometimes I went to school two or three times a week, sometimes I didn't go at all. At one house, all I had to do was walk down two flights of stairs from the third floor, then go three houses down, then right, then down the short street where there were only three or four houses on each side. There were trees, big trees and small trees, in front of the houses, on a strip of grass called the tree lawn.

The tree lawn rested between the sidewalk and street.

In September, right when school began for the year, the leaves were just beginning to change. From deep shiny August green to a duller and dying green. By the end of September, the leaves would be red and orange and yellow, and by the end of October almost all the leaves would be dead and gone from the branches. Kids kicked leaves that lay on the sidewalk. The leaves made dry, scraping sounds.

At the corner, there was a crossing guard. An old man in a lime-green vest, who slapped most of the kids a high five. His name was Joe, and even Maggie said he was a nice guy. All the kids liked him. They liked him a lot.

He had a big nose, and when he smiled, his teeth were perfect. Even and so white that his smile was a flash of bright light.

Mommy said that his grill was beautiful, but she was afraid it was fake. A four hundred dollar set of dentures.

Just past Joe and the intersection was the school. Two stories, red brick, with playgrounds on the front and back of the building.

Peg left me on the playground with dozens of kids, and six or seven parents and aides. Kids were running around and yelling, they were climbing on play structures, they were clustered in small groups, especially the girls.

The girls always seemed much older than the boys. They didn't have to run around and yell so much. They wore dungarees like the boys, and even though many of the boys had very long hair, and some of the girls had short hair like a boy, the girls had beautiful hair that came in so many colors. Girls' hair shined, and girls' hair had ribbons and elastic, and girls' hair was braided. It was always lovely, especially when their hair caught the light.

When a girl's hair was short, it looked like a black or blond helmet.

This was Fall Creek Elementary School. Grades K through five. Grade K was kindergarten. That was my grade when I first went to school. Ms. Deane was the teacher, and she was so nice, like Peg and Mabel without the alcohol and drugs. She was very attractive. She had brown hair that was near to blond, and she wore it in two long braids that were ropes of yellow and light brown.

She was not as tall and thin as Mom, and not as beautiful, but she was still pretty beautiful.

Some days, when I was there at school, Ms. Deane did not have her hair in braids. Her hair fell loose on her shoulders, and it was as though she had just woken up from bed. It took a minute to recognize her, she looked so different.

Ms. Deane liked all the students in her class. She even liked me. She put her hand on my head, and ruffled my hair. She put a hand on a kid's shoulder, or on an arm, and she slowly stroked the shoulder or arm with her thumb.

She stood behind Chloe, a girl with long black hair, and took a thick rope of Chloe's hair in her hands, and began to comb the rope with her fingers.

Kids got calm and dreamy when Ms. Deane touched them. It was like giving a kid a half pill, and watching them drift into happiness. It was like watching a kid float away from the world and enter heaven, or someplace far from the regular world.

Nothing could touch any kid who was touched by Ms. Deane.

Sometimes, in a rare moment when Ms. Deane was not talking or moving, when she was standing still, a little kid would go to her side, and would stand next to her, pressing his or her head against her leg and hip. Ms. Deane's hand would go to the top or side of the kid's head, and the kid would look far away, at some green and flowered valley.

There were seventeen or eighteen kids in our class, depending on if I was in class, and if Wendi with an I was in class. There was a Wendy with a Y too. Wendi with an I was very thin, and Wendy with a Y was fat, though Peg said I should never call a kid fat. They were pleasantly plump. They were husky or strong. They were never fat. Marge said we wouldn't want to give a kid an inferiority complex.

That was when a kid didn't think he was very good, when he thought everyone was better than him.

I was taller than every boy in class, and I was skinny as rope. One girl, Anne, was even taller than me, but all the rest, boys and girls, were shorter.

I don't think any boys or girls wanted to play with me. I ate lunch alone. That was okay in the classroom, because there were so many corners and places where I could be by myself, where I could pretend to look at the pictures in a book.

But the lunchroom was so much bigger, and every kid could see me sitting alone, and no other kid was alone, and every other kid in the lunchroom knew that he or she had chosen to not sit near me.

They didn't look at me, but I knew that every other kid could see me sitting there, and each kid knew that he or she had no desire to sit near me. It was like there was a sign on me that said: Looks Bad; Smells Bad; Is Bad.

A couple of times Ms. Deane came in from somewhere else, and she sat next to me. She was so nice. Ms. Deane was always nice. But that only happened two or three times.

But then we moved, almost overnight, to a basement apartment, and I was supposed to go to a different school. To BJM, and not to Fall Creek. BJM stood for Bonnie J. Morton. She was a teacher who was dead, but who had taught at the school for thirty-five years. Everyone loved Bonnie J. Morton, even if they had never known her.

For quite a while, I didn't go to school anymore. I stayed in the basement apartment, and from the windows, I could see the feet and legs of people walking by. I could see calves and knees and ankles, and I could see shoes and sneakers.

I'd think about lunch at Fall Creek, and it made me want to shudder. Me, and all those kids not looking at me.

9

Dominic and Mitch were Mabel's two favorite boy-friends, though there were other boyfriends she liked almost as much. Dominic was small, and he was completely bald, and he had big muscles for a little guy. There were veins sticking out of his arms, and in hot weather he wore a T-shirt without any sleeves. Dominic often squinted, like his eyes hurt or were very tired, and he had to clear his eyes to see.

Dominic always smelled like baby powder, and sometimes he wore a polo shirt with the collar up. That was called a popped collar. He had pink and white and blue and black polo shirts. When he wore the pink one, he looked at you, waiting for you to say something.

He always wore boots, too, that had big heels. In the middle of summer, in July and August, he wore sandals that had thick soles and black straps that wrapped around his feet. He had toes that almost had muscles in them, and long yellow toenails he never seemed to cut.

When he sat on the couch, he put his feet up on the small coffee table, and we all had to notice his feet. His muscled toes, his yellow toenails.

Wearing shorts, Dominic had way more hair on his legs than on his head.

Dominic worked at a job installing carpet. He made good money, he said.

The other guy Mabel liked was Mitch. Sometimes Mabel called him Mitchell, and sometimes she called him Pudge. But almost all the other times, he was just Mitch.

Mitch rhymed with stitch and hitch and witch and bitch, Mabel said. There was no end of names.

Mitch was almost as short as Dominic, but he was nearly as wide as he was tall. His shoulders filled a doorframe, and when he walked down a hall his shoulders seemed to touch the walls on both sides.

Mitch was beefy. He didn't have veins in his arms and muscles in his toes, but Mabel said Mitch could pick Dominic up and carry him across the street with one arm. No problem. Mitch worked construction, and that was hard, heavy work. That was work that left you exhausted by the end of the day. He might look like a pudge, and he might answer to Pudge, but don't be fooled, Mabel said. He was one tough hombre.

Mitch had big, dirty blond hair, and it was sometimes tied back in a ponytail. Unlike Dominic, who probably shaved twice a day, Mitch might have shaved once or twice a week.

Mitch wore boots like Dominic, but they were dirty and scuffed, and there were cuts in the toes and sides of the boots from work. Dominic's boots were polished.

Mitch never put his feet up on the coffee table, and he wore plaid flannel shirts most of the time. In summer, he wore T-shirts that had arms, and he smelled like a hole someone dug in the backyard. It smelled dirty and clean at the same time.

Dominic pulled me on to his lap on the couch, and squeezed me hard with his steel cable arms. He squeezed so tight that almost right away, it was hard to breathe. He had boozy, minty breath, like gin and Tic-Tacs.

He was shaking a little from this quiet laugh.

But it wasn't funny. Not at all. My chest, my arms, my back. Dominic's cable arms around everything.

Then his hand went down to the bottom of the zipper on my pants. He grabbed my package, my dick and balls, and moved his hand back and forth.

I wasn't old. I was maybe seven, maybe eight, and this was when Mother was away somewhere. In New York City or Buffalo or Rochester. Maybe all the way to Boston.

This was her last chance, Peggy said on the phone. This was her last chance at a new life, and at love.

You don't have love, Mag said, and you've got nothing.

You hear me, Ollie? she asked. Am I making sense?

You could have all the things in the world, put together, but no love, and you're the poorest person anywhere, she went on. That's how simple and basic it is.

We were on the phone, Marge and me. I could hear her breathe between sentences, the same warm breath I felt when we were sleeping next to each other on some nights. On nights when I wasn't sleeping on the couch, and when there were no boyfriends taking my place on the bed.

She breathed a little more, and I could nearly feel the heat of her breath. There was ice, I think, clinking against a glass, and I pictured her raising a glass to her lips, and sipping the clear liquid.

Always gin or vodka, or dark heavy beer from a bottle, or white wine. Never red wine, which gave you a ferocious hangover. The brutal headaches and awful depleted feeling afterward. You still got some of that from white wine, but not nearly so bad as you got from red wine.

Either way, Peggy said, you always had to pay the fiddler. The man or woman who played the music you danced to.

I didn't know what she was talking about sometimes. Like, who in the name of God was the fiddler? What did a violin have to do with drinking and dancing?

There was more breathing and more clinking ice, and Margaret's voice got lower and slower. She was getting like poured syrup.

Then Mitch bought me a small, powerful radio. Shiny black, with an antenna that could be very tall. It was AM and FM, and it worked by batteries or it worked by electric if you plugged it in.

Late at night, moving up and down on the dial, you could hear stations from Boston, Columbus, Cleveland, New York, even Chicago if it was real late. There was music and talk, there was news, there were ads for everything in the world.

People got shot, planes crashed, giant sinkholes opened in the earth, and cars and even trucks disappeared into them.

When it was so, so late, and I still couldn't sleep, I'd keep the volume low, and turn the dial slowly, and I could go almost everywhere, the radio pressed to my ear.

A car pulled into Sylvan Homes, and you could see the headlights moving softly past all the trailers. You could feel the lights going past each trailer, pausing, and you could feel the eyes of the driver looking at the windows and doors.

There was bright light in the living room, and you could feel how the walls of the trailer were so thin. Even in the middle of summer, in July and August, the air seeped in through the cracks, and the damp from the puddles and from the creek— that was everywhere too.

A dog barked, three trailers down, and that was old Mr. Green, who was bald, with a fringe of white hair around the bottom of his dome. His dog was called Doctor, I don't know why. Mr. Green and Doctor were okay, Mabel said.

Me and Mabel, we were frozen for a minute or two while the big lights of the car shined in the window. The only other light came from the television. The sound was so low. It was always low, and Mabel said TV was like a nightlight, only in the day it was a daylight too.

On television, the people had perfect teeth, even the junkies and hookers and alkies.

The light from the car began to move away from the window. Then it paused and the light came in at an angle.

Peg said she missed me very much, and loved me more than the moon. I said I loved her too, and she asked me to tell Mabel that she'd call her, call Mabel, in a day or two.

After I disconnected, and gave Mabel back her phone, I began to think about love and the moon. The moon was very far away.

Mabel put a yellow tablet in the palm of my hand. She gave me her glass of white wine. I took the pill, and sipped a tiny sip of wine.

The pill went down smooth as glass.

This was late. This was one or two in the morning. It was July and very hot, even that early in the morning.

The light in the window was gone, but a little way away we could hear a car door open and close. We could hear boots on gravel outside.

Then bang, bang, bang on the kitchen door.

Then nothing. Then just the flickering light from the television.

Then more silence. Then we waited.

10

From in here, from this distance and this time, everything from the past is really far away and really long ago. Like all that happened to somebody else. In a different world. And in a very different time.

But it's all so close, too, like it happened a month ago, a week ago, possibly even earlier today. Maybe because it happened so long ago and somewhere else, and this has been a hard gray fog for weeks and months and years, a lightless and loveless stay in purgatory with all us sinners, we recall those old days, those former times and things, much more intensely. Because if we didn't remember, if we couldn't still feel it and hear it, see it and taste it and touch it, we honestly wouldn't have anything.

We'd be shells, not that we're not already shells, but we'd be emptier shells, scoured by the years. We'd be dry and as useless as an empty cup. Soiled and more dead than dead.

The first year or two I got a few postcards, and made a few phone calls. Maybe to or from Mabel.

Margie was gone by then. I don't remember when exactly she was gone, but it was a little before I came here. When I went through the back yards and empty streets, always at two or three or four in the morning, always in that thrilling window of darkness.

A little later, at five in the morning, say, a few people would always be awake, in their kitchens, making coffee. Getting ready for work, or school, or something.

I'd see them at their kitchen sinks, doing things with water. Then I'd see them at their kitchen tables, or in a den or living room, sipping from a cup, eating cereal, yawning, waking up.

Just by watching them from out in the darkness, seeing them eat and drink and wake up, I was part of them. I could see how much they were in their lives, and how such a small thing as cereal or coffee or a warm, clean house, could give them satisfaction. Tiny things made their lives worth living.

It's almost two in here. Two in the morning. We're locked down and locked in. There's just snores and mumbles and yips and brays. Somebody, somewhere in these tiers of men, calls out Morton or Jay or Tompkins. They might be the names of people or streets or neighborhoods or counties. Usually, you hear the single word and nothing else. Just a slurred word.

I have moments, almost every day or night, when I think that I can't keep doing this. Everything speeds up, and I remember that I've been here almost forever, and that I'll be here at least a little while longer. I don't know anything about the world, and even if I do get out, or when I get out, I'll have no place to go. I'll have no money, no job skills, no social skills. I have no friends or relations.

Maybe I'll have a rented room with a hot plate. A single bed narrow as a prison cot. A little metal dresser with cigarette burns on the top. A bathroom down the hall with a tin shower, a plastic shower curtain, a stained toilet.

The closed doors in the hallway on the second floor muffle the sounds of televisions and radios. Nobody visits anyone else, ever.

In the beginning of this, when I was in Gladiator School, I didn't think of much.

Nothing bad had ever happened, nothing that I had done. People got hurt because they made the wrong moves. They got out of bed, they turned on a light, they came in the kitchen. They took a knife from the kitchen counter.

What were they thinking? What the fuck were they fucking thinking?

It was three-thirty in the morning. It was the witching hour.

I was six-foot-three. I weighed almost two hundred pounds, back then, all of it coiled muscle and rage.

She wasn't even five feet tall. She was eighty-some years old.

WTF? What the fuck?

In all my nights, in the years of nights, I had learned to creep and crawl in the dark. I wore black, down to my sneakers and socks. I wore a black balaclava.

There was just that strip of blue eyes, bright in the darkness. If someone had snapped lights on, it would have been like poking every nerve in my teeth. It would have been electric and searing. I would have gone to the ceiling and through the roof.

Someone, I think Gates, says, Merse, in his sleep. That must be mercy. He's asking for it. Demanding it.

But you can't demand mercy. It has to be freely given, doesn't it?

You can't demand love, I don't think.

I don't remember precisely when I began to creep and crawl. When I began to wear black and go out in the very early mornings. At nine or ten or eleven years old. At twelve, even.

So many of the places we lived, not counting the single wides, were only a few streets over from nice neighborhoods. Sometimes, all you had to do was walk a little ways down the same street, and the houses became nice. The yards had bushes and trees and flowers, and some had fences that were easy to climb.

There were garages in some back yards, there were tool sheds. Sometimes there was a sandbox, or there was a rope swing hanging from a tree. A tire, a thick length of rope.

There were bicycles, and there were cars, shiny in the night light.

Once in a while the lights would click on as I moved through a yard, and at first, I ran. Then I realized that the lights came on because of motion detectors. Nobody had seen me. Almost never.

My goal became to be invisible. To be silent, still, deadly. At first it was silent and still. Then I added deadly. I don't know why. I was eleven or twelve. I thought it sounded cool.

I didn't know. I had no idea.

I knew, though, that there was something astonishing about being out at that hour of the morning, in those neighborhoods and yards. The air was so different then. So clear and cool, even in the dead of summer. Even in July.

They might have a back deck or a screened-in porch, with lawn or patio furniture. There might be a tub with flowers on the deck or floor of the porch. The moon might be so bright that it cast shadows on the lawn. After a while, I'd creep silently onto the deck, or in the door of the porch. I might see a book, an empty glass, a pack of cigarettes and a lighter.

I was so close to these people. I was in their lives, I could almost smell them.

I took one of the cigarettes—a Newport—and I lit it. I leaned back on the chaise longue, took a drag, pulled the smoke in, blew it slowly out.

This is it, I thought. This right here.

11

She came home after seven and a half weeks. Mother came home, and the first thing she did was to find us a new place to live. Half the ground floor of a big old house that was way up the hill, near the university.

The three rooms were large, especially the kitchen. Mom said it was the original kitchen of the huge house, and she said this must have been beautiful in its time. There were blue and white tiles in a wide line, all the way around the walls, above the counters, and there was an old-fashioned sink, a double sink that was made of stone or concrete or something. The faucet leaked a little, all the time. It made plop, plop, plop sounds, in the morning, the evening, at two and even four in the morning.

I wouldn't be able to sleep, and it went plop, and I started to. like the sound, I started to need it and count on it. Without the plop and drip, the night was empty and almost completely soundless. It would have been so lonely without the drip.

I also began to like the pills, although there weren't that many of them. At the beginning I just got half a pill, or maybe one of them. Pills that were called benzos, or once in a while, pain pills. The benzos made you relaxed or a little bit sleepy, and they were all tiny pills. Yellow or white, once in a while blue. Mostly round and flat like a small aspirin. They made it so you didn't worry about everything, all the time. You could sit back or lie back and just enjoy the warm, loose feeling.

The pain pills might be round or oval, and mostly white, but they were usually fatter than benzos. A few of them—one called Dilaudid, the other hydrocodone—were real small, and one was blue, and the white one was so tiny it was easy to drop.

They made your skin prickly in this lovely way, and they made you feel happy, even if you weren't happy at all. You could lie on the couch and scratch small itches on your skin, and like the benzos, pain pills made all the worry and loneliness go away.

The worry and loneliness bounced back twice as strong, once the pill wore off, but while it lasted it was pretty close to heaven. It felt so happy, so deeply happy.

Peggy and Mabel got their pills from doctors. They both had bad backs, and trick necks, and knees and shoulders that didn't work too well. So they were nervous and in pain so often that it didn't feel worth living sometimes. People didn't understand that most of the time. They had no idea, Mabel said.

I could almost see the pain in her face, though I don't think her face hurt. But maybe it did.

They both had three or four doctors, and though most doctors never listened to their patients, they tried to find the doctors who would actually listen. They were harder to find than you'd think, Marge said.

Sometimes, too, and more and more as the years went by, they'd get bottles of pills from their boyfriends. One guy named Floyd wore a suit, and when he came in he'd toss a small white bag onto the couch, and you'd hear the pills rattle inside, in the little bottle.

Mother put her arms around Floyd's neck and kissed him on the lips.

When she came back, after her long search for love, Mom was thin and her face and hands were gray. She had lost ten or fifteen pounds, and she lost weight when she'd been drinking and doing a lot of drugs. She also looked like she hadn't seen any sunlight in months.

She said the first month with Glenn, the guy with the black beard, had been great. A honeymoon, Maggie said. Strawberries and cream.

In Buffalo or Rochester. She wasn't sure sometimes. Maybe in Albany or Syracuse.

Glenn got up real early. He got dressed in the dark, and then he went to the kitchen and made coffee, carried it to the couch in the living room, and sat there, sipping, in the dark.

He had two or three cups of coffee, all in the living room, all on the couch, then he ate an apple or orange or pear. He made a peanut butter and jelly sandwich, got another piece of fruit, and tied them in an old plastic bread bag for lunch.

Glenn said he liked sitting in the dark, in the quiet, and watching the night turn from deep blue, to a paler blue, then to gray. He liked when the birds began to sing—first far off and faint, then loud and near. They went chirp and cheep, whir, whee, and caw, caw, caw.

Glenn told Mother that he often felt as though he could sit there all day and night, sipping coffee, looking at the dark, and listening to the birds.

But he put on his big dusty boots, pulled a dirty hoodie over his head, and went out to his car and to work.

Late in the afternoon, he came home from work, tired but happy. Glenn took a shower, they watched news on television, then they went out somewhere to eat. They were home in bed by eleven, and that was so healthy, Mom said. So reasonable, so sane. They could and should have gone on like that forever.

After she'd been there for maybe a month, he started to go out in the afternoon with his work buddies. He wasn't going to meetings anymore, he was going to bars instead. He came home around dinner time, not exactly drunk, she said, but pretty happy and buzzed. He smelled of beer and whiskey.

A week later, he'd be out all night, and he said he had spent the night at Cole or Bud's house, on the couch. Even at six or seven in the morning, he still smelled of booze.

He began to miss days of work, and he'd be around the apartment almost all the time. He'd yell and slap her, trap her against the side of the refrigerator and lean all his weight against her.

He never hit her with a closed fist, but the slaps landed on her face, hands, arms, on the top of her head. He called her a slut, a whore, a prostitute, and she knew now that he not only didn't like her, but that he disliked all women, even if he didn't know them.

He said that if she tried to leave him, he'd cut her head off and feed it to pigs. He said a few miles out of town, he had a friend with a pig farm, and pigs ate everything. They didn't give a shit. They ate tin cans, and they ate human bodies.

Peggy got a friend named Willow to pick her up at three in the morning, at the corner of two streets, Ash and Twenty-First, and drive her back here.

She said that all the way home, looking at the darkness and the countryside outside the windows, she wondered if there were the bodies or bones of women, buried on the sides of hills, under trees, in the dark basements of farm houses.

She took a few pills, but her hands kept shaking, and she couldn't stop thinking about things she never wanted to think about, ever again. The dark was full of so many things.

12

Most of Mommy's friends came to the new apartment with the big rooms. Bug and Doc, Mr. Gleason and Speed and Gus and Dub. Once in a while I called them the wrong name. I called Mr. Gleason, Doc. I called Stretch, Fat. Dub, for some reason, became Bud. Then I thought for a second and Dub was Bud, reversed. Once in a while, things made sense.

By then, by the time Margaret came home from being with Glenn, I was nine, I'm pretty sure. I hadn't gone to school in months, maybe in years, but that was okay with me. The day-time apartment was probably the best of all possible times to be in the apartment. Nobody was there but me. It was empty as the sky.

I had grown tall. Not as tall as Peggy. Not yet. But she always told me I was going to be one big sucker when I grew all the way up.

Everybody, she said, will have to look up to you.

Then she laughed.

Most days, I woke up around nine or ten, and there was no noise. Just a few ticks from the refrigerator and clocks, slight groans from the wood in the frame of the house, and some muffled sounds, far away, from the street and neighborhood. About half the time, Margie had spent the night somewhere else.

I'd never know till really late that she wasn't coming home. I'd wake up at two or three or four, in the bed, and the red numbers on the clock said that it was two-forty-seven or three-nineteen, or four-fifty-one. In the summer, the sky was already turning less dark at four-fifty-one. In the winter, it was another thing.

If it was two or three in the morning, and Mommy wasn't home, I turned the radio on low, and moved up and down the dial, trolling stations. There might be a classical station in Albany, or a golden oldies station in Cleveland. The Platters, Buddy Holly, Chuck Berry, the Four Tops.

And all over the place, there was talk radio. Men and women talking about everything. Listeners calling in. Women with cigarette voices, old men who lived alone.

Some old people lived in single rooms and lived off the checks from social security. Teenage boys and girls were in ruined relationships. One girl said her boyfriend told her what to wear, and grabbed her arm so hard that his hand left bruises.

In Boston or New York City, or maybe Pittsburgh, there was a guy on every night during the week, from midnight to five in the morning. His name was Jimmy Summers, and everybody called Jimmy. Cabdrivers and cops, nurses, sex workers, drunks, people who couldn't sleep. Jimmy talked to all of them.

He had a slow voice, a low voice, a voice like dark velvet. People would tell Jimmy Summers just about anything. And I would listen to hours of the show almost every night.

The other half of the time, I wouldn't listen. Mother would be home with me, having a smoke and a drink and a pill, and she'd give me a Valium or a Vicodin, and I'd fall asleep on the couch. I'd wake up, now and then, and hear noises from the bedroom, and I'd wonder when her boyfriend, whoever it was, had come over.

I'd stay on the couch and sleep, and a few hours later I'd wake up, cold, wishing I had a blanket. Even in summer, the nights could get cold at three or four in the morning.

Dub never looked like his name. He didn't have torn jeans and shit-kicker boots and a red-and-black-checked flannel shirt. He wore tan khaki pants all the time, winter and summer, and a button-down dress shirt that was yellow or pink or blue. He wore brown loafers with tassels.

Dub was going bald on top even though he wasn't old, and he wore small wire glasses that slid down his nose.

Bug was the same, with his muscles and boots, and he was as mean as ever. Doc was no older than Dub, and he had short dark hair, and glasses with dark frames. Doc smiled almost all the time, and he always took a few minutes to sit next to me, and ask how I was, and say that my mom was a good woman, that she was doing the best she could for me.

Around that time, I think when I was about nine, I began to go out very late at night. It was so much easier to get out from the first-floor apartment. I didn't have to walk down stairs, and through hallways, past the doorways of other people.

I could step out the front or back door, stand in a small hallway for a half minute, then open the outside door.

And always, every time, there was the beautiful, dark, night-time air.

There was a weak light bulb on over the front door, but when you went ten or fifteen feet, you were out of the pale yellow light, and in the shadows and darkness on the front lawn. At first, the dark was a little scary because you didn't know what it was, or what was in the dark. Then in a minute or two, and away from the light, you could see in the dark, you became a part of it, and it became a part of you.

You were almost invisible. Nobody who wasn't in the dark could see you.

The first few times were in September, and all the students at the university were back for classes. The campus was real big, and went for a mile or two, in each direction, at the top of the hill. There were gorges and waterfalls on both sides of the campus, and every few years a student jumped into a gorge and died.

Everybody would say how sad that was—that if only the student had waited an hour or two or three, had talked to someone, had waited a few days, then things wouldn't have seemed so hopeless and bleak. The dead person would not have died so young.

And it always happened, it seemed, late at night or early in the morning. In the dark, and with the burble of creek water far below.

Our house was on a street of big houses that must once have been beautiful. They had porches that went all the way around the front of the houses. They had gables and turrets, and some had carriage houses in the backyards. That's how old they were. Now the big houses were rundown. They needed paint, or they were missing a few spindles in the railings, and there were five or six or seven mailboxes next to the front door. Some had sagging couches or easy chairs on the porch. But as you moved down the street, away from the university, the houses became nicer. There were more trees and front and back yards. There were flowers, and shiny cars in driveways. You could tell that the owners lived in the houses. They had porch swings and Adirondack chairs. There were kids' toys on the front lawn and walk. A big-wheel tricycle, a hula hoop, chalk drawings on the concrete of the walkway.

This was exciting, to see the houses of normal people, regular families that owned houses and shiny cars, where things were not falling apart. This was so different from anything I'd known.

At first, in those early days, I was so stupid that I didn't even wear dark clothes. I might have on a white T-shirt, tan shorts that showed off my skinny chicken legs, and white sneakers. I wouldn't learn about wearing black until later.

As I think I said, these first few times, when I was nine or ten, were in September, when the students were back. It was still summer, the end of summer, but it was also the fall. It got quite cool in the late hours, at two or three in the morning.

There were streetlights every few hundred feet, and cars reflecting the light on the sides of streets. Then I was near the nicer houses, the houses with families, and I went down the driveway of a house where there were no lights in the windows.

There was a beautiful little garden in back. There were trimmed bushes all along the fence that lined the yard. There were woodchips in the beds of the gardens.

I went to the middle of the yard, and looked up at the clear dark sky. I could see Venus, the brightest thing in the sky, not counting the moon. I lay down in the grass, and it was all there, up above.

Then a light in a small window on the second floor flicked on. A bathroom, I thought.

This was two or three in the morning, I was pretty sure. I was nine years old, maybe ten at most.

I was so close to other people. I was so near the center of life.

13

Bevan Ray Eliot sits down across from me in the chow hall. Bevan Ray doesn't nod, look at me, or say a word. Bevan almost never does. Not with anyone. No nod, no look, no word.

Then Gates, who's old and lives next to me, he shuffles this way and sits down two seats over on my side of the table.

Jesus, I think. What a crew. What a collection of charmers. The Men's Club.

I nod at Gates, and say, Bevan, to Bevan.

Gates nods back at me, and Bevan, of course, says and does nothing.

We've all been here at least twenty years, and Bevan and Gates will be here till they die. We all wear glasses too. Thick glasses with black plastic frames. State issue. No style points.

Bevan Ray Eliot is kind of famous all over this place. Everybody knows his name, knows who he is, knows something of what he's done. Not that he's told anyone anything. But you hear things, from the guards, the staff, from other inmates.

A few inmates work in administrative offices out front, and they use computers. They go online and read about other guys in here. They read about Bevan.

That's all we have to do in here, or almost all. Gossip, hustle, tell stories.

Bevan's average height, and he's pretty lean. But he's strong lean, like a farmer. Ropy muscles in his neck and arms and hands, slabs of muscle going from his neck to his shoulders, and bowed legs.

And a hatchet face. Big narrow nose, lean lips, small dark eyes set deep in his skull, looking out from behind thick glasses.

He's also completely bald on top, shiny, cue-ball bald, but he has long wiry white hair on the sides and back of his head, and he keeps that real long, as though he's making up for the baldness on top.

Bevan's in his fifties, middle to late fifties, and unlike most guys who first come in in their twenties, Bevan got here in his mid-thirties.

He liked, and probably still likes, boys. Nothing so wrong with that, as things go, as long as you do nothing about your likes. But he picked boys up hitchhiking, hanging out on corners, on bicycles and on the sidewalks near parks. He'd offer them rides, drugs, booze, girls.

He was a charmer, the stories go, though that's hard to believe. But people say he could talk his way around or through pretty much anything.

This was all near Rochester, in upstate New York, though a few times he branched out to several suburbs of Buffalo. He'd get the boys in his car. He'd drive them to a remote location.

The lunch today is baloney on white bread, applesauce, a few carrot sticks, and a cookie that looks like a lump of dough. And red or purple bug juice. Bevan eats carefully. Small neat bites, and discrete spoonfuls of applesauce. Then sips of bug juice, like he's drinking tea.

The bug juice stains his lips red.

Gates and I eat in gulps, like most of the guys in here. We're seagulls. We almost make seagull sounds. Sometimes you hear soft grunts from a few guys when they eat. Like they're having sex with their food. It's kind of disgusting. It's something you don't want to hear when you're trying to eat.

Bevan Ray Eliot grew up on a farm west of Rochester. He was one of nine children, second to youngest. His mother and father both drank, and they both slapped and punched the kids. His mother sometimes used a belt or stick, his father used his hands and fists.

His father left when Bevan was ten or eleven. Then things got worse.

The drunk mother tried to take care of nine kids. Or maybe

there were fewer kids. Some of them got older and left. One went to prison for selling crack and for armed robbery. A few of the older sisters were pretty nice to the younger kids. They tried to find food for them. They helped the bunch of them move from apartment to apartment, from house to shabby house.

There were gunshots in the night. There were screams at all hours. Teenagers in hoodies moved through the streets in small bands. Platoons and squads of feral kids. Kids with knives and guns and box cutters. Kids with pieces of chain they'd wrap around their fists.

Bevan Ray Eliot lived through this. His mother's hair grew long and gray and wild. Her eyes were dark stones. Her teeth were falling out. She always had a cigarette in the side of her mouth, the smoke gathering around her head.

She sucked at a can of beer the way a baby sucked a breast. She yelled at the kids, because it became harder and harder to get out of her chair to hit them. She was smaller and unsteady, they were getting bigger and faster by the day.

All those kids. Unwashed, smelly kids. Kids with stringy, greasy hair.

Alex, who was fourth in line, had two broken teeth in front. Alex was a jack-o'-lantern. Marcie, who was fifth in line, called him Jack, and Tiffany, who was third from the bottom, called him, Teeth.

Sometimes Alex got mad and punched Marcie and Tiffany, but mostly he ignored them. He sneaked sips from Mom's cans and bottles, and stole her nerve and pain pills.

Bevan Ray finishes his two sandwiches, his applesauce and cookie and bug juice. I push my cookie across the table to him.

So fast that I hardly see it, Bevan grabs the cookie, shoves it in his mouth, then slows down to chew. Three, four, five times. Then swallows.

He still doesn't look at me.

He touches his lips with a tiny napkin, then stands up, leaves his tray and cup and plastic spoon on the table, and walks away. Guys at other tables, dozens and dozens of guys, look at him as though he's a zebra walking past.

I want to say, Bevan, get the fuck back here and bus your table.

But I don't. I'd be fighting five times a day if I did. Guys here do this shit all the time.

All of us can be real assholes. That's why we're here.

So Bevan got older and bigger and he had a room somewhere. A room with a bathroom down the hall. A toilet he probably never flushed.

He delivered packages from a van, and he had his own car, an old blue Volvo that had two-hundred-thousand miles on it. At night he drove around, sipping from a bottle or can, never going much above twenty miles per hour in the city.

He watched, and he could see through the dark like a cat. He watched the sidewalks, the front of video arcades, the malls. He saw teenagers along the sides of roads and streets, and in the suburbs, he saw small groups of teenagers in skinny jeans, in hoodies, in sneakers or high black boots. He stopped at the bus station near downtown. He parked and watched, and it was amazing how many teenagers came through, or loitered. Some of them weren't even teenagers yet. At least it looked that way. They might be ten or twelve.

He had plastic flex cuffs, a hunting knife, a small steel pry bar. He looked through the darkness, the street in rain and snow and spilled neon light.

14

Maybe I was eleven by then. I think I was eleven. We were still living in the first-floor place with the big rooms, and for a little while I went to middle school, for sixth grade, and the school was four or five times bigger than Fall Creek Elementary, where I had gone, briefly, before.

Mother still had quite a few boyfriends, and she still drank and took pills. Sometimes she gave me a pill or two, and sometimes she'd say that pills were bad for me, and for a week or a month she wouldn't give me any.

But she was out of the house, for hours, or now and then, for days. I'd look through her closet and her dresser, and the brown plastic bottles with the white caps were always in the small top drawer on the right. Five or ten bottles and they were mixed in with her underwear. All that silky stuff that made me nervous.

She also kept cash money in the drawer, in back. There were small bunches of twenties, rolled up like thick tubes and held with elastic bands.

I never took money, but I did help myself to pills. All of the brown bottles had labels with Maggie's name and the name of the drug, and once in a while, the name of the boyfriend who got the pills for her. Just looking at the bottles, picking each one up, hearing the small clicks of the pills inside, made me feel happy and calm and excited, at the same time.

There was clonazepam, hydrocodone, oxycodone. There was diazepam, lorazepam, codeine #3, alprazolam, zolpidem. There was Dilaudid and Norco. They were called opioids, or benzos. Almost all of them. The labels said they were for pain, for anxiety, for insomnia.

Anxiety was worry, only worse. Insomnia was not sleeping.

Pain was hurt, was suffering, was something that ached or stabbed or throbbed, or took over everything.

Almost nobody liked pain. And everybody, sooner or later, felt pain. Even being lonely was a kind of pain.

Around then, somewhere in there—and I knew because we were living in the big rooms—Mom went out on a Saturday night, wearing her cowboy boots and a thin black and red scarf, loose around her neck. She wore a worn jean jacket, and she looked beautiful.

Her hair was short then, cut like a helmet around her head. It was like a boy's haircut, though nobody would ever mistake Marge for a boy.

When she kissed me goodbye, I could smell shampoo and perfume. Vanilla, lavender, lemon, strawberry, lilac. Mom always smelled wonderful around then.

That was early April, and for the first time in many months it had been warm outside, maybe even seventy. Mommy opened windows, and the air was like no air we'd smelled in many months. It felt like being on a mountain in the summer, at least the way a mountain should smell in summer. It was sky and brown earth, and maybe a stream too. Flowers and fruit.

The air made Peg happy. I could tell. She even hummed a little. In the middle of the afternoon, she made me eggs and toast, then she made some for herself.

She talked on her phone a bunch of times, and she sat with me on the couch for a while, and we watched television. A black-and-white movie with cowboys and horses.

She told me she'd be going out later, and that she might not be back until the next day.

Then, of course, she did go out, wearing her black and red scarf.

I was by myself, but I'd almost always been that way.

There were brown bottles of beer in the fridge, and I knew there'd be the pills in their own brown bottles. A lighter brown than the beer, but still good.

I had a whole bunch of time. When Maggie said she'd be

late, that really meant that she'd be gone until at least noon the next day. And if she said she'd be gone overnight that would probably mean she'd be gone at least for a day, but more likely for a few days.

She didn't see or call Mabel so much anymore, at least that I could tell. They used to talk on the phone every day. Mabel was always visiting us, or we were at her trailer. But now it seemed to be different, like so many other people who came in and out of our lives.

They were your best friends, and then they were someone you passed on the street, going the other way. And you didn't smile, you didn't nod, you didn't even look at them. They were a parking meter, a telephone pole, a street sign.

The three big rooms of the apartment were quiet, but it was late afternoon, very early evening, and this was April, I'm pretty sure. There was all this sunlight pouring in, and sometimes, in the living room especially, the light sifted in from behind a really big tree, and it made pretty patterns on the walls and floor. Leaves and thick branches. The branches never moved, but the leaves hardly ever stopped moving. They trembled and seemed to spin and dance, then they were still for about two seconds. Then it started again, and there didn't seem to be wind out there, but I guess there was always air, and air always moved, I thought, even if just slightly.

I mean, didn't the whole earth move? Wasn't everything in motion, even if we couldn't see it?

The light kept seeping in, and it was almost liquid. It showed the worn arms of the easy chair, and the dark tops of the arms, where people left sweat and dead skin and grease from their bodies.

I sat on the couch a while, and so slowly that I never noticed moment to moment, the sun was less bright, and the room was a tiny bit darker.

The beer was very cold, so cold it almost hurt my teeth. It tasted a little sour, but it grew warm in my stomach. I sipped slowly, because I didn't want to get sick or fall asleep. I knew already about trying to control things. Don't drink fast, don't take too many pills.

About halfway through the first bottle, I got up and went to the big bedroom. There were clothes and shoes on the floor. There were bunched up sheets and blankets and pillows on the bed.

I stepped around and over and on the clothes, and could feel even a half beer in my blood. Slightly relaxed, and not so scared, not so nervous.

I took out two pill bottles, and read the labels in the light from the window. Diazepam, oxycodone.

For pain, for anxiety.

I took the white caps off, and tapped one of each into my palm. Then I put the bottles back where they belonged.

Swallowed them with beer, sat on the couch.

I watched the light some more, and the leaves were way less clear. They didn't seem to move much, and then I started to hear cars and people on the street. A voice, then two, a bicycle, three or four cars.

Everything tingled, and there was so much warmth in my body. I loved everybody and every thing in the world. All the people I didn't know, all the places and things I had never seen.

Maybe I fell asleep. I think I fell asleep.

And there was a dream. I'm almost certain it was a dream.

Margaret came in, and I was lying on the couch.

Peg had been crying. Her makeup was smeared and her face was distorted somehow.

Her left eye was swollen, and was turning dark colors.

I couldn't tell for sure because the light from the sun was finished for the night.

Peggy sat down on the edge of the couch, and she pressed her wet face against mine.

This had to have been a dream. Because right then, at that exact moment, I felt so happy that right there, on that couch, I would have been happy to die.

15

By then I was more and more tall. I had to have been twelve years old, at least, and I was as tall as Peg. A little taller, even. But skinny as string. I was legs and arms and neck. I was wide shoulders like a hanger, but with no meat on them.

Big powerful hands, the only strong thing about me.

School was sixth grade at the middle school called Boynton. I hadn't been to school, hardly at all, for a few years. Maybe for three or four years. But I knew how to read and write, and I could add, subtract, multiply, and divide. I knew a very little about planets, especially Mercury, Venus, Mars, and Earth.

Saturn had the giant rings, Mercury was very hot, you could see Venus up there in the night sky, and Mars was the red planet. Earth was us, it was our planet. It had people and oceans, it had mountains and rivers, and ice at the North and South Poles. The ice was melting because the earth was getting warmer and warmer, and there were floods along the coasts, where land met ocean.

Everything out there was immense. From one star to another, one solar system to the one behind it. When you looked up at night and saw a star, you might be seeing something that was many millions of miles away. They measured it in light years, which was the distance it took light to travel in a year. And light travelled faster than anything.

So when you saw a star, you were seeing light that had been emitted years and years ago. Something like that. When I was out late at night, and saw the sky, saw Venus and stars, saw the moon, I always felt almost dizzy, like I had to lie on my back on the grass in someone's yard and breathe slow and deep for a while.

Sometimes I almost liked school, liked how many things

there were, and how much there was to learn. I didn't love the kids, although the teachers were mostly nice. The kids were loud. They shouted and sang, they called each other names. They shoved and pushed and slapped each other, they grabbed one another's hands and arms. Some boys grabbed other boys in a headlock, held it a few seconds and let go.

Kids had so many names, names I'd never even imagined. Amber, Tiffany, Brandi, Bonnie, Leigh, Murphy, Luka, Delaney, Eamon, Belle.

There were no Marks or Johns, Nancys or Ruths anymore. I mean, a few, but not many.

The halls were crazy when classes changed, and all the kids moved at the same time from one classroom to another, from one teacher to another. English to math to biology to chemistry, to computers to social science to history. That was real different from elementary school, where you stayed with the same room and teacher pretty much the whole time.

Twice a week there was music and physical education.

Lots of kids got bullied. Kids would call other kids names. Asshole, faggot, slut, whore, dickweed, pizza face, retard.

In the first week some kid with no neck, named Butchie, called me pencil neck in the hall, between biology and computers. I went over, put my hand on his shoulder in front, near the neck, and pushed hard with my thumb, just below the collar bone. He squirmed, breathed hard, wriggled away, and stood there. This was all real quick, and nobody bothered me after that.

I was very tall, one of the tallest kids in my grade, and I had no friends. I was also wicked thin. But I was also strong, I think, much stronger than I looked. Especially the hands.

When he called me pencil neck, I could have called him a name. No neck, or cock sucker, or shit for brains.

But I didn't think, really. I just went over and grabbed him. He put his hands to his shoulder, and looked like he might cry. But he didn't cry. He just stood there, and I moved along.

Sometimes there were girls in a class, a girl here, a girl there, and I didn't know why, really, but I almost couldn't stop looking at them. I'd be looking slowly across the room, at the different people, and some girl, sitting and maybe staring at her desk, at her fingers, looking around the room herself, would arrest my attention, when I didn't even realize what I was doing. Something about their beautiful shiny hair, about the ribbon or clamp or elastic thing tying the hair back or holding it to the side, just grabbed me.

It didn't matter if the hair was black or blond, brown or red, long, short, curly, wavy, straight—but something about it made me stop. Once in a while they must have felt my eyes on them, the way you can feel a stare. They might turn and catch me looking, which was always embarrassing. They might make a face. Creep, they might say to themselves. Weirdo. Spaz.

One girl named Elissa, a short, slight girl with dark frizzy hair, with red ties on the sides of her head—she smiled at me, and that made me warm inside, all over, like a pain pill.

I didn't want to move, didn't want to break the spell, for what felt like a long time. Even when class ended, I stayed in my seat and watched her stand, gather her things, and join the throng at the door.

I don't think that she was beautiful. I don't know. Maybe she was. I don't know if any of the girls I looked at were beautiful. They could have been. But they could have been plain or home-ly, or simply weird like me.

Almost every kid had friends, or people they hung out with, even if they really didn't like each other. At least they weren't alone. That was the worst thing to be. Especially in the cafeteria, this big open space with a wall of windows, where everybody could see everyone else. Where I sat alone at an almost emp-ty table, until two dweebs, both wearing glasses and cardigan, grandfather sweaters, sat down opposite each other at the far end of the table, and began talking, about computers, I think.

Almost all the other tables had nearly a dozen kids, talking over each other, laughing loud, grabbing each other—a hand, an arm, a shoulder—smiling and talking more. They had each other, this pack, and they were basically safe.

The whole middle school, it seems, had sharp edges everywhere. It was so easy to get cut, in almost any way you could imagine. Practically every kid in the school was bleeding, in one way or another.

There were times I wished I wasn't so tall, because I stuck out so high above the packs. I wished I had never hurt Butchie, because most of the school heard about it, and it made me both weird and a little scary. Like I had a disease, a virus, and people had better stay back, stay away, or they might catch what I had.

They'd have to sit in the cafeteria by themselves.

Sometime around the middle of November, Peggy said that I should stay home from school for a while. She wasn't feeling so hot. She coughed all the time, and had a slight fever, and told her boyfriends not to come over.

She didn't know what it was, but she had something. I told her that I wanted to go to school, and she said that for a while, I couldn't. I needed to be at home, with her, to do a little cooking and cleaning.

When she went to take a shower, or when she was deeply asleep, I'd check her pill supply, and she had enough to last a month or two. I'd take one each from three or four bottles.

Then I'd swallow an oxy, an Ativan, and I'd stay on the couch a long time, while Mother was back in bed, sleeping some more.

Sooner or later, I'd picture the girls in classes with the beautiful hair. The wisps of hair at the back of their necks, soft, transparent, luminous. I'd picture their heads, tilting forward, looking at the teacher. Long necks, shoulders, ears, earrings that looked gold and silver. Sometimes they'd reach up with their long fingers and touch an earring, touch some strands of hair.

They had no idea I was thinking of them. Here on the couch, the drugs moving through everywhere.

16

In here, the guys call their cells, My house.

On D-block, because most of us don't have to share a cell, and we don't get moved around so much, we accumulate more stuff than guys on the other blocks. Most of us have a small television. We all have at least a shelf of books, sometimes two shelves.

We have a toothbrush and toothpaste, soap and shampoo, deodorant, shaving cream. We don't have razors, of course.

One guy on the block is very old, almost eighty, and has long, thick white hair and an enormous beard. His name is Ryan, Thomas Ryan, but all the guys call him Moses. He looks like Moses, or at least the way Moses would or should have looked, all that time ago, in the Bible.

Moses is all stooped over now, and he's lost muscle to the years. But even in his day, he couldn't have been a large man. Five seven or eight, a hundred and fifty pounds shower wet. Big Roman nose, piercing eyes, full lips. And the dark eyes, which have to be black or brown, peering out from behind all that white hair.

Moses looks Biblical, looks like an Old Testament prophet, looks like someone who would bring the Ten Commandments down from a mountain. But instead, he's been in here since 1976. He'll die in here.

He killed his mother and father, in their home. He stabbed both of them, over and over and over, while they slept. They were in their sixties, at least, and Moses, Thomas Ryan, had lived his entire life at their house.

This was near Albany, I believe.

Now he's in the DOC, the Department of Corrections, forever. He's been at this facility for at least twenty-five or thirty years. Moses has been here for all the time that I've been here.

In all these years, he and I have exchanged maybe twenty or twenty-five words. One word a year. I don't know anyone who's talked with him more than me.

Jesus, that's sad. That's what I think when I think of him. Thirty some years at his parents' house, the only place he ever lived, and then the rest of the time he's inside. He's in here.

A lot of the time I try not to think of these things. I try not to imagine how he continues to take a breath, then another, and another. I hate to imagine how he gets out of his bunk in the morning.

Does he think of dying in here? Does he think of the night when he wasn't sleeping? When he went downstairs at his parents' house, moonlight streaming in the windows? The hum of a refrigerator, the red glowing numbers of the clock on the top of the stove?

How his whole body trembled and shook? How he felt, at the same time, very hot and very cold? How his brain was frozen and still, and raced so fast he couldn't keep up, all at the same time?

Then the kitchen counter, deep blue, and edged with unpainted oak, I imagine. Canisters of tea, flour, coffee, a wood breadbox, and the wood block to hold knives. How he slid one knife with a seven-inch blade out of its slot, and how the silver blade did not gleam in the dark and moonlit room. It did not glitter or shine.

The blade was just a blade of a knife. It cut cucumbers, celery, tomatoes, apples, potatoes, onions.

The parents of Thomas Ryan slept upstairs in their bed. There were slivers of moonlight falling in from the edges of the curtains. Deep, slow breaths. Darkness.

His father was sixty-nine, and mostly bald on top. There was a band of white hair on the back and sides of his head, and Moses' father, Thomas Ryan's dad, grew this band of hair long, almost like a scarf.

His mother had more hair, though it was cut short, and it

was colored blond-gray. She was sixty-five years old, and she went to the hair salon every five or six weeks.

Both of Ryan's parents were thin, and for an older couple, they were in good physical shape. They hiked together at least every other day, wearing sweatpants and sneakers, wool sweaters, light jackets, hats and gloves. They both wore glasses. They were a familiar sight in the town where they lived in upstate New York, near Rochester.

A small lean couple, moving briskly along. Sometimes even holding hands for a block or two.

Many of the people in the town somehow knew about the couple's son. Knew about Thomas Ryan, who had not yet become Moses. Knew that he was well past thirty years old. Knew that he still lived with his parents, and that he delivered food for local restaurants. Chinese, Indian, pizza, sandwiches from a deli.

People seemed to know that he had very briefly gone to State University of New York at Buffalo, but had been sent home by the administration two months after he arrived. At the time, nobody in town, not counting his parents, had any idea why Tom had been sent home.

Later, there were rumors that on several occasions at least, he had somehow snuck in the dorm rooms of girls and stole their panties. And one time, he had gotten into two girls' rooms and hidden in their closet.

The police, people learned, had never been involved, so it couldn't be that serious. At least they thought it couldn't be.

Nat Kunitz taught high school mathematics, had twice had Tom Ryan as a student, and he said you couldn't find a nicer kid anywhere. A small compact kid. Handsome, bright, polite, considerate. Didn't seem to have many friends, but the other students seemed to like what they saw in him, if they saw him at all.

Tom was a basic, regular kid as far as Nat knew. Though Nat would add that he had no clue whatsoever about where Tom went after high school. Those are tricky years, Nat said.

Late teens, twenties, even into the early thirties. A lot of things could, and sometimes did, go wrong. Alcohol and drugs, mental health issues. Depression, bipolar, even schizophrenia, God help us.

So many things could mess up a person's life, especially if you were twenty-one or twenty-eight or thirty-four.

At night, everyone saw Tom Ryan's rusting blue Civic, with decals in the back windows, move around town. Going as slow as a prowl car, looking for streets and addresses, looking for lit porch lights. The Civic was a dark, almost midnight blue.

A few people said, though they weren't exactly sure, that the car occasionally moved without its headlights on. And this, on very dark fall or spring nights.

In his parents' house, Tom moved slowly and very quietly. Through the downstairs, and then carefully up the stairs. In moonlight, trying to not let the stairs creak.

He thought it was one or two or three, at least. His mother was a light and jangled sleeper, his father slept as deep and heavy as stones.

The hallway on the second floor was awash in moonlight. Outside, the moon had to be at least two-thirds full.

Tom had been in this house for such a long time. Pretty much his whole life. He had, he really had—to do something.

He went even more slowly down the hall. This would change everything. A few minutes and the world would be different.

He paused outside their door, which was open maybe ten inches. He could hear slow, deep breaths, the breaths of deep sleep.

He stood there for what seemed a long time. He stood for what felt like forever.

17

Pretty close to thirteen years old. I was. Or maybe a little bit past thirteen. A teenager. An early teenager. The land between child and grown-up. We had been in the big-room apartment for a long time by then. We liked it up there, on the hill near the university. Three big rooms. Kitchen, living room, bedroom. Big trees outside, in the back and side yards, and the street just twenty or thirty feet away from the front windows.

Students all over the place. Couches on front porches, bicycles chained to the railings. Then just a few feet over, regular citizens in big beautiful houses. People on the faculty, and doctors and lawyers. Indian chiefs, though in our city they would be Native American Chiefs. A person in a wheelchair was differently abled. Every word, every phrase, could be a bomb.

Watch out, Marge said.

For a long time, for months or even a year or two, we hadn't seen much, or any, of Mabel. I don't know why. Something had happened. Words were said.

And I, for my own part—I missed Mabel a lot. Mabel was so nice. She was generous and funny. She was the closest thing we had to a friend. Not counting the boyfriends, but they really didn't count as friends. They were business associates, Peg used to say.

You give something, you get something.

That was straightforward. That was clean and uncomplicated. Unlike most of life, which was nearly always messy. Full of roots and strands of spider web, making it hard to move most of the time. Catching and snagging—your feet, your arms, your head and hands.

Then, there she was. There was Mabel on the front porch, and Margaret wasn't in the least surprised. As though we had seen Mabel two days ago, and not two years ago. As though no time had passed.

She came in to the big living room, and you could see Mabel looking around, checking out our apartment.

Very nice, she said. Way better than that third-floor place.

And that's how long it had been. Last time we saw Mabel, we had been living on the third floor of the big house, and all the ceilings were slanted. Now the rooms were sort of huge, and there were no slants.

Mother and Mabel gave each other a big hug in the middle of the front room. They held each other a long time. They thumped each other on the back, and they both cried a little, I'm pretty sure.

Then Mabel saw me, and Oh boy. Oh my, she said.

This isn't, she said. Not possible.

Probably I blushed. I kept feeling her eyes on me.

Mabel had new lines on the sides of her eyes. She wore a jean jacket and maroon scarf. She wore black boots and tan pants. She wore glasses, which she used to only wear when she was watching television.

She was a little bit older than she used to be, and she looked a little bit tired.

Mom might have said, The bloom is off the lily.

Mabel kept looking at me, and she said, Ollie? Is that really you?

I smiled and smiled more. I didn't know what to say.

Ollie? she said again. Are you? Really?

I finally nodded, and we hugged, Mabel and me.

She was solid, and she smelled like oranges and lemons, and she was crying.

Mom said, A drink? And Mabel nodded.

I was way taller than her. It felt like I was a head taller than Mabel, if that was possible.

So much time had passed. A huge amount of time had gone by. But there we were. Not the same as before, but pretty close.

Mommy came back from the kitchen with two tall glasses

full of ice and clear liquid, with a slice of green lime floating at the top of the glass, above the ice.

Mabel said, Oh yes, took a glass, and after one sip, she said, You didn't spare the gin.

Never, Peggy said.

Mabel smiled, and I noticed that her teeth were much whiter than Margie's teeth. It seemed, too, that Mabel had gained a few pounds on her thighs and ass. The flesh under Peggy's upper arms was getting loose, a flap. A sag.

They both lit cigarettes, a Newport and a Marlboro. I asked if I could have one, and Mabel slid the pack of Newports across the little table to me. I took one, torched it, and sucked in and blew out.

Can I have a sip? I said, and looked from Margaret to Mabel, back and forth, back and forth. They both looked at me, looked at each other, looked back at me again.

I handled my smoke like a veteran. Sucked in and blew out.

Finally, Mommy said, Sure, and Mabel slid her glass on the table. I sipped, smoked, sipped a second and third time.

I felt relaxed and happy almost at once. Slow and sliding, moving toward painless.

I watched Mabel as she and Mother talked. Mabel was definitely a little heavier, and she looked a little tired and sad. I don't know how I saw that in her, but I did. Maybe in her eyes and mouth. Tiny lines, something in the cast and color of her eyes.

She still lived in the trailer, and she still saw Mel, the trailer park owner, once in a while. She didn't see either Keith or Kevin anymore. Keith had moved to Indiana or Illinois, and was working at something out there. She wasn't sure about the work, and she wasn't sure about the state, just that it began with an I.

We finished the first two drinks, and Peg moved to the kitchen to make more. Mabel went to the powder room, as she called it, and I got up, went to the front windows, looked out. There was the usual stuff—street and sidewalk, parked cars, a few people walking, trees, bushes, scraggly lawns. Other houses, almost all of them big and broken up into smaller apartments. A young woman went by on a bicycle, a big orange cat with white stripes sat on the front stairs, two houses down. I turned and went to the bedroom. Mom was still in the kitchen, and Mabel was in the bathroom. I closed the door as if I was changing clothes, and then I went to Mommy's drawer. I tapped one pill each from two bottles. An Ambien for sleep, and a Dilaudid for pain. Both, As Needed.

I had learned to swallow a pill without any liquid, and I took the Dilaudid first, and put the Ambien in the watch pocket of my jeans.

Then we were settling down again, the three of us, with three glasses on the small table now. Margaret asked about Kevin, and something tiny seemed to happen to Mabel's face.

Mabel said that she thought things were pretty okay with her and Kevin. She knew that Kevin sometimes saw some girl, some twenty-one-year-old, who was a waitress somewhere in town. But, you know, men were like that. They went where their dicks led them.

Then Mabel was in Syracuse, at Upstate Medical Center, for fuck's sake, with her mother, Lillian. Lillian had stage four breast cancer, and this was it, this was the end, they were pretty sure. The cancer was in the lungs, lymph system, bones, and brain.

I mean, Christ, Mabel said. This was the full shit show.

So she's in the room with her mother, on the seventh floor at Upstate, and they've got her mother on a pain cocktail so strong that her mother's in way less pain than Mabel.

Right then I began to notice the Dilaudid in my lungs and bones and brain. Dilaudid and gin. Jesus.

And in the room, Mabel said, her phone pinged, and there was a text from Kevin.

He was gonna marry the kid, the twenty-one-year-old. Kevin was gone.

18

If I went to school, I would have been in seventh grade by then. Over at Boynton, the middle school at the south end of the big lake. All those kids. Way bigger than grammar school. Right near the high school, which was a few sports fields away from Boynton.

Baseball, football, lacrosse, and soccer fields. Chain-link fences here and there. A dark red track around the football field. And up on a high hill, above the track, a cemetery to the south and east.

In the other direction, across a highway, was Lake Cayuga. Bigger than God, almost, as gray and chilly as the tundra most days. Except for July and August, when the lake water got warm enough to swim in. When you'd see power boats and sailboats. Moving fast or slow.

The lake was almost forty miles long, and at one point, almost halfway up, the lake was three and a half miles wide. At its deepest point it was four hundred and thirty-five feet deep. People drowned there. Maybe bad guys dumped bodies there.

Who knew.

Mother said there was always more to things than you thought. Every person and every thing held secrets. You just had no clue at all, she said.

In school, at Boynton, they taught us a little about Cayuga Lake. How long, how deep, how wide. And that it had a surface area of sixty-six square miles. Only once in recent history, according to legend, had the lake completely frozen over, in 1912.

Once in a great while, every two or three years, Peggy and I would drive over to Stewart Park, which faced the lake, and we'd park the car. We looked out at the water, through the willow trees, and we looked at the hills that cradled the lake. You could see the water for six or seven or eight miles, and then the lake jogged left, and you couldn't see it any more.

It kept going, for miles and miles, and you couldn't see it even though you knew it was there. It was a huge stage, but there were curtains blocking most of the view.

The lake didn't have waves as the ocean did. I'd seen pictures of oceans and beaches. I'd seen pictures of people surfing.

But looking out at miles of water, there at the south end of Cayuga Lake, and knowing the lake went for almost forty miles, and was hundreds of feet deep, made you feel small in a nice way. It was all so much bigger than you—the water, the hills, the trees and rocks, the roads snaking around and over the hills, that you stopped worrying about being erased or melting away like mist or vapor, into the pale air.

You didn't have to do anything. Just look and think.

Marge and I sat in the front seat, and when I looked over at her, I could see, and not for the first time, that she was no longer a girl or even a young woman. Her hair didn't shine, and the skin of her face was less tight. There were tiny lines at the outside edges of her eyes, and her teeth were a little dingy.

I'm pretty sure she was thirty, then. She had just turned fifteen or sixteen when I was born. I'm almost positive of that. And I believe I was thirteen that day, the day we went to the park by the lake.

I looked out at the water, and I heard Mag fumbling in her purse. She lit a cigarette, cracked her window an inch. Then she sipped from her travel mug, which was silver and had a black top. She didn't have coffee or tea in the mug, but gin or vodka, and tonic and ice. You could hear ice clink against the sides of the mug.

She passed the cig to me, and I took a deep drag. Then I put my hand out, and she passed the mug to me. She lit a second cig, and I sipped.

It was vodka, which I didn't like as much as gin. But she had put a slice of lime in there, and it was cold and good.

That was strange, because even though it was at least the

middle of April, it had been cold and overcast for a week or more. There were even stray snowflakes falling. She started to talk, holding her smoke in one hand, her silver coffee cup in the other. She asked if I remembered sleeping in the car overnight, and I said that I thought I did.

That was a long time ago, I said. Wasn't it? I was a baby then.

If you were a baby, you wouldn't remember it, Mommy said.

She took a deep, deep pull on her cigarette, all the way down to the lowest part of her lungs, and held the smoke for what seemed like a minute. It couldn't have been that long, but I wondered how she could breathe.

Finally she blew it out in a cloudy stream. I reached over, took the cup, and sipped. It was at least half full. Maybe it was half empty. The lime, the vodka, a splash of tonic water. All of it was good. Already, I could feel the warmth.

If only, I thought. If only.

I was not the person I was.

I lived in another country.

I had a father.

I was rich.

I had friends.

I had two parents who were regular. Who were normal.

There were two times, she said. The first time was in January. Middle of January or something.

She held the silver cup in both hands, and pressed it to her chest. Her cig was burning in the little glass ashtray on the console. I picked it up and took a long drag, then I blew the smoke at the windshield and watched it crash and swirl, gray streams of smoke.

I think you were four or five, and it was January. Right in the heart of winter, she said. Before you had ever gone to school, I'm pretty sure. Not that you've ever gone to school much.

I fished a cig out of the pack in her purse, lit it with a small pink lighter, watched the lake. Still big, still gray. Hills on both sides. Tons of trees. A few houses here and there.

There was a guy, she said. One of her boyfriends.

A john, Mother said. Let's face it. Let's get real.

Roger, she said. A skinny, scrawny little dick. Worked at a huge supermarket, stocking shelves. Always talked about "my store" and "my team," as though he owned it, as though he ran the place.

Roger Placo, I think his name was. Placo, Plado, Prado. Something like that.

Prado seemed nice enough at first. Always brought me presents. Cartons of cigarettes. A bottle, some Vikes or Percs.

Brought me a leather jacket at one point. Nice jacket. Black, soft like butter or cream. Really nice jacket.

But almost all of them did something like that, just not as often and not so much. No leather jackets at least.

Once a week, maybe, she said. Maybe twice a week, a few times.

Then he'd start calling, one night a week, then twice, then more. Then he'd call during the day, and a few times he'd call in the middle of the night. Three or four in the morning. You'd think someone had had a heart attack or died, for God's sake. I mean, What the fuck?

He'd tell me he loved me, but a lot of them did that. You paid attention to them, you were nice to them, and they were grateful. They thought you loved them, and that they loved you.

Then he wanted to know what I was doing, who I was seeing, what I was wearing. He hoped I didn't wear that black top with anyone but him.

Then he was showing up, all hours, but never when other johns were there.

Then he hit me. First a slap. A hard slap. Then a few days later, he punched me.

He said he'd kill me, and he asked why I made him do these things. Why I made him be that way.

He said he had box cutters from work. Box cutters for when he sliced open boxes and stocked shelves at the supermarket with his team. And he said they were incredibly sharp. That he could almost not imagine what they'd do to somebody's face. To a pretty face, or to the face of a little kid.

She said that afterward, she called some people she knew. A construction worker, a police sergeant, a lawyer. They said to get out of the apartment, at least for a few nights.

It was amazing, Margaret said, how cold it was. You could feel the cold and the wind blowing down from Lake Ontario, and then down Cayuga Lake. Like the Arctic had come to upstate New York.

You could hear the branches in trees snap from the cold. The air whistling into small cracks in the car, almost searching you out. How big and black the sky was, with pinpricks of stars. You could feel so clearly how close you were to dying.

19

There's no moon tonight, there are no stars. Opposite the cell block there are giant windows in the big wall, and day and night you can see the sky from the windows, through the heavy wire mesh and the dirty glass. But tonight there's pretty much nothing to see. Just blackness, just mesh and smeared glass.

Once or twice a night, if you happen to catch it, you might see an airplane slowly cross the sky, way far up and way far over. A single white light, and a winking red light. One on the underbelly of the plane, one on a wing.

It takes a few seconds to figure out that it is an airplane, and not a star, and not a UFO.

Twenty-five or thirty or thirty-five thousand feet in the air. Five or six miles above the world. Traveling at five or six hundred miles per hour. Five-seventy-five mph, which is how fast the typical commercial airplane travels. I heard that on television or the radio. Maybe I saw it in a magazine. Those little facts snag in my mind. They never go away.

I've never been on an airplane, as old as I am. Not once.

But I've seen photographs and film, and I know what the inside of an airplane cabin looks like. The seats with high backs, all packed closely together, the people sitting comfortably and patiently. The small windows, the clouds or city lights or neat fields outside and down below.

Mostly people with some kind of money. Because if you have very little money and you have to go fairly far away, you drive your beater car, and hope it won't break down, or you take the bus. The Skinny Dog. Greyhound.

Some guys in here have flown, sometimes quite a bit, and almost everyone has ridden the Skinny Dog. Even me, from

Ithaca to Albany, then Ithaca to Buffalo. Those long boring trips, with stops at every third town on the way. Those trips almost never end.

When I look at the black sky, through the window, the plane has moved without me knowing. From the upper left corner of the cell block window to the middle right side of the window. It's like the trees and plants grow most at night, when nobody notices. Like cars and trucks move most on highways, late at night. When almost everyone is sleeping.

The plane in the black sky is moving, I'd guess, between Toronto and San Francisco, or Montreal and Seattle, or Boston and Los Angeles. Many of the passengers will sleep, at least a little. They'll press the bottom on the side of their seat, and will lean back. They'll feel and hear the big engines.

A guy in here, on D-block, has books about UFOs. His name is Dewey, and he's in his fifties. He's not tall, but quite wide and fit, and he's in here for something having to do with the docks in New York City. Racketeering, or something like that.

He has an enormous head, and thick glasses, and when he gets going, he can really talk, about UFOs, and corrupt prosecutors in New York City.

In the chow hall he eats like every meal is his last meal, until he starts talking. Then his food is untouched.

They're everywhere, Dewey says. The UFOs. Even the Navy and Air Force, the fighter jets, they're releasing footage, video of these objects flying at terrific speeds, usually at night. White lights, or patterns of white and blue and red lights. Going at inhuman speed, then stopping abruptly, hovering, then going in some crazy direction, at that insane speed, sideways, backward, up or down.

Dewey looks at me and says, This has been going on for centuries, everywhere in the world. People all over have witnessed this, and they're always called crazy.

You've got to think of it, he says, and throw off the cultural bonds. All the shackles and chains that direct you to think of the world in a certain way. That up is up and down is down.

I try to do that for a while. Try to throw off the cultural bonds. I try to think, Well, Dewey's a pretty smart guy.

He has beautiful white, even teeth. I know they must be fake. The best that a dentist can sell you. A whole new grill.

Dewey was vice president of a union, then he was treasurer, then president. Over the years, funds and people disappeared. Nobody knew where or how or why. Once in a great while, a body would be found in southern New Jersey, or northeast Pennsylvania. Badly decomposed, missing a head or hands. The head or hands might be found without the rest of the body. Or an arm or leg might be in a large black trash bag, ten feet off a path.

A jogger, a hiker, a hunter, would be out with a dog, and the dog would get a little frantic, sniffing and pawing and nipping at the bag. The bag was under bushes, and would never have been found if not for the dogs.

Dogs were fucking amazing. Noses like you wouldn't believe. Noses that could smell a hundred, no, a thousand times better than a person. They could smell a body five feet down in the ground. They could sniff out a cadaver hundreds of yards away. In the summer, in the heat, they could sniff it out a half mile away.

The winter, everything frozen, Dewey said, not so much. Had to wait till spring, to May maybe, June at the latest.

So Dewey, he went for long drives sometimes, mostly at night. He went north and west of the big city, just to get away from the noise and stink. From all those fucking lights burning every hour of the day and night. Cars and trucks honking their horns. The cabs like sharks, moving on the black streets.

He went through the tunnel, went through all the industrial spill, the sodium lights in long lines, giant parking lots, great squat buildings, and in a half hour, in an hour for sure, he was out of it. There were more and more dark trees, roads snaking over the hills, and suburbs, the towns and villages that might have two stop lights at most.

Everything got quiet, and darker and darker. Then there were farms even. Silos, fields, farmhouses. Hard work. Honest lives. He couldn't hear anything, just the hum of the car, the wind, maybe, once in a while, a dog woofing.

Then he was past Monticello, on small county roads, and there were really small towns or hamlets called Cooks Falls, Downsville, Beerston. He didn't know any of the routes, the route numbers, anything. Just that he was north and west of New York City, and a ways past Monticello by then. He was on some odd route, sixty-seven or twelve or one-thirteen. He guessed it was one or two in the morning, roughly. He'd left the city around midnight, and he was probably a hundred miles from home. Maybe a hundred and fifty. He just didn't know. He kind of lost track of time and space.

Then there was a long clear stretch of road, a valley, Dewey thought. No hills, just fields on each side of the road. And he noticed really bright bright lights, violet and green and red, blinking fast in his rearview mirror.

He thought it was a cop car, even though the lights were strange. But the lights came incredibly fast, went over his car, and then moved over the road a mile ahead. They hovered over the road, and Dewey saw that he was going nearly seventy, and the lights had gone past him as though he was standing still.

I would not shit you, Dewey said, and I would not pretend that I wasn't scared. There was nothing out there. Just trees and hills in the distance, fields, some power lines.

It seemed fairly cold out. This was early April in upstate New York.

I slowed way the hell down, Dewey said. Down to thirty, twenty, even less. The ship, or whatever the hell it was, it hovered and hovered, and made no sound. The lights changed to all blue, and they rotated around the outside of the ship. The closer I got to it the more I felt something like a magnetic pull, not too strong but steady.

All the time it just hung there, a hundred, two hundred feet in the air.

Like God. Like nothing in the world I knew.

20

This was when I was twelve or fourteen. Maybe when I was eleven or thirteen. In around there. When I was getting taller and taller, but still skinny as sticks. Size thirteen shoes, hands and wrists like a broom handle. Unsightly as sin. Gawky, goofy. Tripping over rocks and roots, over the corners of carpets and chairs, over a stray shoe.

Walking down some sidewalk, I'd catch my toe on a crack in the concrete, and down I went. Hitting my side, my shoulder, an elbow, a knee.

One time, much earlier, when I was five or six, I was leaning out a window without a screen, and I went too far. I fell to the driveway which was concrete, and bashed my forehead hard. It was only the first floor, I'm pretty sure, but it was four or five or even six feet, and I landed square on my forehead. No hands to break my fall.

I remember how astonished I felt. The power of pain. How dead hard the concrete was, and how it didn't give, not even a sliver of an inch.

This huge pain, right in the center and sides, the top and bottom of my brain. Then very quickly, the moon and sun whirled and spun in my head, and then all of it went black. Just lightless and loveless. Just nothing anywhere, for a long time.

A while later, and I don't know how long a while, I was blinking, and the concrete was pressing against my cheek and side, and the pain in my head was bigger than any pain I'd ever known, by far. Like I was gonna die. Like this pain was infinitely bigger than me. Was a thousand times bigger. The pain could do anything it wanted. Like I was a tiny person in the face of a mountain. I was bobbing in an ocean.

There was a bird singing or calling somewhere. A crow, a

bluebird, a redbird. I didn't know. An eagle was the same as a sparrow. The bird went tweet, tweet, tweet. Or it whirred or cawed. For five or ten seconds, then was silent. Then started again. Over and over and over. My head was like hammers in there. Like steel-toed boots kicking. When I opened my eyes, it was daggers. Then a car or truck out front. Rumbling, purring, then a little dog yipping, right through my brain. Then again, the bird. Tweet, tweet, tweet. I started to stand up, and fell down. Started again, fell down again.

When I did stand up, I was dizzy, and there were black spots in my eyes. I threw up against the side of the house, and it was all green liquid. And my head. Oh my God.

Peg was somewhere, but she wasn't there, not then. I think it was late afternoon, and possibly spring or fall, getting dusky.

I got back inside. The door must have been unlocked. Then I was in bed with ice cubes in a facecloth on my forehead. And I don't know how long I was there. Sounds of cars and trucks, of dogs barking, of two or three different kinds of birds trilling and tweeting and cawing.

Long thin needles going in and through my brain. So at twelve or fourteen I'd still remember that. A smash to the brain. Blunt force trauma. A severe insult to the brain.

There had been a giant lump at the time, and then I had two black eyes.

And I heard later that head trauma in childhood predicted all kinds of dark and menacing behavior later on.

But I didn't know really. I didn't know much of anything.

I thought I understood what women were like, because I had spent so much time with Mother and Mabel. I knew they liked to spend a lot of time in the bathroom and in the shower. They liked to be clean. They went in for a shower, and they might come out of the bathroom an hour and a half later, a towel wrapped around their wet hair. Wearing a loose bathrobe, their beautiful breasts unrestrained.

I didn't know why their breasts were so beautiful, why I couldn't take my eyes off them, but they were. Like very few things in the world. And the small bulge at the tip of them. Like the eraser on a pencil. My gosh.

It felt weird with Marge, because she was my mother, and she was still so beautiful, but it was as wrong as wrong could ever be. I could understand why she had so many boyfriends, and why they all wanted to be with her. But still, you did not feel that way about your own mother, and I tried not to.

Sometimes, especially in summer when it was very hot, she walked around the house in a T-shirt and panties and nothing else. You could almost see everything.

By the time I was twelve or thirteen, I'd ask her to put more clothes on, and she'd smile. She'd look at me. She'd keep smiling.

Really, Ollie, she said, still looking at me, and smiling in this funny way, as though she knew what I knew. As though we both knew the same thing, and I imagined she sometimes looked at her boyfriends the same way.

You don't want to see these? Peggy said, and she lifted the front of her T-shirt, and there they were. I looked away, but I had seen, and I was on fire. I had a huge fever all through me.

Mom, I said, but my voice could barely escape my clogged throat.

She laughed again. She got up and went to the bedroom. I heard drawers, the closet door, some pills rattling. She came back a few minutes later, and she was wearing a black bra under her T-shirt, and grey shorts. Her legs were long and smooth and white like milk.

She held my wrist and put a pill in the palm of my hand.

She said, I'm sorry, O. I don't mean to make you uncomfortable.

I was gonna say, That's okay, but didn't because my throat was so clotted.

But I did take the pill, without liquid. I was getting good at that. Another half hour and the clogs and clots would be gone. I'd be a well-oiled boy again.

Jimmy Summers was talking on the radio, late at night. It was me and the dark and Jimmy Summers. And the people called, all though the night. A man called from Erie, Pennsylvania. His name was Vince, and he had a small black dog, a mop of a dog, named Gus. He'd had Gus more than ten years. Vince and Gus. They were a team. They did everything together.

But now, Vince said, now, and his voice broke. Gus was real sick. Gus only had a month or two to live.

Vince was crying, I think, and Jimmy said he was sorry. He said it made him sick to think of it. To think of Vince losing Gus.

Jimmy said it was terrible.

This was at three in the morning.

Around this same time, say when I was eleven or thirteen or maybe twelve, a girl my age, more or less, moved in with her father to the apartment on the other side of the first floor. Her father was Henry, and he was tall and thin and mostly silent. He wore green work pants and shirts, and boots that probably had steel toes.

She was tall like her father, and even thinner. She always had braids or plaits in her hair, black leggings, and a dress that was loose and came down mid-thigh. She also wore a soft hat like a shapeless beret, but most of her hair—the braids and plaits and loose light hair—fell to her shoulders.

Her name was Ivy. She didn't talk much, but she had a sleepy smile, and she seemed to have come from somewhere far away.

She whispered in the hall that her dad was away for two days, driving a truck.

She said, Come over, Oliver, and when I crossed the hall and went in, the place was like ours, but completely different.

I'd been in so few other apartments or houses, only our own and Mabel's, that I had nothing to compare it to. But this was neat and clean, and there were beautiful smells. Lavender and mint and cloves.

There was a big vase of orange lilies on a side table.

Ivy said her dad had brought them home after his last road trip.

He was a truck driver, she said. He went all over.

21

Ivy was one year older than me, so if I was twelve she was thirteen, and so on. Her dad was often away on road trips. He went to Memphis and Omaha, to Sacramento and Seattle and Tucson. He had a little compartment behind the front seat where he could sleep, and he had a tiny TV, two radios, even a small burner where he heated water.

Henry pulled into truck stops, after driving for eight or ten hours. He'd eat at the cafeteria, take a shower, and then he'd sleep as long as he could. Two hours, six hours, ten hours.

He told Ivy that even when he lay down and closed his eyes, he could still feel the vibrations from the engine and the road, and he could see the broken white lines of the highway rushing at him. Mile after mile, almost forever.

Henry said that the country was huge, and was growing every day. You could drive from New York to Miami, to Houston and San Diego, to Bellingham, Washington, to Chicago, then New York or Boston. You could drive from Philadelphia to Nashville to Missoula to San Francisco. Thousands of miles of blacktop. Thousands of bridges, millions of pieces of broken white line.

Back when Ivy was a little younger, when her mother first got sick, but before her mom died, Ivy would sometimes go on the road with Henry. She loved to sit up so tall, so much higher than cars and smaller trucks that she could see inside the cars they passed. She loved the constant noise and the vibration of the big truck's engine.

She got tired at all kinds of odd hours. At nine in the morning, at noon, at three or four in the afternoon. And she loved climbing into the bed compartment, and pulling up the quilt, which smelled like her dad, and closing her eyes.

Then she felt so safe and cosy, with her dad driving. She felt as though she was in a sunlit farmhouse, and her dad was out in the fields, and her mom was in the kitchen baking cinnamon-raisin bread, and the wonderful smell was filling the house.

Ivy fell asleep to the noise and vibrations, and sometimes she could sleep longer than she'd ever sleep at home. It might be very bright when she fell asleep, and then it might be deep dark and the roads empty when her eyes blinked open.

How long did I sleep? she asked Henry.

He smiled at her as though she'd done something special.

A long time, honey, he said, and patted the side of her face.

She loved how that made her feel.

Then her mom died, on account of the cancer, and Ivy didn't go on the road with her dad any more. She stayed home in the apartment for anywhere from four to ten days. He called from all over everywhere.

And around then, Ivy and me, we became friends.

If I was twelve by that time, I'd probably been going out late at night for a while. So many times, at Ivy's house or at mine, I nearly told her about going out. How dark it was, how deep the shadows, how thrilling to walk in the yards of rich people, to see tiny pieces of the lives inside. People reading books, or looking at a screen, or eating things in their kitchens or dining rooms.

Looking in the windows of their beautiful shiny cars. Seeing a red coat in the back seat, a child's sneaker, a coffee cup, a wallet, a sweater. One person left a laptop computer on the passenger seat. An Apple. They had so much money they could be careless.

If Ivy was with me, I could have shown her things. The black night sky, the stars, the moon. A scudding cloud. An airplane. Venus, the planet.

I could show her the rooftops of houses, chimneys, and how to avoid streetlights, or the lights of a passing car.

Once in a while I saw a police car, with a single cop driving. He or she would be looking, looking, looking. Into the darkness and shadows.

All I had to do was be careful. I had to be watchful. I had to be mindful every minute. Every second.

There was a big research university on East Hill, and it was so big that you could get lost there easily. It went for a few miles west to east, and for well over a mile from south to north. There were deep gorges on the north and south sides of central campus, sixty or eighty or a hundred feet deep. Fall Creek and Cascadilla Creek ran down below, and from the bridges that ran overhead, the water looked like a roiling, rushing snake. After a big rain, the creeks were white foam.

Collegetown was on the south side, a collection of stores and apartment houses, mostly for students. On the north side there were some fraternity houses, but mostly the neighborhood was called Cornell Heights, and there were big houses where doctors and professors lived, and vice presidents of the university and deans.

A quarter mile past the apartment houses in Collegetown, you were in a neighborhood called Belle Sherman, and it was kind of like Cornell Heights, only a little bit less fancy. Our house, with the big rooms on the first floor, was kind of between Collegetown and Belle Sherman.

At first I only went to Belle Sherman, because it was so close to our place. I could walk there in five minutes, and I could be in the backyards of houses within six or seven minutes.

Margie was out a lot of the time, at bars downtown, and once in a while at the bars in Collegetown. I saw her once on the sidewalk in front of a bar on College Avenue, holding a drink and laughing and talking with two college guys. She wore a short yellow skirt, her jean jacket, and red high-top Converse sneakers.

From a distance, Peg looked like she might be a student. She looked pretty, looked like she was having a wonderful time, looked very much like she belonged at this college bar.

I passed on a cross street, stayed in shadows, and I'm almost certain she didn't see me.

After exploring the yards in Belle Sherman for almost a

year, I began to explore the campus. There was an arts quad, an engineering quad, and an ag quad. There were orchards, arboretums, wildflower gardens. There was big clocktower, ten or twenty libraries, three or four gyms, a stadium. There was a huge veterinary school on the east end of campus.

Many of the buildings looked like big fancy hotels, but some were made from old stone. Sandstone, I think it was, cut maybe a hundred and fifty years ago. There was a beautiful old chapel, which looked small from outside, but inside was big, had tons of pews and stained-glass windows, and big stone coffins that held the shrunken bodies of the university's founders.

I liked the feeling of being near these dead people. They had gone before, but now I could visit and be with them. As though they were part of us still.

For some reason, they never locked the door of the chapel. It was open all the time. I could sit in the pews, and pretend to say a prayer, even though I didn't know any prayers. I could sit at one in the morning or four in the morning. I could sit until I fell asleep.

Nobody ever stopped me. In all the time. Maybe because I was pretty tall already. By age thirteen, at the start or finish of my thirteenth year, I was five nine or ten. I was still skinny as string, but if you didn't see me close-up, didn't see my face, you might think I was eighteen or twenty.

I almost always brought along a pill or two, and kept it or them in the watch pocket of my jeans. I'd sit in the chapel, or sit on a bench on the arts quad, or at the top of Libe Slope, looking out over west campus, and I'd take one or two pills.

Then I'd sit and wait. I'd begin to feel the drugs, the warmth and the oneness with everything. With the whole world.

And for a very short time, but a time nonetheless, it was as though I belonged there. In the world, and in that very place in the world.

22

Mellor, Gates, and me have lived side by side for two, three years, which is a long time for a prison. They move guys around so fast in here, and for reasons you almost never know, that stability is the last thing we have. And they move you not just cell to cell but block to block. Not to mention facility to facility. You might wake up in Attica or Green Haven or Sing Sing, and find yourself going to bed in Dannemora or Auburn. Dannemora is way the hell up north, almost to the Canadian border, in the northeast corner of New York State. I think of the winters there, the winds blowing down from Ontario and Quebec, the snows that fall and pile up, and don't melt until May or June. Sing Sing is on the Hudson River, on the east side, and like Dannemora, is very old, and was built well before the American Civil War. Sing Sing was where many of the state's executions took place.

In New York City, when someone was said to have been sent "up the river," that someone was in Sing Sing. Only thirty miles north of the city.

We pass around books and articles in here, on the prisons, and the history of incarceration. Some of us like to know the facts of things. How old is a prison, how deep is a lake.

The oldest prison in the state, and one of the oldest continuously running prisons in the country, is here, is Auburn. The place has been operating since 1818. More than two hundred years. Through the Civil War, World Wars I and II. James Monroe, the last president from the Founding Fathers, was president then.

The first person executed by electricity in the world was executed at Auburn. William Kemmler, an alcoholic vegetable peddler in Buffalo, argued with his common law wife, Tillie

Ziegler. Kemmler was the child of two alcoholics, and on the night before the murder, he had been on a bender.

During the argument, he went out to the barn behind the house, got a hatchet, and went back inside and killed Tillie. He then went to a neighbor's house and reported that he had killed his wife.

William Kemmler was thirty years old at the time of his death. This was in 1890. Benjamin Harrison was president. Late in the year, at Wounded Knee in South Dakota, 153 Lakota Sioux were killed when members of the 7th Cavalry tried to disarm the Sioux.

Almost all the guys in here know about Kemmler. They know about his murder, and they know about his execution by electrocution. They know Tillie's death, and I've heard some guys say, The bitch had it coming.

But that's just con talk, prison bullshit. Almost all prisoners have decided opinions on so many subjects. Pretty much everyone I've met in here feels that he has been badly treated by life, and is very badly treated by the Department of Corrections.

Once in a while I feel that way too. But not for very long.

I've never heard Gates, next door, say anything about being badly treated, and Mallor, on the other side, doesn't have a self-pitying bone in his body.

We're on lockdown this week because there was a stabbing on the yard two nights ago. A guy from the Bronx apparently stabbed a guy from Brooklyn, bad enough to be in a civilian hospital. The cops in here don't know who the Bronx guy is. There are dozens of people in Auburn from New York City, and some guys, the young ones, the kids, don't like dudes from different boroughs.

Maybe they were in different gangs. I don't know.

But we're in lockdown, key lock. We don't go out of our cells, except for guys who work in the laundry or kitchen.

Mellor's been coughing a ton. Not a clear-your-throat cough, not even a bad-cold cough. He seems to be coughing from the bottom of his lungs. Like his whole throat and chest are on fire. I've asked him through the vent a few times if he's okay. He's said he thinks so. He said this two or three times yesterday. But during the night, Mellor's coughing got worse, if that's possible. It got deeper and more frequent. He was wheezing, and I think the coughs made him throw up a few times. I'm pretty sure I heard that.

I kept saying, Mellor, Mellor, through the vent, saying, You okay? Mellor, what the fuck? Mellor, answer me.

Then I said, Please.

Mostly he didn't say anything. He was lying on his bunk, I guessed, based on where the coughs came from.

Then I called him Street, which is his street or prison name. His real first name is Devon.

I whispered, Street, then I hissed, Street.

Ol, he finally said. Just like all.

You okay, I asked, and he said, Yeah.

You don't sound so hot, I said. No offense, but you sound like shit.

Mellor kind of chuckled a little.

Been better, he said.

You got a fever?

I imagined Mellor put the back of his hand to his forehead.

Pretty hot, he said.

Lemme call Yager.

Nah, he said.

We both knew that Yager would have to cuff Mellor up, and take him to the infirmary. He'd see some medical assistant, he'd get his blood pressure taken, maybe his pulse, then they'd give him an aspirin. One aspirin. And send him back to the block.

Yager was the overnight CO, the corrections officer, during the week. He was a big beefy individual. Not much hair on his head, red face, steel-framed glasses. Pretty decent guy for a CO.

Yager had been working at Auburn for twenty, twenty-five years. Used to be a tough guy, a prick, in the beginning, but mellowed into something else over the years. He read books in between his rounds, sitting on a wood chair. I mean, what kind of CO read books?

Mellor was in his bunk, I was in my bunk, and I went to sleep somewhere in there. Light sleep, like slipping into water, the conscious world separating from the sleep world, and moving farther down, under the surface of the water, deeper and deeper, and being able to breathe underwater.

And Mellor going cough and cough and cough, and other sounds—groans, sighs, snores—up above, and cushioned by the water. In that other world, far away.

When I first came inside, I was pretty young. Every time I woke up I saw the bars, and I had to remember that, Oh no, I was inside. This was my life. This is where I had come to.

I tried to imagine, for a moment or two, that the bars and the cell were part of a dream, a slow-moving nightmare, and I had done something terrible which had brought me here. But it was a dream, I imagined, that I had committed an awful crime, and that I was in a cell, with bars, a slab to sleep on, a toilet, and that I would be here for much of my life.

If I could get back to sleep, if I could get below the surface again, I would be in a place where I had done nothing wrong, where there were no bars, no concrete slab, and I could stand up and go out into a life, just like the rest of people.

But it never worked for more than a moment or two. A minute, maybe a little more.

I always opened my eyes. I always heard the crash of cell doors, the yells, the singing, the blast of radios. People walked past, a few people bounced on their toes.

People shouted, Yo. They made loud, weird sounds.

Aaaiiiyyyeee.

Wwwoooooo.

The COs had bunches of keys.

I had to pee something fierce. The silver toilet was about two feet away. My bladder was gonna explode.

I had to stand up, and I had to pee. That wasn't above or

below the surface of the water. That wasn't waking or sleeping. It just was, and it didn't care what I thought, or dreamed or wanted.

And Mellor next door, he was still coughing.

23

Mother was getting friendly with this guy named Wallace. He should have been Wally too, but nobody called him Wally. He was Wallace to everybody, and that was because he was so big, and he had a face that didn't smile hardly at all, and shoulders that were two yards wide.

I didn't know if Wallace was his first name or his last name, and we were pretty sure he didn't come from our city. He came from Syracuse or Rochester, or maybe from the Bronx in New York City. He always carried a small gun, which he kept in a holster that was under his arm, a few inches under his armpit. Usually he left the gun and holster on a table near the front door, and he always checked the door to make sure it was locked.

Wallace was the most careful man we had ever seen.

He was half Asian and half Black, and he was white too, and from somewhere in the Middle East. Maybe from Egypt or Algeria. Maybe China and Korea too. It was hard to be sure. But he was very handsome, Peg thought, and Mabel said he could be in movies if he'd smile even a little.

Yet even though he didn't smile, he was a very nice man. He brought Mother flowers almost every day, and he brought her small plastic bags of pills. He brought me this nice leather baseball glove, and a baseball, and even though I didn't play baseball, and had never played sports of any kind, the glove was so beautiful and so well made, and had this deep, rich leather smell, that I loved to put my face in the glove and inhale. Sometimes I slept with the glove next to my pillow on the couch or bed. It made me think of green fields and summer and sunshine and tall trees waving their leaves in the distance.

Wallace didn't live in our small city, and at first I thought he came from a city nearby, from Rochester or Syracuse, or maybe from New York City. He'd come to town and stay for around a week, always in a room at a fancy hotel downtown, and he always rented a Range Rover or a Mercedes for the week.

Then he'd fly out for Chicago or Philadelphia, Denver or Seattle, and we wouldn't see him for a few months or more. But when he was in town, he spent every evening with Marge, and sometimes with me. He took us to really expensive restaurants, to concerts at the university, to basketball or hockey games, and then back to our place.

Every night he was around, very late, I'd hear him moving softly near the couch, putting on his shoes and gun and coat, and then he'd put cash on the table near the couch. Fifteen 100 dollar bills. One year, right before Christmas, Wallace left fifty 100 dollar bills.

Mabel eventually learned that Wallace was from Chicago, and that he had a daughter who went to the university. He was some kind of businessman, and he always carried a ton of money. That's why he had a gun. Mabel thought he might be some kind of big drug dealer, but Mommy didn't think that.

He was too nice, too polite, she said.

When Ivy saw Wallace in the hallway, they shook hands and said a few things, and Ivy thought that maybe Wallace worked for the government. For the FBI or the Department of Justice.

He always wore either a blue blazer and no tie, or a brown leather jacket that was soft as cat fur. Wallace still didn't smile, even when he met Ivy.

Me and Ivy, we were becoming friends. Better and better friends as the weeks and months went by. I think by then she was fourteen and I was thirteen. She was pretty tall, and she was getting hips and breasts, but not so you'd notice, unless you were looking.

Margaret and Mabel both liked Ivy, though they both mentioned that she didn't talk much.

I said that she talked when it was just her and me, and Mabel wanted to know what else happened when it was just her and me.

I didn't say anything, and Peggy said to ignore Mabel, and

Mabel laughed. Sometimes grown-ups said embarrassing things that a little kid might say. Even when they weren't drinking and on drugs.

This was definitely when I was thirteen and Ivy fourteen, because Ivy had her fourteenth birthday in early October, the sixth or ninth, I'm pretty sure. Henry, her pops, took me and Ivy out to a place called Spicy Asian, on the strip, toward the south of town. We had chicken with broccoli, General Tso's chicken and kung po tofu. Half the people in the restaurant were Asian, and Henry said that that was a good sign. That Asians would know good Chinese food.

Ivy gave me a taste of kung po tofu, but it was white and rubbery, and had no taste aside from the sauce. Plus it was like chewing rubber bands. I thought that would also be like trying to chew an eel.

Henry had a beer, and he asked Ivy if she wanted to split a beer with me. She looked at me, I nodded with my eyes, and Henry asked the waiter—a small thin man dressed all in black—for another beer and two glasses. The waiter smiled and nodded, and said, Okay. He didn't seem to have been in America for very long. He mostly said Okay when we were ordering, and wrote the orders in Chinese on a small pad.

Henry said the written Chinese looked like chicken scratches, and Ivy said there were thousands of characters in Chinese calligraphy.

Well, Henry said. We weren't in China, we were in America. They should use the English.

We're not in England either, Ivy said. Plus, where is it written that everyone in America needs to speak English?

Henry laughed. He said to me, She's always saying that. Where is it written. And then she says, Plus, and buries you with another argument.

Ivy looked at her dad, then she smiled at me.

I had never gone out to dinner with anyone who was not Mother or Mabel, and Ivy had tried hard to convince me to join her and her dad. I told her I had never gone anywhere with strangers, and she said that I wasn't a stranger, that I was a friend.

Even though I knew we were friends, even though I knew Ivy was my only friend ever, and that she didn't have friends either, we had never said anything about this. I liked her as much or more than I liked anybody, except probably Marge. We were so much alike.

We were only about a year's difference in age. Neither of us went to school very much. Ivy was being homeschooled, and she had a few tutors who came in to teach her math and science. She read books and wrote little papers. She lived with her single dad, I thought, because her mother had died of infection of the brain or blood.

Ivy and me were both tall. Really tall.

The small waiter in black came back with a bottle and glasses. Then I watched Ivy pour, and both glasses had a head of foam, and brown liquid underneath.

Henry said to be careful with this stuff, and I kept watching Ivy's hands, her long, beautiful fingers on the sweating bottle, and her face, which looked intent on making sure that we both got an equal share of beer. Her eyes were brown, and her tan hair was braided into small cords that were pinned up on her head. Her ears were like seashells, I thought, then I thought, Don't ever say any of these things out loud. She'd laugh, she'd run away.

In the car on the way home, Ivy said she wanted to take a walk when we got back. She asked if I wanted to join her, and I said sure.

Henry said, You two sure you won't be afraid walking around in the dark.

Ivy laughed, and I said, No.

Lot of creeps out there in the shadows, Henry said.

In the back seat, I started to wonder if Henry was joking. Joking, because we had so little crime in our city. I felt two pills in the watch pocket of my jeans. I wanted to take one, there in the darkness of the back seat.

But I had to wait. Wait until Ivy and I were walking around in the black night.

Then I started to think that Henry was only partway joking, about walking in darkness. But the other part was the fact that Henry lived in the same house, on the other side of the hall. He often wasn't around, but when he was he kept weird hours, just as he did when he was on the road. He might sleep all afternoon, and then be awake for much of the night.

Maybe Henry saw me or heard me. At two or three in the morning.

Maybe he knew everything. About the night, and about the things, the people, who moved in shadows, in the dark.

24

Wallace hadn't been around in weeks and probably months. Two months, Mother thought. Over two months.

He was in San Juan and Los Angeles. He was in Seattle and Miami. Mostly sunny places. She was sagging. Mom was tired, and she looked gray. The skin on her face, the skin on her hands and arms and legs. It was weirdly white, fish-belly-white, and leaning to gray. There was nothing pink on her, and though I didn't know a thing about death, had never seen a dead guy, I could tell that she looked a little dead.

There was no shine in her eyes, no sparkle, and no light in or near her.

She still more or less looked like Margaret. The same nose and mouth, the same shape of the face, but it was like a drawing or statue, very like her, but not Peg, not Marge, not Mommy.

I had found some needles in a bag in a kitchen cabinet, with the clear plastic push-thing on the top part, and I had asked her what they were.

She said the obvious, that they were needles, that Bug and Doc had left them, that they were for IV drug use. Intravenous, and that meant into the vein. People did that, Peggy said. Right into the vein on the inside of your arm. That way you got a hit of the drug like you couldn't believe. A hit, a rush, a slam.

In like three seconds. Zero to sixty in three seconds. You got the full weight of the drug, the full heat, the lift, the bliss before you even got the needle out of your arm.

Most of the time the drug was heroin. Scag, they called it too. Junk. And heroin addicts were junkies.

You had to be ridiculously careful if you were a junkie. You had to use clean needles all the time. You could never share needles, or you could get AIDS, you could get hepatitis, all kinds of awful things might happen.

The quality of the heroin varied. Sometimes it was almost pure, sometimes it was cut with powdered milk or baking soda, or some sick fuck might cut the package with rat poison or a laxative, or who knew what. Junkies got sick all the time, and sometimes they died if they shot too much quality junk all at once. People would find them on the floor of the bathroom, the spike still in their arms.

Instant death, in two or three seconds. Their last act was pushing the plunger on the needle.

Boom, Mother said. On the floor, their head half underneath the toilet bowl.

Junkies died ugly deaths every day. Dozens and dozens and dozens of them. And nobody gave a shit. Almost nobody.

Mommy said there was no such thing as an old junkie. None of them lived very long.

Are you a junkie? I asked, and she looked at me a few seconds, her tired, red-rimmed eyes, and she said, Of course not, Oll. What gave you that idea?

I didn't say anything, but I knew she was lying. I'd seen the red marks on the skin on the inside of her arm, near the elbow. She was lying to protect me, so I wouldn't have to worry. But she had it backward and upside down. I worried all the time by then.

I was pretty sure that Peggy would die young. There was no such thing as an old junkie. Marge herself had said that.

Ivy was going to school for a little while, at the big high school. She thought she'd do it for a few weeks or months. She wasn't sure. Every year or two she'd try school again, but she'd leave pretty quickly. She said there were too many dicks, students and teachers, at school.

Maybe Ivy would like school this time and she'd find a new friend. Someone named Chloe or Nat. Someone who's mother was not a junkie or sex worker. Mom said we no longer called sex workers prostitutes or whores. It wasn't polite.

But me and Ivy still hung around a lot of the time. Not during school days anymore, but on the weekends and later at night on week nights, especially when Henry, her dad, was on the road.

This was September, late in September, and the weather was changing, especially long after the sun had gone down. Even if the temperatures had been in the upper seventies or eighties during the day, they always dropped into the sixties, fifties, and forties after the sun had finally gone down and we moved into the deep darkness and stillness of night.

This was the best part of the year for me. The temps, the leaves changing, the clear blue fall sky, which seemed very high, like the dome of heaven. People playing football all over the country, people wearing sweatshirts and wool sweaters, people kicking fallen dead leaves on the sidewalk as they walked, which made a swishing sound. Almost the sound of someone diving into water.

The summer was pretty good in some ways. It was better than winter, which was real cold up here. Summer was open windows, screens, cool night air that smelled of grass and earth, the smell of somebody cooking hamburgers and hot dogs on a grill.

You could hear sounds from a long way off in summer, especially at night, especially through an open window. You could hear cars and sirens, you could hear dogs barking, especially the small yippy ones, and you could hear voices—a yell, a whisper—from way far away.

I'd hear Chicago on the radio, and Cleveland. Atlanta was very hot, and so was Baltimore. A young woman who said she was nineteen, but sounded like fifteen, called Jimmy Summers. Her name was Vanessa, and she said she was being stalked by a man she used to work with at a convenience store. He called her on the phone twenty times a day. He showed up at her apartment, and left notes on her car.

Vanessa wouldn't say what city she lived in. Her voice was flat, but she still sounded very scared. Sometimes it was hard to tell with callers, was hard to say if they were telling the truth. Vanessa was telling the truth, I thought, and Jimmy seemed to think that too.

Sometimes it was hard to tell how near or far a sound was. Two streets over, or half a mile away. I'd hear a siren or two, and it sounded like it came from the street outside, in front of our house. Then over a minute or two, it got closer and closer, and then you'd know that it came from the firehouse on Green Street, downtown. That was at least a half mile from here, and down the big hill.

But the heat in summer could be brutal, especially late at night, especially in the apartment, the air thick and choking like wool.

Ivy and me, we walked for a long time that September night. The air was cool as ice cream almost. We didn't say a lot, most of the time. We were walkers, hikers, kind of old friends. We were both pretty tall, even there in our early teens. Ivy was a year older, but I was taller, though not by much.

She had one of her black-knit hippie hats on, her light hair in dreadlocks that fell around the sides and back of her head. She wore leggings and one of those loose dresses, and a jean jacket over everything. She wore low-cut white canvas sneakers, and you'd think it looked goofy, this outfit, but it didn't.

Maybe she was confident, or maybe Ivy didn't care. Maybe it was because she was so smart, but she definitely made it work. She looked interesting, and she definitely looked cool.

We went over a few streets, and then we were in the good neighborhoods, with the nice wide streets, with the big trees, and the houses with fences and lawns. Almost all of them had front porches with Adirondack chairs and porch swings. And even though it wasn't a holiday, a bunch of the houses had tiny white or blue Christmas lights strung along the top of the porch.

The lights might have been out of season, but these people didn't care. Every day was a holiday to them.

Those lights, Ivy said. They look sweet.

I thought, but didn't say, You're right. They do look good. Then we were on the street of the house with the back porch. The one where I'd smoked a Newport. I really wanted to tell Ivy. I wanted to tell her everything. About going out very late at night, and walking the empty streets. I wanted to tell her about the back yards, the bushes and fences and trees, the back porches, the decks, and how amazing that felt.

I didn't know why it felt that way. The feeling of transgression. Of trespassing. Of dipping into some new world. The danger and excitement, the joy of doing and seeing and hearing this forbidden thing.

I didn't think that I was hurting anyone, not that I could see. But nobody in the world knew what I did. And maybe they never would. But maybe if I told Ivy, I might begin to understand why I went out.

Not that I was going out every night, or even every week. But I went out often enough. And each time I loved it even more.

Then I thought of Maggie and her needles. I thought of her skin, and what she said about junkies.

Ivy, I almost said. My mother.

Ivy might have stopped and turned to me. In the strange, silvery light of the moon. On a late September night.

Needles, I might have said. Heroin.

That was a thing I might have done.

25

J uly in here is worse than the middle of January, and by a wide margin. If it's ninety outside, it's ninety-five or a hundred in here. If the humidity is seventy-five or eighty outside, it's ninety percent in here. It's that heavy, wet wool blanket people talk about, and there's nowhere inside to escape. It's on you. It's snug, and you can't do anything.

The hot days start in May. Just a few ninety-degree days strung together, but suddenly you're back to the feel of summer. Something you know well, you know intimately, but you haven't seen in a while. Then in June it's more than a few days strung together. It's a week, it's ten days, all of them around ninety and the humidity's over eighty percent. By July it's pure ugly.

Guys get impatient, get mean, get aggressive. Almost everyone. Guys trudge from place to place, or sit in their houses in undershorts. They sweat and breathe through their mouths. We get fights, but nothing that lasts very long. It's too damn hot.

There's nothing natural green in here. No trees or bushes, no grass, no plants. There's not even any wood.

There's steel and concrete, there's bulletproof glass. I think of it all the time.

We all wear green work clothes, the pants and shirts, and we usually wear boots. We wear white socks and white underwear.

Years ago, someone gave my mother an air conditioner, and we put it in the window of our third-floor apartment, in the bedroom. I remember that now. It made the room cool, it made it even cold, but after a few days my mom took it out.

She said it sealed the room in this creepy way. You had to keep the windows closed all the time, and you couldn't get fresh air into the room. She said she started to feel as though we were sealed in a coffin, in a tomb, or under the ground in a grave. She said it made her want to jump out of bed and run to an open window in the kitchen or living room, and kneel. It made her want to breathe deep at the window.

Plus the noise of the air conditioner. It was constant and loud, and my mom said it was like hearing someone on a vent in a hospital. Someone who was about to die. Someone who was about to be put in a coffin, and then in a vault. Someone who wouldn't be seeing any more sunlight.

Kind of like us in here. Sealed in. For weeks and months and years. Almost like forever.

A couple of years ago an old guy named Buck was about to be released on parole after twenty-five years, at Attica, Green Haven, Sing Sing, and here. I didn't know him much. I was early then. He was well into his sixties. Sixty-six, sixty-eight.

A week or so before his release, Buck attacked a correction's officer named Carter. Carter was a big young dude. A couple inches over six feet, two-twenty, two-forty. And like most of the young COs, Carter was a weightlifter.

Buck did this in the chow hall, and it was ridiculous. Buck swinging his arms at Carter's head, and Carter was seventy or eighty pounds heavier, and at least forty years younger.

Buck went to the hole, of course, and his parole was cancelled. And everybody knew what was going on. The guys and the staff.

Buck didn't want to leave. He had no idea how he might live in the world. Buck was terrified.

We got Bevan Ray Eliot, and Gates, and Moses. We got me too, for that matter, and we've all been in a really long time. Those three have been in longer than me, and I think they're older too. None of them is getting out ever. They've already got their tomb.

Say the prison's the tomb, the cell is the coffin.

And so many in here, they have a new name.

God, the names. They're fantastic.

I've known Bar, Lumumba, Patrice, Eyes, Cats, Feet, Chon, Wallika. Guys named Ice, Heat, Ride, Sticks. A Jacques, a Jack, a Jan. A guy named Jaws bit someone's ear off in a fight. It goes on and on. Names like weeds, growing everywhere. Guys with time. A little time. A life of time.

A guy named Mal killed his sleeping wife with a hammer. He was forty-seven, she was forty. They had four kids, ages four to thirteen. This was in a town named Greene, upstate.

A guy named Arturo sexually assaulted at least nine women in city parks over a period of two and a half years in Albany. He used a butter knife, the same butter knife each time, to press the skin at the carotid artery in the sides of their necks, to threaten and subdue the women.

A guy named Adler trafficked boys and girls, one who was seven years old, and manufactured and distributed child pornography. There was no proof that Adler himself had sex with children.

A guy named Naem shot a twenty-one-year-old clerk in the face at a gas station convenience store. She was a college junior, majoring in psychology, and she died less than two hours later at an emergency room. Naem got two-hundred and thirty-eight dollars in the robbery, and three packs of Marlboro longs.

You see them—Mal, Arturo, Adler, Naem—in the yard, in the halls, in the chow hall, and they look like everyone else. They wear the same white underwear, the green shirt and pants, the boots and sneakers. Maybe they're a little older than some guys. They might be balding or bald, they might have more wrinkles or more graying hair. Some wear glasses. But they all look very far from monsters.

Then you hear shit about someone. Somebody else, a trusty who works in one of the administrative offices, who was cruising the internet, googled Mal or Adler, Arturo or Naem. Holy shit, they whisper to you on the yard.

You won't fucking believe this, they say.

You know Mal? they say. You know Arturo? Little white guy on the fourth tier? D-block? Bald?

And you think of them, you try to picture them. Little white guy? D-block? Bald? A third of the guys here are white, maybe a quarter of the white guys are bald. But we all wear the same drab clothes. We're all shadows of one kind or another.

Guys do things with their hair and beards, they have tats on their necks and sometimes on their faces. You see guys with real bald heads or shaved bald heads, and huge beards like Moses. You see tats on the tops or sides or backs of their heads.

You see snakes and roses, swords and daggers, vines, trees, skulls and gravestones. Lightning bolts, clouds, the face of Jesus or Hitler. You see words: ALL-ONE; PRIDE; 4EVER; LOVE next to HATE.

You see women. A woman robed, a woman naked. You see names. VAL; EMMA; FAYE; NADINE; SORIAH.

Sometimes when the man is over fifty or sixty, and he's bald as a lacrosse ball, his huge beard will have turned a yellow-white color, and he braids the bottom of his beard with beads and strings and bands.

And the tats on his neck, the snakes, leaves, vines, the face of Buddha, the number 88, an eagle holding a lance, the letters A.C.A.B. Two lightning bolts.

88 is HH, Heil Hitler. A.C.A.B. is All Cops Are Bastards. The lightning bolts are for the S.S.

There are three dots in a triangle near the outside edge of his eye.

One guy, Pinky, has all this stuff. He's wide as the state of Nebraska, and nobody knows why he has the name Pinky. He seems to go from one prison to the next every year. This is at least his third stay in Auburn.

We hear that he's done four or five stints in Southport, near Elmira, at the state's maxy max. When they can't control you at a maximum-security facility in New York, you go to Southport. It's pretty much total lockdown. I've never gone there, but know guys who have. It's supposed to be very nasty.

I'm sitting with Gates in chow, in the whites section, and

it's gotta be ninety degrees in here. This is dinner, starting at three-thirty in the afternoon. Breakfast starts at four-thirty. Mallor's across the aisle, one table in, in the Black section. The Latin guys have their section near the front.

The really old dude, Moses, comes shuffling away from the food line, and he sits at our table, two seats down, on the other side. Gates says, Moses, and Moses nods slightly without looking up from his food.

Gates, who had been telling me about Mal a few days ago, says, There, Al. Three tables down, on the far left.

A guy in a white T-shirt stands in the way for a moment, and I can't see.

Mal's only been here seven or eight months, when he was transferred from Dannemora. Until a few days ago, nobody knew what he was in for. There wasn't an inmate in here who wasn't dying to know.

We're like middle school or high school. We breathe gossip.

The white T-shirt guy steps away, and I can see the guy on the far left. I can see Mal.

He's sitting alone, his green shirt buttoned to the top. You almost never see that, especially on a hot day. He's got short white hair, and he wears thick glasses with black rims. He's small and very skinny. His hands seem to shake badly. He's in a deep cloud.

Know what I'm saying, Al, Gates says.

I keep looking at Mal. I don't think I know what Gates is saying.

Fucking hammer, Moses says, and he's staring down at his food. Make your fucking kids fucking orphans.

Then we hear from a CO. We're on key lock again.

Bevan Lee Eliot has been stabbed. In his cell on D-block. He's at the hospital, and they don't think he'll make it.

Bevan's a pedo, so anyone could have done it. Hundreds of guys wanted to do it.

Any of us, anywhere, anytime. We could get killed. We could die. The blink of an eye.

26

Mother got worse and worse. She'd close the bathroom door and lock it, something she never did if she was just taking a shower or having a pee. I'd hear little movements in there—the bent spoon, the tiny glass tube, then the scrape of the lighter cooking her dope.

Then it might be five minutes or an hour, but the clack of the door unlocking, the door opening, and she'd be in the doorway to the living room, where I was sitting on the couch, doing I don't know what.

Listening to the radio, reading a magazine or one of the books that Mabel had left for me.

Marge walked slowly, and she always wore a long-sleeved shirt with the sleeves rolled down to hide the marks of the needle. She smiled at me, but it was always a slow, sloppy smile. You could tell, any idiot could tell, that she was slammed. Those glassy, tired eyes, and the pale gray skin, and wearing long pants and the sleeves rolled down, even if it was July or August, and eighty-eight degrees out.

I don't know if she actually thought she was fooling anybody, though there was not much of anyone to fool. A few of her johns, Mabel, me, herself. None of us were fooled, except for maybe Peg thinking she was fooling us.

She might say, Hey, Ollie, but even those two words were kind of slithered like a snake, covered with moss, in deep grass. She was coated with dope, with heroin.

I mean, how was this gonna end up? Where was any of this going?

To a hospital? To a prison? Where else?

Then Marge sat in the one big chair, and she slouched so she was almost lying down. She looked at me, but just from the corner of the eyes, then she closed her eyes. She didn't go to sleep, not that I could tell, and her breathing didn't slow because it was already as slow as a dead person, almost.

Maybe I shouldn't have minded. Who was I to criticize Margaret? I'd been drinking and popping pills for years. But at least I was a little bit moderate. That's what I thought. I didn't shoot fucking heroin. I wasn't a junkie.

She stayed in her chair for a while. That's what she did. For fun? For something. Her eyes blinked open for a second. They were slits of glass. Then she kind of sighed, kind of hissed slightly, and I thought she must have done a double, two tiny tubes.

Maggie was snowed.

She went into the slow-motion itching and scratching. She scratched her hand, arms, cheek, nose. She reached slowly behind her and scratched her back. She hit her thighs, breasts, shoulder, neck.

Almost every part of her.

She stopped after a while. Her glassy eyes opened, and she looked some more at me.

She said, All, then she didn't say anything else. Not for a while.

I didn't know what I wanted, or what I might say. Tell her that this had to stop, that she was a junkie. That she was going to die. That she was going to die ugly. On a bathroom floor, her face pressed to the tiles. The rubber tube she tied herself off with on the floor. The needle still in her arm.

She was already skinny, and getting skinnier. Cheekbones sticking out, the bones at her wrists sticking out. Her knees were knobby, her elbows sharp.

Mom was still good-looking, I thought, but in a stranger, corpse-in-casket kind of way.

Even her johns were thinning out. There had always been tons of them. Almost in a line. Now, there were whole days and nights when she didn't have a customer. Now and then there were two in a day. Doc still came, and a guy named Larry who had a ponytail and a skull tattoo on his upper arm. Larry rode a motorcycle, a big beast of a thing. A Harley that rumbled. Larry always had a leather backpack with him.

Larry smiled at me and said he was a garden-variety redneck. A piece of white trash that washed up on the smelly beach of life.

I was still thirteen, as best as I can remember, and Ivy was still my friend. She had been in school for a few months, then she was home, then it was summer.

We went for walks, day or night, and we played video games, and we talked a lot, but I don't remember what we talked about. I think she told me about school. The kids, the teachers, the halls and classrooms.

Even the walk to and from school.

Down the big hill on Dryden Road, then on Williams Street. Across the gorge bridge on Stewart Avenue, then down the twisty Cascadilla Park Road, past all the cool bungalow houses that looked like California. Then north on Lynn, cut behind Fall Creek School, through a parking lot, then on to Lake Avenue. She saw other kids walking to school, kids going to Fall Creek, kids going to Boynton Middle school, kids like her, going to the high school. But she never walked with them. Once in a great while one of them would nod or wave to her, and she'd nod or wave back.

Classes were more or less the same. Maybe some eye contact, a nod, a wave, but that was all. The classes themselves were fine, because everyone was in his or her seat, and sort of paying attention to the teacher. But before and after class was crazy. Lots of milling around, yelling, talking, bumping into each other, pushing, grabbing.

And this one kid, Anthony, a small pudgy kid, sat behind her in biology, making grunting and hissing noises. Now and then he'd kick her chair.

Mostly Ivy ignored him, but the last time he kicked her chair, she said, loud, Stop kicking my chair, you worm.

He turned red, and Mr. Wohl, the teacher, made Anthony sit in the far back corner of the room.

Mr. Wohl said, That's your new permanent seat.

Sometimes late at night, lying in bed, she'd hear Anthony's grunts and hisses. Almost as though this little pudge with the black eyes and brown bangs, was under the bed or in the closet or just outside the window. She didn't know why he made noises, she said.

Maybe Anthony was lonely and was trying to make contact with her. Maybe kicks and grunts and hisses were the only thing he knew. His only form of speech. Maybe he lived in a foster home where nobody was nice to him.

He smelled musty, as though he or his clothes had been packed away in a basement for a long time.

Like her, he didn't seem to have any friends. He wore two different shirts, a white one and a blue one. White on Monday, blue on Tuesday, white on Wednesday, and so on. Ivy wondered if he was from a poor family, and then she felt bad that he was sitting alone in the back corner of biology.

But the weirdest thing was Mr. Pollard, her global history teacher. He was a big, bald guy, who always wore the same coat, and one of maybe three ties, to class. He had a peculiar red mouth that was rubbery, and he had small yellow teeth. He hiked his pants up to his belly button and cinched his belt tight on his round stomach.

Mr. P.—that's what he asked his students to call him—wore thick glasses with black frames, and they magnified his watery blue eyes.

When he laughed, Mr. P. snorted. The first time he did this all the kids in the class looked at each other, as though to say, Did you hear what I heard?

He seemed very old, a good deal older than any of the other teachers. He might have been seventy years old. Maybe he was only sixty, but probably he was somewhere between the two.

Then the weird shit started happening, Ivy said, and it made goosebumps rise on her skin.

They were taking a pop quiz, about England and their colonies in the eighteenth century. Everyone was quiet.

Ivy was in her seat by the windows, and she looked up, and Mr. P. was looking at her. He was smiling with his red rubbery lips and small teeth, and then he winked at her. With his right eye, and his yellow teeth showing.

She looked down at her desk, tried to go back to the quiz. But she kept seeing his big bald head, his eyes and teeth, the red lips.

Who was he? What was he?

And what did he want?

She felt as though a warm bucket of drool had been poured down her back and over her legs.

She wanted to run. She needed to take a long shower.

Ivy needed all the soap in the world.

27

Mother was so erratic and eccentric that I usually never knew what to do or say to her. I had never really known, not much anyway, but now I had no clue.

Some days and nights she would just sleep, on the couch or chair in the living room, in the big bed, or a few times, on the toilet or on a kitchen chair, her head on her folded arms on the table. The times I found her on the toilet, I thought she was dead. Her head was hanging down, she wasn't wearing anything, and I could see the needle marks, the tracks, on her arms, thighs, feet, even on her neck.

Then I could see that, shallow as a puddle, she was breathing.

I helped her from the toilet or kitchen chair to the couch or bed.

Then I thought that if she breathed any more shallow and slow, she wouldn't be breathing at all. That scared me at first, the idea of her death. The ambulance and the cops, wheeling her out on one of those stretchers with folding legs, her body wrapped in a white sheet, or maybe a black tarp.

Then I'd get shipped to a foster home, where both parents were fat and jolly. Until they sat at the kitchen table drinking, and then they weren't so jolly. They told me my mother was a junkie and a whore, and that I had made her that way. She was so upset with her useless son that she began drinking and whoring and shooting dope. Those were the only ways to escape this awful, ugly child.

I'd heard or read about this somewhere. On the radio or in a book.

The foster parents, the ones with red faces from the booze, the ones who were so fat that they barely had necks, they had two sons who were sixteen and seventeen, who were Matt and Mike. Matt and Mike were not fat like their parents, but they were big and blond. They played football for the high school. They played hockey and lacrosse. They wore baseball caps backward, as though that was clever and unique.

They said, Hey, bro.

They said, Dude.

They said, Lame, so loud that the glasses and dishes in the cabinets shook.

But Marge didn't die, not then, and I didn't have to go to foster care, not then and not ever.

I watched over Peg pretty carefully. I was there all the time. When she slept through the night and then all day, curled on a corner of the big bed, I went in to check on her every hour or two. She wore a T-shirt and sweatpants, and her hair was all over the place in dark ropes. I'd put my ear close to her mouth to see if she was still breathing, and her breath was sour, like rotting fruit.

She was skinny as string, as skinny as a line on a page. She couldn't have weighed more than a hundred pounds. Margaret was cheekbones and elbows and sharp knees. Her butt was flat as a boy's. Her nose and ears seemed big, and her eyes, when she opened them, were enormous. Her pupils were tiny.

One night Ivy came over so we could go for a walk, and Peggy was lying on the couch, uncovered. I had never given it any consideration, how Peg would look to others. I saw her all the time.

Ivy looked, and without thinking, I believe, she said, Jesus.

Then she stopped. She didn't say anything else. She stood and stared.

We went out, and started to walk the dark, as we called it, and for a long time, it seemed, we didn't say anything.

My mind was going sixty, at least, and my emotions were going way faster. There were so many things I had wanted to tell Ivy, but had never said a word. I had almost told her about going out alone, late at night. I'd almost asked her to join me.

A few times I had almost told her about drinking and taking pills, and had nearly offered her a Percodan or oxy or benzo.

And once or twice, I had wanted to tell her about Mag. About her boyfriends, her johns, her tricks, and all the booze and drugs she consumed. Mostly, I wanted to talk to her about heroin.

I didn't know how long she'd been doing the heroin. She had started so slowly and silently. I noticed the needles in a kitchen cabinet, and I saw baggies with little glass tubes of white or brown powder. Dozens of tubes with red or blue or purple caps to hold the dope in.

She'd disappear into the bathroom, and close and lock the door. Or into the bedroom, as though she was changing clothes, or as though she was with a john.

She had no interest in food, and she didn't talk much. She slept way more. Sometimes whole days and nights and on into the next day.

I noticed in her underwear drawer that there were at least twenty fat rolls of cash, and the pill bottles were all full of pills and stayed full a long time. Margie wasn't taking pills any more.

All this was going on, and even though I thought I was paying close attention, even though I thought I was looking closely and carefully, I wasn't seeing anything. Nothing that was important, nothing that might kill Peggy, and take us down.

Two guys, one named Grover, the other named Tommie Lynn, came by with their backpacks. Both of them were skinny, but Tommie Lynn was taller, and had wild curly hair. Grover's hair was so short it looked like he shaved his head every week or so.

They both had tattoos on their necks. Snakes and daggers, and Tommie Lynn had the letters AB in front, at his throat. Tommie Lynn had a big mustache that covered his upper lip and went down on both sides of his mouth.

Neither one said much. They'd come in, nod at me at the most, then they'd go to the bedroom with Mother and close the door, as though they were having sex. But they weren't having sex.

There were just low voices saying low and secret words. I never knew what they were talking about. Then I figured they were talking about red caps or blue caps or white caps. Each color had its own batch of heroin.

Ivy and I walked a long time that night. By then I believe it was very late summer and early fall. We were in September, somewhere in the middle of the month. The summer had been brutal hot, especially July and August.

You could never get away from it, unless you put an air conditioner in, but then you'd feel sealed up in the chill, almost like a dead person. Margaret hated that. So we had a few fans going, and they moved the curtains a bit, and mostly swirled the awful air from one side of the room to the other.

Ivy was walking pretty slow for her. I was walking the way she walked.

We passed the chapel, but Ivy didn't want to go in. Then we walked by the two big libraries and the giant bell tower, and beyond them we were on the arts quad, the oldest part of the university.

The buildings were big and old and beautiful. Some of them had domes on the roof, or towers or turrets, I think they're called. There were paths through the great fields of grass, and big old trees, mostly oaks, I think, but I'm not really sure.

There were some lights on in some of the buildings, but pretty much all of them were lights in halls and stairways. Nobody was around.

We sat on a bench in front of a long building that had giant pillars. It was called Goldwin Smith.

There were crickets and a few lightning bugs. There was almost no sound, just the faint hums of machinery somewhere, from air conditioning or water or something.

Ivy said, All, softly. She didn't look at me, and she didn't say anything else.

I was still thirteen, and in another month I'd turn fourteen, which would make me the same age as Ivy for a little while.

That was the thing, how nothing anywhere stayed still. How you couldn't hold anything, not really, and never for long.

Ivy said, All, again. Then she turned to me.

I was staring across the quad, between buildings, at the valley and the hills way past the valley. I could see little pinpricks of light, maybe on a house or barn or street. Miles away.

I turned and she was looking at me. With sadness, with attention, with affection, with worry. I didn't know which, and how much of each.

Then she lifted her hand to the side of my face. So lightly I could feel her fingers, her palm, the heel of her hand.

Jesus, All, she said.

Then she was pushing my hair back behind my ear.

So sorry, she said. So fucking sorry.

28

Johnny Lee Wales is around forty years old. He's got gray-blond hair that's short, and a gray goatee. Blue eyes that are very clear and very blue. He's average height, maybe five-nine, five-ten, and he's extremely fit. He has the slabs of muscle that run from the bottom of the back of his head to his shoulders, and arms and chest that are so big his arms can't hang straight down at his sides. They stick out. Usually, Tommie Lee has his arms crossed over his chest, whether he's sitting or standing.

He's got tattoos everywhere except his face.

He's on D-block, and that's surprising because he's far from a model prisoner.

Johnny Lee Wales is one of the three bosses of the Aryan Brotherhood inside, in Auburn. The others are on A-block and C-block, to keep them apart.

Johnny Lee gets moved around a lot, at least once a year, sometimes every six months or so. Every second or third stop for him is Southport, near Elmira, the state's maxy max. When they can't control you in a maximum-security facility, you go to Southport.

If you stab someone, if you attack a CO, you go to Southport.

Johnny Lee will never do something that obvious or stupid. Tommie Lee will order someone else to attack his target.

His tats say it all. He's got vines on his neck, curling around his Adam's apple. His arms both have sleeves, with double lightning bolts. He's got a small swastika on each bicep, and 666 for The Beast, from the Bible. On the back of his right hand he's got a small three-leaf clover in green, on the back of the left hand he's got AB.

Johnny Lee seems to be very bright and very disciplined. He

seems real serious, and the blue of his eyes, when you look into his eyes, is unsettling.

A few times, Johnny Lee has nodded to me, and I've nodded back. But he nearly always hangs with people like himself. Big guys with lots of muscle and lots of tats. Guys in white T-shirts. Guys who, like Johnny Lee Wales, seem smart and disciplined.

There are lots of other gangs too, but it's hard to tell if they exist in Auburn. The Mexican Mafia, the D.C. Blacks, the Black Guerrilla Family, the Dirty White Boys.

Sometimes in the yard, I'll see ten or twenty guys grouped together according to race or ethnicity—Black guys, Latin guys, white guys, and I think there's some kind of meeting. But I never really know.

I'm thinking of Johnny Lee Wales because he's a scary guy, and a few times he's nodded to me, and he's always seemed to be a decent guy, even though I know he's not.

He's in for the manufacture and sale of methamphetamine, and for manslaughter. I don't know if he's from upstate or downstate, or from one of those little cities in between. Horseheads, Watertown, Rome, Utica, Geneva.

I think all these towns must have meth problems, and all of them must have a murder every now and then.

Nobody, in here, has been charged with the stabbing and murder of Bevan Lee Eliot. Maybe they're not trying too hard to find the killer. Bevan Lee was a pedo.

So I was in the yard two nights ago, doing what I usually do in the yard. Walking a little, stopping to talk with someone every few minutes, then standing and leaning against the wall. I've been in a long time, and I don't cause trouble, and people leave me alone.

But I was standing there, with maybe twenty minutes to go in yard time, my back against a wall, which is how you want to stand around in prison.

Then Johnny Lee Wales came walking toward me, walking slow and deliberate, and I thought, Oh shit.

Johnny Lee walking slow and deliberate created a path

through the guys in front of him. When he reached me, we did a fist bump, and he stood next to me, almost touching.

He said, Oliver, which almost nobody calls me.

I was surprised he knew my name.

Johnny Lee, I said.

How you doing? he asked, and then I asked him, and we both said we were pretty good.

He asked if I was in for murder, and I said, Murder, aggravated burglary.

How long you been in? Johnny Lee asked.

Twenty-eight, twenty-nine years, I said.

But who's counting, he said and smiled. His teeth were so white and perfect, I thought they must be fake.

All of D-block was in the yard. About three hundred guys, and maybe ten COs. Plus, as usual, maybe a half dozen guys with the high-powered rifles in the perch, in the guard towers. They were always up there, and they were always looking. They were all marksmen, at least that's what we heard. They could hit a nickel in someone's hand at fifty yards.

The yard wasn't huge, but it was still pretty big. It was between the two enormous blocks, A and B on one side, C and D on the other. At the top of the yard was a twenty-foot chain-link fence, topped by razor wire, and at the bottom of the yard was a series of smaller buildings.

There were at least a dozen big halogen lights illuminating the yard, so in the dark it looked like noon on an Arizona day.

The yard was maybe fifty yards long, and probably thirty yards wide. And there were clusters of guys, talking, laughing, telling stories. All dressed in the prison green work clothes, in sneakers or boots. Some guys carried clear plastic or string bags. One old Black guy collected small bits of paper, and another, an old white guy, had pieces of cloth in his bag. The white guy had a huge white beard that was so old it was almost yellow.

Johnny Lee said, You got a board date?

I said no. I said that the murder charge was thirty years, solid. Aggravated murder was true time, real time, natural time, whole life. It was worse than simple murder, murder two, and it was way worse than aggravated manslaughter.

Then I got aggravated burglary. Fifteen years, to run consecutive to the murder. I was still in my first sentence.

Oliver, Johnny Lee said. You had a shit lawyer.

I laughed. I said, I've thought of that. More than a few times.

He said, You could have a board date before too long. In the next year or two.

I just looked at him. He looked at me, and I thought that maybe he knew something I didn't know. I was willing to bet that he knew way more than I would ever know.

Then I saw this really big guy moving toward us. He was a giant, almost.

Snowy Russell. He was pretty well known around the prison, and not just because of the name Snowy. He was Johnny Lee Wales' closest associate.

Snowy was at least six and a half feet tall, maybe more. Maybe six seven or six eight. And he had to weigh three hundred pounds. Huge muscles everywhere. Muscles in his toes. Tats on every muscle.

Snowy worked out with the weights half of every day. And the weird thing was, Snowy worked out most days with a Black guy named Johnson. Johnson wasn't as tall, but he was even wider than Snowy.

How did that make sense for an AB white supremacist to hang with a Black guy? Sometimes I'd hear that the AB was working on deals (usually drug deals) with the Mexican Mafia, with the D.C. Blacks, and often with the Dirty White Boys.

Snowy's hair was shaved around the back and sides, and was long and gelled on top. It was white-blond hair, and that wasn't from age. Snowy looked about thirty, thirty-five. Snowy had earrings in both ears. A cross in one ear, a shamrock in the other.

He came toward us, and the sea of people parted, like Moses or something in the Bible.

I'm not small. I'm six-three, and I weigh one-eighty,

one-ninety, some times of the year. And I guess I'd have to admit that I'm a killer. I'm a murderer. I don't think it's the biggest or most important part of me. But it's there. Big as a lie. Bigger than my forehead, my nose, my mouth. When I saw Snowy coming toward us, I thought, Oh shit. Snowy and Johnny Lee. And me. What could they want from me? I had done nothing. I was nothing.

Then he was right in front of us. Snowy gave Johnny Lee the prison hug, shoulder pressed to shoulder for about two seconds.

Then Snowy turned to me and we bumped fists.

He said, Ollie, as though we'd known each other for years.

Then we stood, backs to the wall, for twenty, thirty minutes.

There in the yard, with hundreds of guys around us, I felt safer than I had felt for three decades.

29

I walked the dark, as Ivy and I called it, but at least half the time Ivy wasn't there. It was just me and all that darkness. It was just me and those empty streets, those sleeping houses. A stray cat, a raccoon, a quiet dog. A wind chime on a porch quietly tinkling in a slight breeze. A car moving several streets over. Then a guy on a bicycle, down the street, moving fast downhill, tires whirring, his helmet reflecting streetlights.

Then me, and I was a shadow. A tall, thin fourteen-year-old boy, and back at the house, Marge lying on the couch, itching and nodding, scratching her junkie dreams.

A few of Mother's boyfriends had talked to me about her. Doc and Matt, Mabel and A.J. They said she was not well, and Doc said she needed to get to a rehab, before she landed in the morgue. He said a rehab would mean a thirty-day stay.

I said good. I said fine. I think I said whatever, and Doc stared at me, as if to say, Don't you care?

Of course I care, I wanted to say to what I thought about what Doc might have wanted to say. But he didn't say and I didn't say.

Doc said he'd make some phone calls.

Mom kept disappearing into the bathroom or the bedroom, both doors closed, and shooting her junk. She'd come out scratching her face or head or arms, pretending that I didn't know and that she didn't know what was really happening.

In four or six or eight months, Mag had become a full-blown junkie. A big-time dope fiend.

I hadn't noticed anything almost. Just a box of needles in a kitchen cabinet, just the brown rubber band or belt to tie herself off. She didn't take showers very often or wash her hair very much. She slept a ton, and she hardly ate at all.

Peggy's cheeks got hollow, and her eyes and nose and ears

got really big, I guess because everything else was shrinking back. This was strange, all of it. This person who was my mother—this mom, this Peg, this Margie, this Margaret—she was disappearing almost while I watched.

Most of the boyfriends had disappeared too. But a few kept coming, and they brought her bottles of pills, they left money on the coffee table. I put the money and pills in Mother's underwear drawer, and the boyfriends, the johns, they never went into the bedroom with Maggie and closed the door. Or if they did, they were only talking, as far as I could tell. There were no squeaking bedsprings, there was none of the headboard banging the wall.

I think they were telling her that she was all fucked up. That she was gonna die unless she got help. Doc kept saying rehab, then Matt was saying rehab, then A.J. and Mabel said rehab too.

Back outside, on Myrtle and Maple and Mitchell Streets, it had to be one or two in the morning. On Irving Place, the streetlights glowed like the eyes of giants. This was a nice neighborhood, only two or three streets over from our house. There were some fences in back yards, but almost none in front or side yards.

There were big bungalows, big Victorian houses with porches all over the place. There were Tudor places, and Cape Cod houses, I think they were called. Just about all the houses had garages, for one, two, or even three cars. But most people left their cars in the long driveways.

A bunch of the houses had skylights on the roof, and you could tell that there were playrooms or studies or bedrooms on the third floor.

In some houses, there were kids. You could see bats and balls, nets and sticks, in the yards. There was always at least one SUV in the driveways, and there were swings hanging from trees in some yards.

Other houses were different. The lawns would be cut and the leaves raked by a lawn service. There would be just one car—usually a little bit old—in the driveway, and there were never toys anywhere. In the evenings there were only two or three lights on in windows. A window in a den on the first floor, a low kitchen light maybe from the stove, and a hall light on the second floor. Only one person lived in each of these houses. The widow or widower of a retired professor, a man or woman who had been divorced, someone who had raised their kids, and the kids now lived somewhere else. They might live in Missoula, Montana, or Urbana, Illinois. Pretty much everyone was far away now. They had their own lives.

Now and then, and sometimes with Ivy, I walked the streets of Belle Sherman, the neighborhood near us, during the afternoons and early evenings. I looked and watched. I watched closely and carefully. Who had kids. How many young men lived in a certain house. Did a single woman live alone in a house. An old man, solo.

If a house had two cars in the driveway, it was certain to have two adults. If there was just one car, and the car was more than five years old, only one old person lived there. If there was an SUV and a regular car, then you had the full family.

Sometimes when I—or Ivy and I—were walking, we'd see a neighborhood person in the driveway or lawn, maybe on the porch, and they'd nod or wave. They might say, Nice day, or, Beautiful afternoon.

They seemed like such nice people. They seemed like people who voted, who gave to charity, who served on the PTA when their children were younger. They were good parents, they paid their taxes. They signed their kids up to take tennis lessons, to go to language camp, to spend a year abroad, in Spain, in France, in Argentina. Some of the kids went as far away as Japan or Russia or South Korea.

I read about this. I heard about this. Sometimes Mabel told me things.

The kids came home changed in some subtle way. They were quieter, they were not so quick to judge. They had belonged to somewhere else for a while.

Irving and Kenyon streets seemed to have far fewer houses with kids. One or two on each street had the SUV and the toys in the driveway and lawn, but most had the look and feel of deserted houses.

Many were deserted, especially during some of the weeks of summer, and during Christmas break. They went away to warm places—the doctors and lawyers, the professors and deans and vice presidents at the university. They went to the Mexican coast, they went to the Bahamas, the Virgin Islands, to countries on the north coast of South America. In summer, they went to Asia or Europe. They could go anywhere in the world.

So could I. That's what I thought when I was finally fourteen, and I was finally over six feet tall, and still growing. I could go to all kinds of places. And tall as I was, I was almost invisible. That was another thing I believed, at least some of the time.

They were tall too, the people in these houses. Some were short, it seemed. Of course there were short people. Most of them seemed tall, though, even the women and children.

So out alone. A Monday or Tuesday night, I believe. Very late. Maybe two or three. Maybe even four.

Very dark. A porch light on, here or there. The stove light on in the kitchen. But nothing else.

Just me in dark jeans, a navy-blue T-shirt, a black hoodie. Low-cut black sneakers with soles as soft as cloth. I went on the front porch. No creak.

The front door locked, the front windows on the first floor locked.

But no dog, no lights on the porch, the backyard, inside.

Just a quiet and dark house. Just a house where the people were away, somewhere nice.

I checked the windows. They were all locked, every one of them.

But people forgot things. People were always forgetting things.

The yard was big, the yard was covered with leaves in the fall, because if there were all these leaves, it had to have been

November or even December. Nobody had called a person yet to come and rake up the leaves.

There were flowerbeds along the back fence, and along the borders of the yard on the sides. There was a three-car garage, but no cars that I could see.

Then I checked a door on the side that was ground level. It probably went to the cellar and the upstairs. I turned the knob, and it was, Holy Shit.

The door was unlocked.

I could feel my heart, and my brain—they went very fast. I thought that I should run away.

But I waited maybe a minute. There was no sound anywhere. Not even a hint of a sound.

I pushed the door open, and there was that basement smell. Kind of musty, kind of like the air had been there for years.

I stepped inside to the landing on the stairs, and it was half-way to the basement, halfway to the the first floor.

I was fourteen then. This was my first time.

30

Mother, by then, was a full-blown, full-bore dope fiend. She had been that way for more than a year, and it had gotten worse in the last few months. There were scars and scabs and bruises all over her body, far more than before, especially on her arms and legs. There were needle marks all up and down her arms and legs, on her neck, even between her toes.

She was so skinny it almost hurt to look at her. Her eyes and ears were big. Bones stuck out on her wrists and ankles, her elbows and knees. And her face. God. It looked like her face had collapsed. Her face was all bone poking at skin. Gray skin, big dark circles around her eyes. A large nose.

She looked at least fifty or sixty years old, and more than half dead. Her skin was not just gray, but waxy. Like a cancer victim, like a dead person in a coffin.

Doc, A.J., and Mabel had been saying for months that Marge had to break this cycle of addiction. She had to go to the hospital, or she had to go to rehab. She lost weight, and then more weight and then more weight. Her ears and nose and eyes kept getting bigger and bigger by the day. Her hands seemed enormous, and her toes were long as fingers.

Her three friends, and these were the only ones who were left, kept saying that this had to stop, that she was going to die. And I'd find her on the floor, in front of the kitchen sink, on the bedroom floor, half under the bed. She'd nod off anywhere in the apartment. Naked on the toilet, the belt or brown rubber hose around her bicep, the needle in her arm or thigh. Sprawled in a big chair in the living room.

She peed the couch and the bed, defecated in the shower, threw up on the kitchen table. I cleaned up as best I could. I'd

half drag her to bed, and I checked at all hours to make sure
she was still breathing.

I didn't want to lose Margaret. I didn't want her to die. The
thought almost put me in a panic. Would they put me in an
orphanage? In jail? In an institution for bad teenagers?
But I had already lost her. She went away a long time ago.
She had always been gone now and then and here and there.
For an evening and for overnight. For a few days, for a week,
for a month or two. But I could always try to call her, and she
might call me. We talked once in a while.

Now I didn't know who she was. Peggy left for somewhere
else. She left for the far side of the world. She left for somewhere near Tahiti or Pitcairn Island, or the shadowy side of
the moon. I'd look in her eyes and they were dead. There was
nothing there.

Finally Doc sat down with me, A.J., and Mabel. He said he
had made phone calls. There was a rehab about twenty-five
miles north on the west side of the lake. There was a place
called Lake Breeze, and they had thirty- and ninety-day pro-
grams.

Doc had reserved a place for Mom. She could go in two
days. Two days and a wakeup.

Mabel could drive her, and A.J. would go along.

When A.J. and Mabel came to pick Peggy up, Mabel brought
me four bags of groceries. Mac 'n' cheese, ramen noodles, cans
of soup, and apples. I hugged Margie, and she stumbled out
between her two friends. She didn't say anything. Her mouth
was open, as though there was something to say, but there was
nothing.

We were all very tired. Especially Mother.

Once I was alone in the apartment, I could feel all the emp-
tiness. If Mommy died now, it would not be my fault. It would
be on the rehab. There was an alarm clock, an old battery pow-
ered alarm clock, on a shelf in the living room, and it made
really loud ticks that I hadn't noticed before.

I could suddenly do anything I wanted, but I had always

more or less done anything I wanted. I hadn't been going out late at night, especially since I had gone in to the house on Irving Street. And I hadn't seen much of Ivy either. I didn't know where she was, or where she had been. I thought maybe it was because she sensed or knew that something weird, something scary was going on with Margaret.

Once in a while I read a book because Mabel would bring me bags of books to read, along with ther stuff. There were all kinds of books. Books about UFOs, books about crazy conspiracies, books about killers. Plus there were romance novels, about guys named Lance or Max and women named Chloe or Zarelda. They were beautiful and handsome, and they had secrets, though we never found out the secrets until the third to last page.

Lance and Max almost always had a scar on their cheek or chin or forehead, but the scar only made them more handsome and mysterious. Chloe or Zarelda had come from—nobody knew where she came from. And sometimes at the most peculiar times, Chloe or Zarelda would fall into sadness, but she would never say what saddened her.

Lance or Max wondered about her past, and her sadness, and Chloe or Zarelda wondered about his scar. But neither of them would talk about these secrets, these mysteries. Because if they did talk, we wouldn't keep reading, would we?

And they were in a castle or a great manor house. There was a cook, a driver, a gardener, a maid. The cook knew everything, and the maid was very thin, almost gaunt, and she was always standing just outside the door to the bedroom or drawing room. She was always listening, though she said almost nothing.

The grounds were vast, had fields, lawns, a lake, a forest. They rode horses, though some days they rode along the roads of the estate in a little sports car, with the top down.

One afternoon, at dusk, they returned from a drive, and pulled into the enormous garage, which smelled of old wood and oil and gasoline. Lance or Max stood next to Chloe or Zarelda. They stood facing each other. Their faces were flushed and their hair tousled from the drive.

For a moment, for two moments, their faces were only a foot apart. They looked deeply into each other's eyes. They looked for what seemed a long time. He was about to kiss her, she thought. He was about to declare something. His interest, his devotion, even his love.

He winced briefly, as though remembering something. Something he had never told anyone. Then he turned away.

Late on a Tuesday or Wednesday, at midnight or maybe at one, there was a soft knocking on the door. Mom had left for the rehab on Monday morning, with Mabel and A.J., and I had been alone since then. I barely heard the knocking. I thought it must be the branches of trees scraping a window or the side of a house.

Nobody knocked on our door in the last six months, unless it was Doc, A.J., or Mabel. And they knocked hard. They made the door shake, as though they were trying to reach Marge in her stupor.

The soft knocking came again. One, two, three, four.

Maybe the sound came from one of the apartments on the second floor. Maybe it came from across the hall, though nobody visited Ivy and her father this late.

I was on the beat-up couch in the living room, and everything in here was dark. There was just a little shadowy light from the windows, from streetlights and cars passing. Nobody could see or hear me. Nobody knew that I had gone in the house. Even with special security cameras or drones, nobody had seen me.

From ten or fifteen feet away, the door was big and dark and scary. Who in the world would knock, even softly, at this hour. There were voices on the street, young and loud, for maybe a minute, but then they passed away.

Then I thought that someone like me was at the door. A weird, creepy guy in a dark hoodie. A short squat guy with major muscles, or a guy with thick glasses with smeared lenses.

What could he want, I wondered. What could we possibly have?

Then I remembered the bottles of pills. Fifteen or twenty bottles, all full with benzos and pain pills. And money. Rolls and rolls of money. Hundreds and thousands of dollars. Ten thousand dollars, thirty thousand dollars.

Margaret had always been careful with money, even when she was far gone. She got the johns to bring drugs, she spent almost nothing.

We had everything a burglar could want.

Tons of drugs, tons of money.

I kept sitting, and I didn't move or anything. The knocks paused sometimes, and then I'd think the person was gone. But just when I was going to move, they tapped again.

One, two, three, four, five. Still soft, still quiet as a creeping cat.

They knocked again, and the reason they knocked so softly was because they wanted me to think that the knocking person was soft and small.

Then I heard, All, All, in a high voice that was as soft as the knocking.

I stood up slow, and moved as soft as if I was in someone else's house. I stood in front of the door.

Then there were knocks, and it was Ivy, saying, All. All.

Ivy, I said, and it was her.

I unlocked and opened the door, and Ivy was no longer as tall as me. I didn't know when that happened.

Where's your dad? I asked, and she said he was away, for more than a week. He was gone to Indianapolis, then Kansas City, then Spokane in eastern Washington state.

I got her to come in, and she sat on one end of the couch.

She said, Your mother?

I shook my head in the darkness, and I knew she could see me. I was on the other end of the couch. She kicked off her sandals, and put her legs and feet up next to me. I put my feet up too, next to her, and this was as close as we had ever been.

She seemed really warm, and she was wearing one of her hats, with the frizzy hair spilling out behind her. She wore one of her hippie dresses.

Where's your mom, All?

Gone, I said.

Then I went into the kitchen, and got us a can of beer. When I came back, she took my hand for a moment or two.

I'm so sorry, she said.

I looked at her face, at her eyes, and I could see them clearly in the darkness. Shiny, almost lit with something. They seemed to glow a little.

You wanna tell me, she said.

Then she said, All, please tell me.

I cracked the beer open, sipped, then handed the can to Ivy.

I could feel her thigh and calf against my leg. Then I thought that she could feel my leg.

She sipped and sipped some more.

Outside was really quiet by then. It might have been one or two in the morning.

I said, My mother, her name is Mom or Marge or Peggy. She has so many names.

I could feel Ivy's eyes.

She's an escort, a prostitute, a sex worker, I said. She's a junkie, a heroin addict, a dope fiend.

Her eyes, Ivy's soft and quiet eyes, were on me.

31

There are days in here that last a week, or sometimes, even a year. We might pause during the day, on a catwalk outside the cells, and realize that we've been here ten, fifteen, or thirty years. On the way to the mess hall, we go through doorways that we've gone through a thousand times. Down hallways, past walls with the same chipping paint, with little spots of rust on the steel doors and wall, and on sections of concrete.

The screws, the guards, the man, the corrections officers, they're mostly the same. We might see a new one every six months or so, maybe two a year. Young, very green guys with short hair and big muscles. Once in a great while, a woman. The women may not be tall, but they're almost always wide.

They all have batons and a ton of keys on their belts. I think they have pepper spray and a book of tickets. When they take a prisoner down to the floor, there are usually four of them. When they do a cell extraction, when they need to remove a reluctant or crazy prisoner from his cell, they have a team of six in riot gear, with helmets, face masks, big plexiglass shields, elbow and knee pads.

People get hurt in cell extractions, usually the prisoner. If a CO gets hurt, the prisoner is charged with assault and battery, and goes to court and has five years attached to his sentence. Plus he gets one or four or six months in the Special Housing Unit, the Disciplinary Unit. Also known as the Hole, as solitary.

In all my time, my three decades, in here I've never been hit with batons, pepper spray, or tear gas. I've never gone to the Hole, not even once. But I know a ton of people who have.

At least a third of the guys have been hit or have been sent to the Hole, and they all say the Hole is the worst. It's twenty-three hours a day of being alone. One hour out—to the shower, the exercise cage, for a medical visit.

Guys get sent to the Hole way, way more when they're just in, in the first five or ten years of a sentence. The new guys have the attitude that no screw, no cop, no CO, is gonna tell them what to do. The cops can go fuck themselves. He, they, them, have another thing coming to them. They've never seen a prisoner so tough, so bad, so cold.

But of course the cops have. They've been dealing with tough guys forever.

And the convicts, many of them got to prison because they thought the rules didn't apply to them. Not really, not all the time.

So when they committed crimes, got caught, got convicted, didn't go to jail, they committed more and maybe worse crimes. Until finally, maybe in their late teens or early twenties, a judge sent them to jail. Which was a shock, because they were special, and particularly bad, and the rules didn't apply.

After a year or two locked up, they got paroled, they did more serious crimes, possibly with a gun or knife, this time, and when they got caught and went to court, they came out with serious time, with a long bid, as we say in here. For sexual assault, for armed robbery, for manslaughter, for selling crack or heroin. They were given fifteen to twenty-five, twenty to thirty.

They weren't given four years with parole at eighteen months. This was big boy time. And if they kept fighting the system, if they had to be taken to the floor and cuffed up, if they had to be extracted from their cells with batons and pepper spray, they were getting more years at the back of their sentences. Instead of fifteen to twenty-five they were looking at twenty to thirty. It didn't matter how cold and tough you thought you were.

They almost certainly wouldn't be living on an honor block.

So the year was moving as it usually did. We were in October, I believe, which was my favorite month of the year. There was football somewhere, in all kinds of places, and there was that amazing fall air—crisp as apples and pumpkins—the deep blue skies, and sunsets with orange and purple and red splashed across the western sky.

October is when you could wear thick hoodies and wool sweaters and jean jackets. October was when the students had all returned to our city and were settled into the semester at the university. At night, you could sleep with a blanket, and get up at three or four a.m. to close the window. By the middle of October, you could see, very late at night, a silvery shine of frost on the lawns and parked cars. You could hunker deeper in your warm bed, and imagine the cold night outside.

By now, by October of my thirtieth year inside, the only thing I know about the fall anymore is the things I remember from a long time ago, from more than half my life ago. Along with all the guys in here, I've been buried under a great pile of stone and steel and concrete. And like rats in walls, I scurry along the narrow passages of the pile, looking for light and space.

There are all kinds of rumors about the murder of Bevan Lee Eliot. That he was having dope brought in, that there's a really crazy guy with a shank, moving among us. That he owed someone money. Or that he was a pedo, and guys don't like pedos.

But they haven't caught anybody, and word is that they have no clue. So a guy with a shank is here and he might go after almost anyone. Any time. The whole place is on edge. More than usual.

Then on a Tuesday morning, in the second week of October, I believe, I get a typed note from a counselor, a guy I didn't know named Martin DeMarco. He was a parole guy, a social worker of some sort, and he wants to see me at 1:45 to talk about my status.

I have no idea what that means. I'm finishing my first bid, on the murder charge, but then I'll have fifteen years to go on an aggravated burglary charge. I'm almost fifty, and I've always believed I wouldn't be out until I'm sixty-five. Until I'm at the beginning of being an old man.

The sentences, I'm almost certain, are consecutive and not concurrent. I didn't even know what that meant until Spector, my court-appointed lawyer, told me back then. I liked Spector. He wasn't much older than me, wasn't long out of law school, and he was already half bald on top. He was bright, but this was his first rodeo.

At one-thirty I cuff up, and a skinny little guard named Prelazine takes me through gates, steel doors, down halls, upstairs, and so on. At every gate and door there's a CO watching and counting us.

Then we're at the front of the joint, two stories of offices, the front gate, and steel doors every ten or fifteen feet. Somewhere in here is the warden's office, and at one corner, either the south or north corner, is the big room where they used to execute prisoners, starting with Kemmler. Some guys say it's the north corner on the first floor, and some say it's the room where the warden's office is.

Just about every guy has an opinion about this. Every one of them is sure about where Kemmler died. About where all those guys died.

We go up to the second floor, down a long hall, past all these small offices. There are women in dresses and men in dress shirts and ties, and a few of us guys helping out. These are trusties, guys on the high end of the honor block. Eakes is there, and Walton and Grimaldi and Williams. They have access to computers. They can find out things.

Mr. DeMarco is kind of short and thickly built. His sleeves are rolled up and there are tats on his forearms. He has dense black hair that's going grey, and thick glasses with brown frames. He's got a tie with neat orange stripes on a dark blue field.

Mr. Curtin, he says, and stands up from his desk to shake my hand. He sees that I'm cuffed, and asks Prelazine to uncuff me, and please wait in the hall.

Then I'm sitting, and Mr. DeMarco says, You want a board in February or March?

I just look at him. I don't know what he's talking about.

Mr. Curtin, he says. A board. A parole board hearing.
Mr. DeMarco's got a thick New York City accent. Queens or
the Bronx. He talks fast.

He smiles, and I say, I don't get it. I got fifteen years consecutive to the thirty.

You did get that, thirty years ago, but various judicial reform
bills have passed the legislature. Your fifteen years have been
folded into the thirty years. Your sentence has been commuted.

I stare at him.

Your thirty was thirty to life, so that's why you need a board,
Mr. DeMarco says.

There are pipes in the corner running floor to ceiling. Their
paint is rusting and looks water damaged. A sign on the wall
says, In the land of the blind, the one-eyed man is king.

Are you sure, Mr. DeMarco? I ask.

If you're Curtin, he says.

In the hallway, I turn around for Prelazine to cuff me up.

He says, Never mind, and puts the cuffs back on his belt.

Prelazine says, Fuck it.

32

Then I was alone, except for those odd times when Ivy came over to hang out with me. Or when Mabel stopped by with bags of groceries, and would sit with me for an hour or two. In most ways it was more or less the same as when Mommy was around, only now that she was gone, I wasn't cleaning up after her accidents, I wasn't trying to feed her, and I didn't have to check anymore to see if she was dead.

This was more like the times when she was away overnight, or for a weekend, or when she was gone for a month or two in Rochester or Buffalo, or one of those upstate New York cities. Maybe Albany or Syracuse. There was always a boyfriend in each of those cities, a Walt, a Ken, a Donald, a Cliff. They always ended up telling her what to wear, who to talk to, and that she was a dumb cunt, a liar, a whore, a cheater. Then they'd start slapping her, choking her, bending her arm behind her back, and punching her.

She'd escape at three or four in the morning when her boyfriend was passed out. Sometimes Mabel drove up to Rochester, or Wayne, the Bug, drove over to Albany, and they brought her home.

She'd be real quiet and tired for a week or so. She had bruises and maybe a black eye. She seemed very small and soft and kind of dreamy. She slept a ton, she said very little, and then, by and by, she seemed her old self again.

I didn't know how she'd be after Lake Breeze. I didn't know if she'd be gone for thirty days or ninety days, or even longer than that, but I guess it didn't matter. She'd get home, and she'd either stay straight or she wouldn't. There wasn't much I could do about it.

Even Doc had said that.

It's not on you, Al, he said. These are Margaret's choices. Not yours. I wish it was different, but it's not.

So I stayed in and I stayed low. We had a small television, and a little tablet computer, and I went out and around on the internet a few times. But I didn't know how to use it, not very well at all.

The days and nights were real long or real short. I read a few books that Doc had brought me, and even Mabel brought me a few books when she saw I was reading. Her new boyfriend, Merv, was taking a class at the community college, and she brought me some books he had read in English class.

There was one about a boy growing up on the plains or deserts of Arizona or New Mexico or Utah. He was twelve or thirteen, and this whole thing was in 1880 or 1890, I'm pretty sure. It was him and his big sister, who was always treating him like a small boy or even a baby. Plus his mom and dad. His mom cooked and cleaned, and she rode a horse or buggy.

The boy's father had a ranch where he raised cattle, and he also worked as a blacksmith on the side, making horseshoes and tools and such.

Then a stranger, who wore black and hardly talked at all, came to town and started living in the bunkhouse on the ranch.

I think this book must have come from Doc because I doubted they were reading it at a community college.

Often at night, if Mabel or Ivy hadn't come over, I'd take a pain pill, I'd get a beer from the fridge, and I'd sit on a stool at one of the front windows. The window would be open, but the screen was in place. There were bushes outside that had grown, and from the dark, from behind the screen and bushes, I could see the street and sidewalk.

Our house was between the university and the Belle Sherman neighborhood, and there were lots of big houses that had been broken up into student apartments. So the students were out, at the bars, the restaurants, just walking around. The bars closed by one.

Then it got more quiet. Then it got way more quiet, and there were just leaves in the trees whispering, and cool night air. Maybe a voice from somewhere, a dog, a car or truck or motorcycle half a mile away. All the regular stuff.

I believe this was late September or early October. It always seemed like that time of year because I loved those months. Maybe it was late April, early May. We were moving toward spring rather than fall. One of those threshold times.

By one or one-thirty, a few students would still be out, a single student, a couple, a small group of three or four. Sometimes talking loudly, sometimes talking in normal voices, as if this was a normal time of the day or night.

Looking out, I'd think of those times when Ivy and I walked the dark. We moved quickly, probably a little nervous, and we talked quietly, if at all. We almost whispered.

Did other people who were out wonder about us? Did they think that we were normal individuals or a normal couple? With regular lives?

Students? Who lived together? Or had jobs?

Was someone standing or sitting by a window, looking out? In a dark room? Unable to sleep? Watching us disappear from the cone of a streetlight, into the dark?

Did the watcher think of us after we disappeared? Would anyone, anywhere, remember us? Ivy? Me? Both of us?

I always wondered what a person would see when he or she looked at me. A tall kid, skinny and goofy as a stork. Big nose, long dark hair, sometimes pulled back into a ponytail. And very dark, very black, very large eyes. Nervous eyes, scared eyes, watchful eyes. Eyes that took things in. That noticed stuff even in the dark. Especially in the dark.

Would a person watching me think that I grew up in a family, in a big old Victorian house, with a big porch wrapped around the front and side of the first floor? There would be a porch swing, Adirondack chairs, white pillars holding up the roof of the porch.

On the street, a man and a woman, holding hands, passed

the front of our house. Under the streetlight the woman was wearing a dark blue dress with a yellow collar, and yellow outlining where the pockets would be. The man was wearing a dark suit jacket, and they leaned their heads toward each other.

I watched them disappear, and I could feel the pain pill, I could feel the beer, moving though my body, in the muscles and blood, through the lining of my stomach, in and around my brain.

Then I got up, went to the bedroom, took another pain pill, went to the kitchen for another beer. I wanted to push this feeling, this numbness, just a little more.

By then it was two or two-thirty, and outside the window in front, there were no people anywhere, that I could see. Just leaves moving very slightly in a slight breeze. Just the streetlight shining down on empty parked cars. I couldn't even see a cat or raccoon deep in the shadows.

But I could feel the beer and the pill. They were warm, and they were in every part of me. I could float in the air if I had wanted to.

I wondered again about someone who might see me, and wonder who I was. About the big Victorian house with the porch, and the enormous beech tree on the front lawn.

Inside, the floors were sanded and polished, the windows were clean, and there were Persian rugs here and there. There was a wide, generous staircase to the second floor.

The mother in this house, in this family, was an attorney, and the father was an oncologist. There would be an older brother, an older sister, and then there'd be me. The youngest, the baby of the family

Each night, at six-thirty or seven, we'd all sit down to dinner. To something delicious, balanced, and nutritious. We'd sit down at the old oak table, which was so old and so polished that it looked black. People talked with each other. My older brother, who was a student at the university, talked with my mother about something political or legal or topical. My sister talked to my father about his beard, which he'd had as long as any of us could remember. She joked that he should shave almost all of it, but leave a soul patch below his bottom lip. Dad laughed.

Then there was me, at the far end of the table. I didn't look like any of them, and I doubted I sounded like them.

Hey, Scooter, Mom said. How're things for you?

Yeah, Dad said. What's going on with you?

My handsome brother smiled, and looked at me.

My sister, beautiful as a model, smiled too, and she looked at me.

All of them, my family. They were looking at me.

33

I was only fourteen, I'm pretty sure. Time was not moving, but I was getting taller almost every day. My name was Oliver Curtin, the way it had always been.

Mother was still in rehab, and somehow I knew that she was going to stay there at least three months, maybe longer. They could keep her for three months, or six months, or shorter or longer.

However long, I didn't mind. I was doing just fine on the first floor of the apartment. I had food from Mabel, and I had beer, and I had enough pills for a year. Pills for pain, and pills for anxiety, and sleep pills too.

Late at night, especially when her father was on the road, Ivy came over to hang out with me. She might knock on the door at eleven, eleven-thirty, and I'd whisper her name through the wood of the door, and she'd say, All.

Then we'd hug, and it was as though she was my favorite sister, and we hadn't seen each other in a long time. Ivy was very strong, and held me like a vise, and I could feel the whole front of her, especially her breasts.

We might stand there for a minute or two, and then she kissed me on the side of my long skinny neck. Then we sat on the couch, and we usually drank one beer between the two of us, sitting on opposite ends of the couch, our legs up, feet almost hidden on the sides of our thighs and butts.

The days and nights swam together most of the time. I ate ramen noodles, and mac 'n' cheese, and I drank coffee too, with hazelnut creamer. If I had two or three coffees, I got jazzed up. I got nervous and trembly, and my fingers jumped around as though they were plugged into an electrical socket.

Then I'd take a pill or two, an Ativan and a demerol. Demerol was one of my favorite pain pills. It was strong and clean.

They didn't put Tylenol or anything else in in—just demerol, and twenty minutes after taking one, boom, there it was. That sweet, smooth feeling.

If you added an Ativan, and then drank a beer, oh, boy.

So my days and nights, they were pretty much upside down. I didn't go to sleep until five or six or seven in the morning. The sky might be going from black to gray, but in the bedroom, we had heavy shades and thick curtains, and they were always blocking out the light. I'd lie there, in the dark bedroom, knowing the day was beginning, and I'd watch the line of light at the edges of the curtains and shades.

I could hear the noise of the traffic, and once in a while, I could hear a piece of a voice. But the voice was always different, more quiet, than at midnight or two a.m.

Then I'd stretch my feet toward the bottom of the bed, and if I was still wearing socks, I'd take them off and throw them at the window. I don't know why, but I always slept in my jeans and a T-shirt. I kept my sneakers lined up on the floor at the side of the bed.

If I just slept in my boxer shorts and a T-shirt, I'd feel naked, vulnerable. Anyone could expose me. Someone could break down the door, and stand over the bed with a knife or a gun. The cops or robbers. This way, with my jeans on and my sneakers lined up, I was always ready for anything.

Then I'd start to drift under and away. I could feel a veil drop between me and the world, and the traffic and the shards of voices were a little farther away.

Then another veil dropped, and it grew quieter, and my breathing slowed. There were at least two veils between me and everything.

I might have thought that everything out there—the people, the cars and trucks, dogs and cats, birds, worms, ants, even the leaves on trees—was having a life. They were seeing other people, they were leaving their house or apartment, they were waving to other people, they were thinking about their job or class, their girlfriend, their friend.

The world was so big, and during the day the world was bright, even if it was cloudy. More veils had fallen, and then I was asleep, and I never knew where I went when I was asleep. The dreams were crazy all the time. People from everywhere appeared. The girl in the front row from the class at school. An old woman I'd walked past on North Tioga Street. The old woman had smiled at me. A teacher from third or fourth grade who had short black hair like a sailor's watch cap.

How could you love someone you didn't know?

They were in rooms, or they were in long hallways, or they were outside and it was snowing.

For a fraction of a moment or two, I'd float up from the depths of sleep and I'd break the surface very briefly. I'd see two bureaus, a closet door, a door to the living room. I'd see the light at the edges of the window, and I could tell from those thin, thin strips of light what time it was, more or less. It was brightest between one and three, in the summer, and in the winter it was brightest between noon and two. After two or three, the thin strip became less intense, and the sun came in at a lower angle.

If I had had two or more beers the previous night and early morning, I'd have to get up to pee at eleven or noon. I'd stagger to the bathroom, and then I'd stagger back. I'd be back asleep in less than a minute.

Sometimes I wondered what other people's lives were like. I did that a bunch. Often I did it nearly all the time. I'd wake up late in the afternoon, around four, and I knew it was four because the strips of light were from a lower angle, and they were way weaker than at one o'clock.

I always lay in bed a while. I thought about going back under again, gliding down to the depths of unconsciousness, but I was never sure if I could get there. So I lay under the sheet or blanket, and before I even knew it, I was thinking of people on the street outside.

Maybe I'd seen a man in a green puffy jacket, and a gray

watch cap, wearing jeans and boots, and a red backpack. He hadn't shaved in a while, and his hair, at the sides of his cap, spilled nearly to his shoulders. The hair was brown with reddish-blond highlights.

The man walked with almost a bounce in each step, as if he had too much energy, and had to get to some other place fast.

I don't think that I had ever seen him. I saw some people go by pretty much every day. But not him.

I wondered who he was. If his name was Dan or Patrick, Brendan or Mark. I wanted to know what he carried in his red backpack. Lunch, books, papers, notebooks. A camera, a gun.

Was lunch a sandwich and apple? A container of yogurt? Carrot and celery sticks? A few cookies?

And what did he do? Was he a student? An instructor? Somehow, I didn't think he was a teacher because he was unshaven, and I thought a teacher would want to present himself in a more or less professional way. But what did I know.

He looked maybe twenty-five years old, possibly older. He could have been a graduate student, in biology, in chemistry, in physics. He kind of looked like a science type, but I wasn't even sure what I meant by science type.

Because he might have been a law student. He could have been a graduate student in history or social studies, if they had social studies in graduate school.

I wondered if he lived alone, in an apartment or house. Maybe a little third-floor place up with the eaves, the kind of place where Mommy and I used to live. He had a space heater; he had a little boom box for music and radio. He had a desk, a former door set on top of file cabinets. He had bookshelves. One bookshelf if he was a graduate student in chemistry, at least two bookshelves if he was a history grad student.

This guy, say his name was Dwight, could have had a roommate, perhaps a girlfriend. She was Zoe or Chloe. If he was studying chemistry, she was a law student, if he was studying social sciences, she was studying physics.

Dwight loved Zoe more than she loved him. Sometimes late

in the evening, while he was working at the desk in the living room, and she was reading on the couch, she'd look over at him and she'd wonder if she loved him.

Who is he? Zoe wondered, seeing his long brown hair, his round, wire-framed reading glasses, his pale neck.

Is he the person I want to be with? she asked herself.

Then he felt her eyes on him. He looked up and over at her. He smiled. She kept looking.

34

After the first few days of meeting with Mr. DeMarco, everything felt different. The idea of the time inside didn't stretch out endlessly into the future. The concrete and steel, the shouts and bangs, the smell of toilets, didn't seem like forever, the way they always had.

For those first days, everything I saw and heard and smelled, was temporary. I'd look at the cellblocks, at the other guys, and I'd say to myself, those cells are endless, and that guy there will be in for twenty more years.

I kept picturing myself with a big black trash bag slung over my shoulder, holding everything I had in the world. I'd picture myself at the front of the prison, near all the offices, near the warden, near Mr. DeMarco, near the street in front of the prison.

And all the heavy gates, the steel doors, the boxes where one barred gate would open and then close, and a CO behind heavy plexiglass would look at you, make you wait a minute, and then another barred gate would slide open on the other side of the box, and you went through.

You'd go down a set of concrete stairs, and then walk a corridor lined with closed and locked steel doors, past a barred window to somewhere, where the plexiglass was painted black.

Then into another box, with a CO and three sides of barred gates. Then I had to stop thinking about leaving, because I had no idea what the front gates to outside looked like, or where they were, or even if they were the way I would leave.

If I leave.

When I leave.

On the yard, I ask a few guys, older guys who have been here a long time, if they know Mr. DeMarco. Someone DeMarco, in administration. Guy with big arms and some tats.

I ask Smiddy, a Black guy with white hair, who's been here almost as long as me. Twenty, twenty-five years, for murder, of course. Smiddy says he never killed nobody, and that's what most people in here say. I didn't do it. We're a prison full of innocents.

But with Smiddy, it might be true.

He's got thick glasses with heavy black frames.

He asks me where I've seen this guy, DeMarco.

Out front, I say.

Smiddy looks at me through his thick frames. His eyes are watery and dark.

He looks away for a few seconds, and says, Nah unh-unh.

Where'd you see DeMarco? he asks again.

Out front, second floor.

Smiddy looks thoughtful.

No, sir, All, he says.

Then he pats my upper arm.

I ask Dessen, this old white guy, who's got a huge grey ponytail and beard. He wears the standard green pants, and a white T-shirt. He stands by himself at the far end of the yard. Dessen doesn't talk to many people. And Dessen, we hear, admits to killing his wife.

I say, Dessen, and he's looking at the night sky, which you can't really see because of the intense lights on the yard.

He looks at me and says, Oliver, something almost nobody calls me.

Can I ask you something?

He nods.

You ever heard of a guy named DeMarco?

He moves his head slowly, side to side.

One of us? he asks. Or one of the screws?

Some kind of social worker or something. Works out front, second floor, in administration.

He moves his head side to side again.

You sure of the name? he says. DeMeo?

DeMarco.

DeMarco, he says after me.

He looks up at what he can see of the night sky.

You sure you didn't dream this? he says, and we both chuckle a little.

Jesus, I say. God, I hope I didn't dream this.

He giving you money, this DeMeo, Dessen says.

I shake my head, and we watch the yard awhile. People moving and standing. Guys in the green work clothes. Guys with beards, with shaved heads, with huge Afros. Guys carrying string bags, or files of paper like a lawyer.

We got everything in here.

We got walls, and we've got guards with the high-powered rifles up in the perch. We've got maybe ten COs patrolling the yard in their gray shirts and dark pants. Each of them have radios on their belts, cuffs, batons.

About half the guards are buff, work out with weights, same as about half the guys.

I ask a few other guys if they know who DeMarco is, or if they know he even exists. But nobody knows him, and have never even heard of him.

They call him DeMeo and DeMello and Detroit.

They say, Who the fuck you talking about, Ali?

Then I'm back in my house, and the door's locked, and it's late. It's always late in here.

It's quiet too. As quiet as this place ever gets. You might hear somebody calling out in sleep, or muttering something. But not much else. And most of that is the earlier part of the night. Coughing, a smaller bang or ping against a steel wall, sneezing.

Then by midnight, we're silent as death. There might as well be nothing and nobody in here. We are, all of us, nothing. We are a small spot of mold growing on a concrete wall. We are even less than that.

Then my head is resting on the small pillow on my bunk, I've got a sheet covering most of my body, and I can hear people breathing—mostly Gates and Mellor.

Gates sounds like an old person, even in sleep. He breathes

with a rasp, and then he sputters every minute or two. Sometimes he goes to sleep by seven or eight, and he sleeps till four or five, which is late for here. When he sputters, it's like a baby whale who's come up from the ocean of sleep. Mellor's much more quiet. Mellor meditates, and he's always concentrating on his breathing. He tells me that life and time are way easier when you meditate. Then things don't bother you so much. He says Buddha meditated under a giant fig tree in India, and didn't get up until he was enlightened. Mellor has tried to get me to meditate over the years. He's offered me books on Buddhism. One of them is called, *Be Here Now*. I laughed and told Mellor that I certainly was here now, whether I liked it or not. I most definitely was not anywhere but here.

Mellor said, All, you could be somewhere else in Buddhism. You could be more deeply here, and not here, at the same time.

I didn't understand that, I told Mellor. How the fuck could you be here and not here?

That's the thing he said.

Then we didn't say anything else for a while.

My eyes are closed and I'm thinking of Mellor and his contradictions and his Buddhism. Then I hear footsteps, kind of light footsteps, and I open my eye to a slit of low light, and it's the small skinny guy named Glenn, who always works the overnight. We don't know if Glenn is his first or last name, and we see him later at breakfast, which starts at five.

Gates is still sputtering a little, and Mellor maybe turns over in sleep. His sheets make a whisking sound.

I don't know what to think since I talked to DeMarco, and since Prelazine didn't cuff me up. That was highly unusual, especially outside the inner part of the prison. That was a security breach. Only Prelazine, like DeMarco, knew I was on my way out. I think.

But then I think, Why didn't Smiddy and Dessen know about DeMarco? Smiddy even works in an office near the front gates. Smiddy has access to a computer.

Smiddy and Dessen are two guys who really keep their eyes and ears open. They know things.

Maybe I dreamed the whole thing, the whole scene with De-Marco. Or maybe the Department of Corrections is running some kind of weird experiment. Testing things about patience and information on the inmates. Seeing how information affects us.

I don't know. It's so hard to tell about so many things in here.

My eyes are closed and I can feel the sheet on my bare legs, and the pillow is lumpy. It's been a while since Glenn came through, doing his count. That would have been around midnight, give or take a few minutes.

I'm just under the surface of sleep, the water lapping at my face and head. Then I rise, so briefly, for air and light, then I'm under again.

I see DeMarco, and he's wearing a dress shirt and a tie, and his sleeves are rolled up on his thick forearms. He has tats. An anchor like Popeye, the head of a woman with long auburn hair. He wears heavy glasses, and he has a New York City accent. Queens, I think, possibly the Bronx.

You get a board, he said. Early next year. Maybe February, maybe March.

I know he said that, this DeMarco dude. Talking fast, like New York City.

He said my thirty years was just about up. He said I had nearly served my time, and that the extra charge, the aggravated burglary, was commuted.

Then I'm under the surface, five or ten feet down. It's blue and blue, and almost pale green. There are fronds of something, of some fish or plant, down below me.

Then I hear sputtering, sputtering, somewhere in the distance. I look up and down, side to side, but there's nothing there. Just waving green fronds, and vast shimmering water. And me, going deeper, not breathing. Not worrying at all.

35

By then I was fifteen, or just about fifteen, and Mommy was still gone. She had spent six months in the rehab itself, and then she was living in a halfway house run by the rehab. It was called Serenity House, and there were ten addicts and alcoholics living there, including Peg.

I went once with Mabel to visit her. It was a huge old house with fifteen or twenty rooms, and out front, attached to a pillar by the front steps, was a flag with a rainbow, and the name, Serenity House.

We sat outside in the backyard on metal chairs that were rusting. There were a couple of big, beat-up trees, oaks or maples. One had rope and a tire swing, and the rope looked kind of frayed.

The yard wasn't that big for such a huge house. But it was enclosed by a newly painted white fence, and trees and bushes. You couldn't see other houses except for pieces of roof, or a few windows set in dormers on the roof next door. Some of the windows in Serenity House, especially on the second and third floors, had sheets or a pair of pajama bottoms as curtains.

Maggie's chair was close to mine, and she held my hand the whole time, and Mabel smiled at us. Margaret kept saying, You look so tall, All, and I wanted to laugh. She was making a rhyme but I was pretty sure she didn't know it.

She said, You're so fucking tall, and then she said, You're all grown up.

Her face was bright and clear, and she was nervous. Her arms and hands kept moving, and she crossed and recrossed and recrossed her legs. The top leg was always bouncing a little.

Then after waving around some, she'd grab my hand again.

Mabel seemed normal, seemed the way she had always seemed. She looked and sounded like Mabel. But Marge and me—we were weird. We were abnormal. I wasn't sure what we were.

Peg's eyes were clear and very bright, and her skin was pale. Not deathly pale like when she'd been home, with that gray tint, but pale like someone who stayed inside a long while. She didn't wear makeup that I could see, and her hair was untreated, and there were quite a few gray strands that had never been there before.

This was being clean. This was being sober. She said she took a walk every day with a woman named Marina. Marina was only nineteen, and she was a heroin addict and a sex worker.

Like Marge, I thought. Only Marina, she ran away from her junkie mother when she was fifteen, and started on the stroll almost right away. She lived in shitty hotel rooms, which cost thirty or forty bucks a night, and where there were cockroaches and centipedes with long wavy antenna. Sometimes the toilets wouldn't flush, and live coils of shit sat in the toilets for a day or two, and the stink was unbelievable. That was you, your body, and just think how nasty it was, Mom said Marina said. And Marina was so ashamed to even have a body.

Then hookers, sex workers, whores, started getting killed in and around Rochester, and their bodies dumped near the Genesee River. It was as though the river washed the women up on the banks, one by one, every two weeks or every two months. Over and over and over. Till there were more than ten, twelve bodies, and then maybe some more.

The TV and newspapers were full of the news. The bodies, and the terrible danger for sex workers. How some lone maniac was out there, strangling women. Just for. Just for what?

So Marina moved out of Rochester. She moved to Geneva.

Now Marina was Mother's roommate at Serenity House. They had a big room on the second floor. After the lights were out, always by ten, they talked half the night in the dark. They knew everything there was to know about each other.

So Margaret, she'd been away for a while, for two months,

maybe, and I hadn't been going out very much. I don't even know why. I guess because I didn't feel like it. I guess because I had no backup in case I got caught doing something I shouldn't be doing. So around midnight some nights, I'd take an oxy, drink a beer, and get all dressed in black, maybe like a ninja. The black almost made me invisible. Mabel still brought me pills with the groceries. Sometimes amber bottles of pills, sometimes blister strips, sometimes baggies with loose pills.

By then we were somewhere in November, middle November or late November. The leaves were almost completely gone from the trees. They covered the sidewalks, the gutters of streets, the lawns around houses. Very early in the mornings I'd see a skinny layer of white frost on the lawns and on the cars parked in the street.

Some of the houses in Belle Sherman seemed empty. There were no lights in these houses, no cars in the driveway, or there was a porch light, a bedroom light, that seemed to stay on all the time. These few lights were on at midnight, and when I went back in the early afternoon, the same lights would still be on.

I was pretty sure that the people who owned houses and who had gone away, were trying to trick people like me. They wanted to make us think that they were really home. They seemed to think that we were easily tricked, that we were stupid. I guess that they were at least a little bit right, but at the time I was insulted.

So at the end of November, or maybe early December, I was out, and it was maybe two in the morning. I was in my usual black outfit, only I was wearing an extra hoodie, a black watch cap, and black gloves. The sky had begun to snow, real slow, but there was still a half inch of snow on the ground.

It was beautiful to watch the snow fall in the cones of yellow light from the streetlights. All these lone snowflakes, solitary

and languid, dancing and drifting down at a slant, and then settling gorgeously on the ground. For a minute or two, I'd just
stand and watch them in the light.

God, I thought. Boy, oh boy.

That's so lovely, I thought. Then realized I had never in my
life used the word lovely. I almost didn't know what it meant.

I was on Kenyon Street, one street over from Irving, and
there were two houses in particular that interested me. One was
a big Victorian place that was green, with tan trim around the
windows and doors and porches. That place was on Kenyon.
Then on Irving there was this big bungalow, two stories, with
lots of trees and bushes in the yard. The Kenyon place had a
low light on in a side room on the first floor, and the Irving
house had a light on in a second-floor bedroom in front, over-
looking the front porch.

Both lights had been on in the rooms for days. Neither
house had cars in the driveways or garages.

I looked behind me, and my footsteps in the snow, on the
street and sidewalk, stretched back as far as I could see. But
they were also filling up quickly, and would be gone in half an
hour. It was as though I'd no longer exist. It was as though I
had left the world.

I went softly up the driveway to the back of the house.
There was a back door, and three windows. Someone had left
the screens in the windows, and the middle window was unlocked. I took out my small knife, the Swiss Army knife, and
cut the screen in two long diagonals. I lifted the screen out, and
pushed the window up.

There was warm air from inside, and that deep silence of
an unoccupied house. There was a refrigerator humming, and
down below, in the basement, the furnace making a faint rumble. There was water in pipes. But there was no music, no computer or TV, no radio, no voices.

There was a low light on in the next room over, and I looked
at the doorway. There was nobody. So I dropped down onto

the carpet, leaving small clumps of snow. They'd melt in a few minutes.

Everything here was beautiful. Bookcases, a massive flatscreen TV, brown leather couches and big chairs. The kitchen was chrome, and there were marble countertops. A block of knives with black handles, a cabinet with wine glasses that gleamed in the dark. There was a rack of wine bottles.

My eyes got used to the dark. There was an island in the middle of the kitchen. More marble, cloth napkins, silver salt and pepper shakers. There was a cork board with small papers pinned to it. There was a birthday card, to Nicole, but I could only read the name. There were tickets to something, a couple of bills, a small envelope with bobby pins.

The living and dining rooms were big. A huge wood table that shined in the lights from outside. Six wood chairs, perfectly spaced. The long living room had heavy dark beams in the ceiling, and an entire wall of books.

I went up the stairs, and at the top, there were four bedrooms, a bathroom, and a second bathroom inside the biggest bedroom. I went into the big bedroom. There was a cleanly made bed the size of the state of Iowa. A quilt with what looked like a design of peacock feathers.

I sat on the bed, and it was firm. I took my shoes off, pulled the quilt down, then got underneath the covers. I got two pillows bunched up under my head, and took deep breaths.

Closed my eyes, lay on my side.

I thought, These people must be happy. Rich. Educated.

Nobody here was a junkie, an alcoholic, a sex worker.

Then my breathing got deeper still, slower, and that was most of what I could feel or know.

Just breathing, in then out, in then out.

Finally, after not very long, I was under. I was asleep. And the snow kept falling, a lovely, hushed blanket of white.

36

Ivy was sixteen by then, and she got taller, the way I got taller. We were giraffes, we were trees. Compared to most people we could touch the sky. Clouds could pass over and through us.

Her dad was gone so much of the time. For five days, for two weeks, once or twice for a month. He went everywhere—even to Alberta and British Columbia in Canada. In those massive open fields where wheat grew, and then in winter the gray sky merged with gray land at the horizon, and it was all together. It was sky and earth, and snow was all over everything.

Her dad, Henry, liked to drive. Sometimes Ivy thought that he loved to drive. When he was home, she said, he was restless and itchy, and seemed to be jumping out of his skin. For the first few days after getting home from the road, he was real tired. He slept almost all the time.

He'd sleep all night, like a normal person. He got up in the morning. He was unshaven, and he wore an old flannel shirt that had black and white checks and was wrinkled from having been slept in.

He cooked two eggs for her, made toast, made three sausage links. She was sitting at the kitchen table, half asleep, her face in her hands. He was as alert as if he was driving on Interstate-90 or Interstate-80.

I-90, she thought, went from Boston to Seattle. I-80 went from metro New York to San Francisco. Henry, she said, knew those highways like he knew the roads in our neighborhood. He could almost drive them with his eyes closed.

Her dad buttered the toast, got a clean fork and a paper towel for a napkin, and set the plate, the fork, and napkin on the table in front of her.

Then he said, You want coffee? And she said, Sure. That would be great.

More and more, Ivy said, she was drinking coffee in the morning. She always had coffee when her dad was around and he made a whole pot. When he was on the road, she often made a single cup, with a small cone and filter. She liked milk in her coffee, and sometimes she even drank it black.

But the breakfast, the buttered wheat toast, the eggs and sausage and coffee, were fantastic. Now and then, her dad made breakfast for himself as well, but often he just down at the table opposite her, and watched her eat, and smiled.

These were some of her best memories. Her big, shaggy father, his flannel shirts, the quiet of the early morning. And the breakfast itself. God, she said, it was so good.

Now, he was on the road far more. He was taking loads from Canada to Mexico, from Los Angeles to Daytona Beach, from Atlanta to Albany, NY, from Buffalo to Cleveland, Chicago, and St. Paul. The money, he said, was really good, and he was making as much as he could so he could pay for her college.

After breakfast, Henry sat in their living room and watched the Weather Channel. He'd lie on the couch and watch for an hour or more—ridges of high pressure, cold fronts or warm fronts, a massive storm building in the Gulf of Mexico. There were so many states, and so much air, and it was all moving as the earth turned and spun, forever and ever, it seemed.

Her dad could picture the way a highway in Kansas would look, compared to a graph on the TV.

Later, she'd pass through the living room, and Henry was sleeping on the couch. She spread a blanket over him, and hoped he'd get a ton of rest. He worked so hard. He worked so long.

Across the hall, everything was pretty much the same as it had been for months. We still had a landline phone, but it almost never rang. Once or twice, I picked it up and it was always a man or woman trying to sell me insurance, siding for my house, or get me to give money for finding a cure for cancer. I never knew who these people thought I was, but I always hung up.

After three or four days, Ivy's dad was out on the road again. This time for maybe two or three weeks, maybe for as long as a month. She was fine with that, and she told me that probably we should spend most of the time together. Hanging out at her place or my place. I said we should do my place because my mother, I didn't think, would be home for a long time.

Her dad called from Erie, Pennsylvania, from East St. Louis, from Flagstaff, Arizona. The country was so big, Ivy said. There were so many states, and thousands of cities. All of it went forever. He would call, just about every night. From truck stops and motels, nearly always from small cities on the highways, usually at the near or far side of big and famous cities. Just past Denver, or on the near side of Missoula in Montana. Near Spokane on the eastern side of Washington State, or a little south of Topeka, Kansas.

Ivy could hear the interstate noise in the background, on Henry's end, or the crash of silverware and dishes and voices. Probably in some truck stop dining room.

She asked him if he always ate alone, and he said yes, that's what you did on the road. He said that you might ask another driver, who was standing in front of the diner, or who was pumping gas, what the weather was like to the west or north. After talk of the weather, if it was good or bad or just okay, he said they might talk a minute or two.

Where you from?

Where you going?

Drivers were from all over. Putnam, Vermont; Daytona, Florida. They were from Arizona, Oklahoma, and a suburb of Asheville, North Carolina.

They had five kids, one guy said, and the youngest needed an operation on his spine.

One woman had been driving almost four years, ever since her driver husband had died over three years ago. She had two teenage kids, a girl and boy, and she hated that she had to leave them alone for days and weeks at a time. They were okay, she said, but they needed their mother.

The woman was short and thickly built, Henry said. She looked strong.

When Ivy talked to her dad on her portable phone, I could hear his low gravel voice on the other end. I couldn't make out the words, but he always sounded tired. He had gone six or seven hundred miles that day. He had gone across three states and partway into another. That was big miles, Ivy said.

She didn't know how he did it.

Ivy was still tall, maybe two or three inches under six feet, but she had put on a little weight, especially in her bottom and her breasts. She was long and very lean, but she couldn't have passed as a boy anymore.

She didn't smile very much, but when she did her mouth was big and white and her eyes were sparkly.

Once I asked her why six was afraid of seven, and when I answered, Because seven eight nine, she paused for about ten seconds, and then she groaned and laughed, laughed and groaned.

Later, she'd say, What did seven do?

Ate nine, I'd say.

That became kind of our joke.

So we were making mac 'n' cheese, which we had decided on over hot dogs. Ivy didn't like to eat meat, though she did occasionally eat chicken or turkey. We were in my kitchen, and I had boiled water for the macaroni, and Ivy was using another small pot to mix butter, milk, and the orange powder that came in a white packet.

She was wearing this black top that had spaghetti straps over her shoulders, and I didn't know for sure, but I thought that maybe she wasn't wearing a bra. I mean, I wanted to look, I was dying to look, but I kept not looking.

I almost never thought of Ivy that way. I didn't want to. But she was my only friend ever, and I couldn't lose her.

I knew she liked me, but not in any romantic way. I was so

tall now, six-two or six-three, and I couldn't have weighed more than one-hundred-fifty pounds. Plus my nose was immense. It entered a room minutes before the rest of me. If my nose got any bigger, it would need its own zip code. Plus my eyes and mouth were small and piggy. I was definitely nothing to look at. I was ugly as a frog.

After we ate we cleaned up. This was around midnight. I went and got a pill, an oxy, and we had a beer. After a while, sitting on the couch, we talked about going to bed on the early side. Ivy was usually asleep by two or three, and I was usually up till four or five.

Ivy said, Why don't we go to bed?

I said, Okay. Then I asked her if she wanted the couch or the bed.

She looked at me. For five or ten seconds, but it felt like a half hour.

Why don't we both sleep in the bed, she said. I won't be seven.

Seven made me smile.

You sure, I said.

Ivy took my hand and led me into the bedroom.

I went to the far side of the bed. The room was dark. Ivy took her cap off, and her hair was a riot of curls. She unbuttoned her jeans and pulled them off, one leg at time.

I got in the bed with all my clothes on, and she said, What're you doing?

Ivy laughed.

So I took my jeans off. I was all bones. I was as long as California.

Ivy took my hand again.

She smelled like lime and apple. She smelled like lavender.

Ivy was clear and clean. Ivy was late night air.

37

His name is Roger Furey, and everyone calls him Furey. He's in his mid- to late-forties, and this is his second long bid. He came in in his twenties, served fifteen years, and was released just shy of his fortieth birthday. For armed robbery, I believe.

He was in Attica for part of the first bid, and was then transferred to Dannemora, way upstate, near the Canadian border. Dannemora is often called Gladiator School, because it's usually the place where they send young guys, new to the system. Dannemora is also supposed to be the coldest prison in New York State. Even in the middle of summer, in July and August, the stones and steel and concrete of Dannemora stay cold.

Furey was released when he was thirty-nine. He held up a convenience store in Corning less than two years later, and killed the clerk, a sixty-six-year-old man who, like Furey, lived in a rooming house. Furey went into the store at four-thirteen in the morning, and a relatively high-quality surveillance camera caught all of it.

They got him the next day, and he's here for the duration. He was transferred to Auburn from Green Haven about six months ago. Some of the guys know Roger Furey from Attica, Dannemora, and Green Haven. It's like one big closed system, with satellites all over the state.

Furey's a small man. Real small. He's five foot two or three, at most. He's got big shoulders and arms for a little fellow, and his hands look like they belong to a much bigger guy.

He's got long, thick black hair down to his shoulders, with little bits of gray, and an enormous beard, a biker beard. You almost expect him to be wearing a leather vest with Hell's Angels or Satan's Slaves on the back.

Roger Furey almost always carries a small knife, but I don't know how he gets it past the pat downs and checkpoints and metal detectors. You say, Hey, Furey, where's your pick? And if nobody's around, he'll pull it from his boot, from under his arm, maybe from his rectum. He'll smile, these big yellow teeth appearing in the middle of his beard.

Roger Furey's kind of stupid, like all of us. Why else would we be in here? But he's as wily, as cunning as anybody I've met inside.

Some guys think that Furey killed Bevan Lee Eliot.

The two things that are really special about Furey, that make him as formidable as anyone, are his eyes and voice. He's got these black eyes that don't seem to have an iris and pupil. They're big eyes, and when they get hold of your eyes you're finished.

Roger can stare and stare, and then he's got your eyes, and you can't hardly look away, although you should. He pulls you farther and farther in, and you're hypnotized. You almost can't get away.

I don't know how he does this, and I've watched myself when it happens. It's like a fly going to the web. It's like the power of nature. Like gravity. These two dark pools pulling you all the way in.

The other thing that Roger Furey uses is his voice. It's a regular voice with a little bit of twang. He grew up in southeastern Ohio, near the West Virginia border, near the Ohio River, and you can hear that when he talks.

And Jesus, the man can talk when he gets going. He's one of the three or four best talkers I've ever heard. He tells stories—about his life, and his miserable childhood. About the state of the world, about the coming apocalypse, about shit in the prison, about the books he supposedly read.

I may start out having a more or less normal conversation with Furey. I talk, he talks, I talk, he talks. But within ten minutes, it's all Furey all the time. He's a train that starts slow, but pretty soon it's Furey Furey Furey.

You don't even try to get a word in.

I ask Furey if he knows a guy named DeMarco, and he shakes his head. Then he keeps on talking.

We're in a hallway, and there are guys standing and walking real close to us, but I'm in the Furey bubble. He's going on about Buddha and Jesus, and somehow he's found his way to Abraham Lincoln, Napoleon, and Julius Caesar.

I have no idea how he moved from Jesus to Napoleon. I thought I was paying attention. I didn't especially think I was stupid or slow.

But Furey talks fast and talks without pausing to breathe. He has more energy than the sun. He moves his hands as he talks, and waves his arms. At times, it's as though he's going to reach out and hit you, with a fist or a knife. But instead, he puts his hand on your arm or shoulder, on your back or the top of your head. Once or twice, he even puts his big hand on the side of your face, like a mother.

It's weird and warm, especially in here. We don't ever get close to touching each other, not in the joint. For years, for decades, we don't touch or feel touched. It doesn't happen.

He does pause to breathe, and I say, Roger, can I ask you something?

He looks surprised, but stops talking. Someone's about to ask Furey something, to invite him to talk. He almost never needs a prompt, just as fish, I imagine, don't need to be told to swim.

I say, Furey, what's it like to get out of here after a long bid? What's that feel and look like?

He looks at me with those black eyes. He looks for a little while, and I'm wondering what he's thinking. If he's calculating something, because Roger Furey always calculates everything.

All that black hair, on his head, his beard, and his dark eyes looking out as if from a cave.

It's fucking weird, Oliver, he says. He's one of very few people in here who call me by my Christian name.

It's really weird if you've been in a while, he says. Then Furey says, Why? You getting out?

I shake my head.

I wish, I say.

How long you in?

Twenty-nine years, I tell Furey.

No shit, he says. Twenty-nine fucking years.

I nod, and he breaks the taboo about directly asking what another guy did.

What for? he asks.

Stuff, I say.

Stuff? What stuff?

So what was it like? I say. Getting out after a long sentence?

Furey's looking at me. He wants to know what I did, but I'm not gonna tell him. He can find out from a third party, which is how we all find out. From someone else, someone with access to a computer, or someone who was a celly with someone. As I've said, You don't just ask a person directly. We have our un-written rules in here.

He's still looking at me, and I'm not looking back. And he's silent a while. Like I've taken his weapons away. The eyes and the voice.

Finally, he looks down at the floor. I know he must think, I didn't get him now, but later. Sometime.

I think, I don't think so. Not now, and not ever.

We're in the hallway outside the chow hall. We're long past lunch, but a few people are passing, are going in or out. Guys, an administrator or two, and corrections officers. Cops, we call them. Or screws, or guards. The admin people have ID cards with their photos hung around their necks from a lanyard.

Furey and me are leaning against a wall. I'm about a foot taller than him, but that doesn't seem to bother Roger Furey. He's gotta be used to it. But it makes me uncomfortable. Like he's a toy or something. Maybe that's why he always carries a knife.

The screws don't bother us, perhaps because I've been here forever, and I've never caused trouble. Not in all the years. Or possibly because I'm short-time, if I really am short-time. If DeMarco's for real, and not some prankster.

Furey starts up again, as if he's flipped a switch.

Well, Oliver, he says, I'll tell you. He looks up. His eyes, my eyes. His mouth, his yellow teeth. Like a dark, wet cave.

I was twenty-four when I came in. Armed robbery of an old couple in a parking lot, outside a movie theater. Around midnight. They were driving a Mercedes, so I thought they'd have money. Right, he says. Of course.

This was in Binghamton, Furey says. I'd been doing this shit a while. Not my first rodeo. Figured I knew what I was doing.

They were pretty old too. Sixties, maybe seventies.

So the old man unlocked the passenger side door to let his wife in, and then he came around to the driver's side, where I was, crouched down, behind the next car over.

There were plenty of lights in the parking lot, but no people. They'd all gone to earlier movies.

So what? So I showed the old man my .22, and I told him to give me his and his wife's wallets, and that nobody would get hurt.

So he did. His face was white and he was shaking like fuck. But nobody got hurt, like I said. I grabbed the purse from the old lady, threw it back in the front seat.

Then I told them to drive straight home, that I'd be watching. Which was bullshit. I had no way of watching. As they were driving away in their shiny black Benz, I checked their wallets.

A hundred and twenty-six bucks.

No shit, Oliver. A big one hundred and twenty-six bucks.

And the cops, state and local cops, they were pounding the shit out of my door around five a.m.

Fingerprints and security cameras. Fifteen to twenty-five.

38

Mother used to talk about her mother, and the times near Boston when my mother was growing up. Peg said that her mother was quite tall, quite a bit taller than Peg was as a grown-up.

Marge said that she still thought about her mother, she guessed, pretty much every day. Thought about things she said, or about ways she was back then. Her walk, her gestures, the ways she'd move her hands and arms.

Her mother's legs were very long and shapely. Narrow ankles, muscular calves, great knees and thighs. And hips that were not too wide, more a subtle swell and an ass that drew stares almost everywhere. How could you not stare at that woman's ass. The way it moved slightly when she walked in that long-legged, coltish way.

Maggie said this, about her own mother. Like her mother was competition.

And she moved like an athlete. A long jumper, a pole vaulter, a high jumper. Long and loose, but controlled too. All the held-in energy, the balance, the grace.

She had small high breasts, reddish-black hair that fell to the line of her jaw, and an amazing face. Her nose was large and just a little rounded. Her mouth was wide, her lips full and she had large beautiful teeth. The eyes were a little too close together, but they were big like her mouth and nose.

Somehow, despite the off-center mouth and nose and eyes, it all worked in some mysterious way. If the eyes were pushed farther apart, if the nose was smaller and the mouth more narrow, then it might not have come together.

This was hard to know or understand, the way beauty worked. When you saw it, it almost made your knees shake, your heart stop, and you couldn't look away. You couldn't exactly say, This woman had a perfect nose or smile. Shining hair, lovely, whorled ears. This was not just any one thing. It was one feature, and another, and another, all talking together, mixing, drawing things from the ears to the forehead, to the hair, the nose and mouth and eyes. And all together the alchemy turned it into beauty.

You only had to see it once, but then you couldn't forget it. Margaret said her mother's name was Livvy. She had a surprisingly high voice, when you expected it to be low and breathy. She spoke quickly, in bursts of words, and she had a big laugh, and that was as surprising as the high voice. She also had about ten smiles. A laughing smile, a smile where she didn't open her mouth, a shy smile, a quiet smile.

Peggy said they were all just beautiful, and seemed to make your heart go tap-tap. Her smiles flooded your brain with ice and heat. Both at the same time.

She said her mother loved to drink and do drugs, though that wasn't obvious at first. She always had bottles of beer and wine in the refrigerator, cooling. She never drank before noon, but by one in the afternoon she'd be slipping steadily, her gaze on the distance, to something far, far away.

In and around Boston, Mother said, she and her mom lived in small apartments. They lived in Newtonville in Newton, on Pill Hill in Brookline, in West Roxbury in Boston, in Cambridgeport in Cambridge. Pill Hill was called Pill Hill because, years ago, many of the doctors in Brookline had lived on the hill.

Her mom drove a few VW Bugs her entire childhood. When it was time to move, her mom had friends, guys, who had pickup trucks, and they were always there to help. Livvy and she would pack the Bug with as much stuff as it would hold, and they'd throw everything else in the back of a pickup.

Peggy wasn't sure how they lived. Every year or two or three, they had to move. There were maybe a half dozen gentlemen friends, and Peggy thought they gave her mom money, or drugs or a case of beer or wine. They were big beefy guys named Norm and Travis and Teddy.

But there was one other guy, kind of small and thin, and Mommy thought he might have been called Len. She said he was the one guy she could remember for sure. She didn't know if Len was short for Lenny or Leonard. But for a while he seemed to come over pretty often.

He bought her a doll with brown hair and pretty blue eyes, and one Christmas he came over with an entire doll's house for her. It had two stories, and four bedrooms, and bathrooms on the first and second floors.

Len also bought her books. Big shiny books with hard covers and lots of pictures and very few words. They were all called, *The Book of . . . The Book of Trees, The Book of Houses, The Book of Countries, The Book of Animals, The Book of People.*

Margaret could look all day. She could miss meals and not go to the bathroom. She could lie on the floor, her head resting on her elbow, slowly turning pages. She would see elm trees, oaks, and maples. Gingko and pine and ash and baobab trees.

She didn't know it, had never realized it, Mom said that Livvy had said, but books reminded her that the world was huge and so various that it made your brain swim. Mud huts, rhinos, people on the far side of the world who hunted with falcons or eagles.

There were tiny countries nestled among huge mountains. There were countries that were mostly deserts, where the wind blew almost all the time, and there were waves and waves of giant sand dunes that were like an ocean, and changed constantly.

Some people were brown and black, some yellow or red or pink or tan. Certain people were tiny as children, others were tall as trees. Some lived in houses with stilts, near the water, and some houses were made of red or yellow bricks.

For a little while, Len moved into the apartment with Mommy and Livvy, but after only a month or two, Len moved out again because he didn't like that Livvy had boyfriends. Boy-friends was what Livvy called her johns, and even when she told Len that it was all only business, Len said he didn't care. He not only didn't like it, he hated it.

After he left, Len didn't even visit anymore. There were lots of johns coming over. In the middle of the afternoon, and at two or three a.m. When they came late at night or early in the morning, they were always drunk and a little unsteady on their feet. They either talked too loud, or they whispered, as though nobody knew they were there at all.

Marge usually had her own little room, next to Livvy's room or the living room, and no matter how deeply she was sleeping, she was always near the surface of the world, and she always heard the movement of people, and she always heard the voices, even if they were whispering. She half woke up and listened, and her mother's voice was so soft and low that she could never tell what Livvy was saying.

Peggy said she had no idea if any of this was normal. If most kids had mothers but no fathers. If most mothers with a kid or two moved around so often. From Newton to Boston to Arlington to Cambridge. She wondered if most mothers had men friends who visited at all hours. Who closed the bedroom door and made rocking and moaning noises, for a half hour, for an hour at most.

Whose men friends were old and young and in between. Who wore ties or jeans, boots or sandals. Some had glasses, and some had a chain attached to their wallets in the back pocket of their pants. Some were mostly bald, and some had hair so long that they tied their hair back in a ponytail.

Almost all of them were very nice, especially Len. Another man called Gar was pretty old. He must have been fifty or so. He had a lot of hair, and he wore glasses with wire rims, and his eyes were brown behind the lenses. He brought Margie a stuffed brown bear that was softer and fuzzier than anything. She slept with the bear every night.

Gar always wore a tweed suit jacket, and a yellow dress shirt with the collar unbuttoned. He smiled all the time, and had a high soft laugh like a wind chime.

He called Margaret, kiddo and gorgeous and sport.

How you doing, sport? Gar asked, and she nodded at him.

She was doing just fine, she wanted to say, but never did.

Mother liked almost everything about her life, when she was small. She liked waking up and going to bed at night. She liked when they moved and she could explore a new apartment, and see who walked outside on the sidewalk. Neighborhood kids, old ladies, young men with dogs on a leash.

Then it was later. Only five or ten years later, and time passed like a single tick of the clock. Livvy was drinking a lot, every day. She wasn't so nice then. She said things that Mommy didn't want to repeat. Then she lost her looks, pretty much overnight.

One night she was mostly beautiful, and the next day she looked old and sloppy and wrinkly and gray. Just like that.

Then they took Livvy away, and Maggie was on her own. She couldn't pay the rent or the electric, and she was evicted.

Fourteen years old, and staying in these party houses, and she was part of the party.

Shit happens, Livvy used to say. And Mag could only say that it certainly did.

On the radio late at night, Jimmy Summers was still on at three and four in the morning. Vanessa called again, and Jimmy said that he'd been worried about her. He had been hoping she was all right.

39

This was late, I'm pretty sure. This was around two or even three in the morning. The days were short by then. It got dark around five in the afternoon, and it didn't get light until seven.

All the trees were bare, and the thin branches looked like spider legs against the gray-white sky. Plus it was starting to get cold. Not freezing all the time, and not every day. But it was cold at least part of the time, and at night it was almost always cold. Down to the twenties and thirties, and now and then down to the teens.

I had taken the two wool blankets out of the closet in the hall, the big thick puffy blankets that had stripes at the top and bottom. Some john had given them to Maggie. A green blanket and a blue blanket, with red and gold and maroon stripes.

I put one blanket on the bed, on top of a sheet and thin spread, and the other I left folded up on the couch. It was amazing, the weight of the wool, and how warm the blanket was.

The landlord didn't turn the heat on until early December, so I often walked around the house wrapped in a blanket.

So it was two or three, and there were no people out front, in cars or on the sidewalk. This was the very dead heart of night. This was as dark and lonely as it got.

I was half sitting, half lying on the couch, the green blanket all around me. No openings, no cracks in the edge of the blanket to let cold air in. If you felt cold, say, on your thighs or back, and you reached down and felt with your hand, there was always an opening where the cold was, and after you adjusted the blanket, the cold went away in a few seconds.

I believe I was sipping from a can of beer, resting the can on the boxes that served as a coffee or beer table. I had also taken a few pills, a diazepam and a hydrocodone, and I was as mellow as a June evening. Just the usual drug and booze warmth that you got early in a buzz.

All the lights were off, and there were slices of rectangles and triangles coming in and sitting on the walls and floors from the streetlight out front.

Then, just then, there was a light tapping on the door, but so light that I didn't know if I had really heard anything at all. Old houses had these creaks and taps and pings. These tiny groans. You never really knew what was going.

It was a mouse, a cat. It was old wood in the floors of the house, expanding and contracting. Maybe it was a ghost or spirit. People must have died in these rooms over the years.

Maybe someone had been murdered in this house, many years ago. Maybe it was the spirit of the murder victim. A young woman, a lonely old man.

I'd never seen anything, but I had heard plenty. Now, I thought, might be the time. A floating, transparent figure, white and wavering.

Then I heard four taps on the door. If I went and stood next to the door, the spirit would be only inches away from me, separated by the hollow wood of the door.

But the door wouldn't save me from a ghost. Ghosts and spirits could move through walls and doors. That was what ghosts did. The door was useless.

I heard more taps, and I thought, That thing knows I'm in here. I stood up, the green blanket all around me. Maybe the ghost would be covered in blood. Its own blood, from the murder all those years ago. Maybe there was a knife sticking out of its chest or neck.

Then there were more taps, five or six of them.

Then I heard, All, in a soft voice. A murdered young woman? All, the voice said again.

It was a woman's voice.

Ivy, I said, and she said, All, you there?

Is that you? Are you Ivy?

All, she said. Who else would it be?

I opened the door, and there she was. In gym shorts and a gray hoodie, and her beautiful frizzy hair piled up and pinned to the top and sides of her head. I don't think I had ever seen her hair when it wasn't covered by a hat.

Come in, I said.

She looked cold, and she seemed to be shivering a little.

She stood next to the couch, and I stood next to her. I wrapped the blanket around both of us as we sat down.

Our sides were touching, but it still felt cold. Her long legs were bare, and they were cool as marble, even through my pants. Her hoodie was fairly heavy, and wispy strands of her hair brushed my face, like a fine rain that shifted to fog, and then back to rain again. It was so fine and so thin that you couldn't be sure if you were feeling anything.

She asked if she could get a beer from the fridge, and I said that would be good.

Mabel brought over a case of beer every time she brought groceries. Every two or three weeks.

Ivy came back with a cold can, got on the couch, under the blanket with me. We took turns sipping. I'd take a sip, she'd take two sips, I'd take a sip.

The beer was half empty, and I was already feeling the near edge of the buzz. Just a slight warming, just a slight loosening. Her long legs weren't quite so cold.

We had said almost nothing, and I was still a little nervous. So finally I said, You wanna try a pill?

I could feel her head turn to me. If I had turned my head, our eyes and lips and noses would have been an inch apart. As it was, pretty much all of our bodies were pressed together.

What kind of pill?

I dunno, I said. A pain pill, an anxiety pill.

What do they do to you?

I looked at her, and our mouths were maybe an inch apart.

Like how do they make you feel? I asked.

Ivy nodded.

They make you feel relaxed. They make everything sweet and slow.

I'll try, Ivy said. Why not?

I got up and got two pills from the bureau drawer. There had to have been thirty or forty bottles in there, almost all of them full. I took two white hydrocodone. They were oblong, and had a line, an indentation, across the middle in case you wanted to break the pill in half.

I gave one to Ivy. She swallowed the pill with a chug of beer. Then she handed me the beer, and I took mine. We sat there in the dark and silence, and I could feel her leg next to my leg, and I could feel her beautiful hair against my face and neck. Her hair smelled like oranges and lemons and something else. Something like cinnamon, like nutmeg, like warm and flaky pastries.

Her hair tickled a little. Her hair was like the gossamer strands of a web. I could eat or drink the web, I could fall into it.

We didn't say anything for a little while. There was just more darkness and silence. This was the best kind of dark and quiet you could have. You didn't have to feel sad or lonely, you didn't have to wait and count the minutes until daylight began to sift in around the edges of the curtains.

Ivy got up to get another beer, and when she came back, it had probably been ten or fifteen minutes since we'd taken the pills.

I felt my pill a little bit. I felt it at the sides of me. In my toes and feet, my hands and fingers. It was reaching my ears and nose. Just behind these feelings was the sense of something bigger and better, like a larger wave coming in behind the small wave. It would wash completely over me, and ride me out into deeper water, where there was only sky and water, and way off, a glimpse of the land. Hills, boats, tiny cars moving through roads on hills.

Ivy said she had begun to feel it, she thought. In her back and butt.

She said, Damn, this is good. This is really nice. No wonder this shit's illegal. My God.

And Ivy was right. Who would want to go back to the regular world after opioids? Who would ever wait and hope for daylight?

We sipped the beer, back and forth, and then she said, It's getting hot.

It was getting hot.

I said, Yeah, it is.

She said that if I didn't mind, she was getting undressed. She'd much rather do that than not stay under the blanket. Being under the blanket was so cool, so sweet.

She took her shorts and hoodie off, and that was all. She was this shining white spirit in the darkness.

She said, You too, All?

And me too.

So we were these two kids, naked, at three or four in the morning, under a lovely blanket. Ivy was sixteen, I think. I was fifteen, I'm pretty sure.

40

The toughest time of the year in here has got to be the holiday season. Halloween through the New Year, give or take a few weeks. Or maybe Thanksgiving until Christmas. But really, it's the longer stretch, Halloween-New Year, that gets in the bones and brains of the guys.

Maybe because of the weather, as much as anything. How cool it gets, and how cold, even, it can sometimes feel out on the yard.

In June or July, at eight in the evening, the sun streams down, even in here, and you can lean your back against a wall, and it's just delicious, that feeling of the rays of the sun. The days are getting longer, the sun is warmer, and we can sort of be like anyone else, anyone anywhere, feeling the sun on our faces, on our forearms. Making us deeply relaxed, even sleepy.

In the fall, you can't see the leaves on the trees change. We don't ever see trees. We see the sunlight, but it's thinner and weaker than it is in summer. It doesn't seem thick and full, it couldn't make you feel close to sleepy, not even a little relaxed.

By the time we're on the yard at six or seven or eight, depending on the day, the sun has already gone down. It's already passed by. We won't feel the sun again until May or June. But we go to the yard anyway because it has real air, fresh air, and that matters way more than how cold it is.

Even if it's raining, even if it's snowing, we're out there. If it's nine degrees below zero, we're out there. Maybe some guys, the really old guys, stay inside for the coldest weather, but very, very few. We need to be outside of the blocks of buildings.

But in late October, then November, you can feel the holidays. At the end of the October, you can picture the carved pumpkins, the candy corn and chocolate, kicking fallen leaves on the sidewalk. You can picture the kids with their bags. Maybe a plastic grocery bag, a pillowcase, a hollow plastic pumpkin. Kids as a skeleton, a ghost, a princess, a ninja. Kids as a prisoner, in a striped jumpsuit, kids as cops, kids as a box of cereal, as Cheerios or cornflakes.

It might be raining, or foggy, or unusually warm. There were some parents walking with the younger kids, and people carrying flashlights. There might be a hundred kids, a thousand kids, on the sidewalks and streets. And tall, bare, spidery trees, their leaves dead, fallen over everything.

And that air. That late October air. Crisp, cool, smelling of earth and trees, bushes and dying grass. That air was not summer or winter or spring. That air, as certain as flying geese, was fall.

As the evening went from six to seven to eight, the bag, the pillowcase, grew heavier and heavier. And what were the chances that some weird person somewhere was putting pins or razorblades in apples, was injecting antifreeze into candy bars? What kind of person would do something like that?

Maybe someone like the people in here. People who would laugh at the thought of a kid poisoned, of a kid with a pin or razor blade in his mouth.

Take joy, and twist it until it was suffering, was pain, was injury or death.

Some people would like that. Maybe not too many, but a few would be amused, even delighted.

On some days D-block gets an extra hour in the yard. Many of the guys are at work, in the laundry or workshop, or at appointments with vocation counselors or social workers, so only fifty or a hundred of us are out here.

There's an old Black guy name Scobbie, walking the perimeter of the yard. We nod and smile each time he goes by. He has short white hair, receding from his forehead, and a big beard that's half yellow, half white.

He's in his sixties, and I'm thinking that almost everyone in their sixties or older has to be doing life without for murder. If you come inside when you're in your twenties, thirties or forties, and most people come in pretty young, by the time you're in your fifties or sixties, you're out on parole.

Scobbie's not a guy people think about, not someone you notice. He's very quiet, he seems like a decent fellow. What did Scobbie do for Halloween as a kid? Did they even have Halloween where he was a kid?

What about Thanksgiving? Did Scobbie sit down to dinner with his family? Did Scobbie have a family when he was a kid? I've never had Thanksgiving, not in my life, but I've seen pictures and read descriptions. Of young people, young fathers and mothers, maybe with children of their own, driving a good distance on Wednesday of Thanksgiving week. Or old people flying to the homes of their kids and grandkids, and getting picked up by their son or daughter at the airport. In Boston or Newark, in Chicago or Atlanta.

The holiday, I think, was all about food and family. It was about being grateful and counting your blessings.

It wasn't about a tree, or presents. It wasn't about colored lights or candles, or music. Was there even a single Thanksgiving song? I didn't know one.

But the big thing, the center or it all, was Thursday or Thanksgiving afternoon. The big meal, the feast. All these people, eight or ten or a dozen people, maybe twelve or sixteen. Because there was always a stray friend, a lonely uncle, an opinionated aunt or cousin, who had been invited. All crowded around a table, or a few tables pushed together and covered with a giant white tablecloth.

So many faces, so many mouths and eyes and noses. So many years and memories shared by the people.

Someone, probably the mother or father of the host family, would say grace. Bless us, O Lord... And so on.

Then the turkey, the mashed potatoes, the green beans and broccoli, the gravy, the cranberry sauce like a small barrel with ridges from the can. Bread, butter, wine and water, even a little bourbon with water for the older adults.

Someone, usually an older man, sometimes a female cousin,

would get at least a little drunk. His or her face flushed from the booze, talking loudly. Saying things about sex or money that nobody wanted the kids to hear.

I don't know what Mother and I did for Thanksgiving. Certainly no big dinner. I don't think she knew anything about cooking except to boil water or to open a can of tuna or soup. One year, Mabel, Marge, and I went to the Athens Diner, which was open all the time back in those days. Twenty-four seven, three-hundred-and-sixty-five days a year. The Athens wasn't crowded that day, but it wasn't close to empty either. There were two police cruisers parked out front, and four cops at a booth inside.

There were some scruffy people sitting at the counter, and then a well-dressed couple with two small kids at another booth. The couple and the kids looked like they had just been at church.

The waitresses were moving fast, and seemed to be in good spirits.

After we sat down at our booth, Mabel said there was the turkey special. Turkey loaf with mashed potatoes and string beans and a roll. But I ordered pancakes, and Mom and Mabel got eggs with sausage and wheat toast, and all three of us got coffee.

We pretty much never did this, never went out to eat, and we were kind of happy.

Scobbie rounded the far turn, and as he headed toward me, a CO came out of a door of A-block and B-block. He said something to Scobbie, and Scobbie went into the building with the CO.

Had somebody been stabbed or something?

Then there was the big one, of course, and that would be Christmas. Trees and lights. Lots of music. Snow and families, tons of presents that were wrapped in gold or silver paper, or paper with candy canes or sleighs or Santa Claus.

We didn't have a tree, not ever, I'm pretty sure. But for a few years we had a string of pale blue lights that Mom used to hang over the windows in whatever apartment we were living in. You could see the lights from outside and you could see the lights from inside. And you could get Christmas music from just about any station on the radio. You could hear "Jingle Bell Rock," and "O Holy Night." There was "The Little Drummer Boy," "Joy to the World," and "Silent Night."

We hear that music even in here. On little tape decks that have to be twenty years old. On small, battery-powered radios. On tiny TV sets. They hit us like things we used to know, from a long time ago, that used to mean something to us.

But if we had no tree or presents, Maggie still marked the occasion. She always let me drink one or two or even three beers Christmas Day. And I had my first oxycodone on Christmas morning, when I was eleven.

There are four or five scattered guys walking the perimeter. A guard in the doorframe of the cellblock, he waves for us to come in. Come inside, he calls to us. Come inside.

41

Me and Ivy, us two together, we drank a beer and took one Dilaudid each. We had a nice mild buzz on, and it was Monday night, Tuesday morning, a very quiet beginning-of-the-regular-week night. The very beginning of November, and already past Halloween, and most of the leaves that were going to fall from the trees had already fallen.

Ivy's dad was on the road again. He seemed to be on the road much more than when I first knew Ivy. Back then, he was gone three or four or five days, and then he'd be home. Now, he was gone two, three, four weeks. I never really understood where he went and what he was doing.

I mean, I knew he was driving a truck, hauling stuff from one city or another, in the United States or Canada. Vancouver to Los Angeles to Fresno to Daytona Beach. He went up to Newfoundland, and down to Meridian, Mississippi, but I never understood why this took so long. You dropped stuff off, got a new load, went to another city, unloaded and loaded up again.

Why did this take so long?

You go from upstate New York to San Diego in three, four days. Maybe five days. Where was he the rest of the time? I asked Ivy. What was he doing?

She didn't know, she said, and smiled this slow, sleepy smile.

Then we were quiet again.

Finally, I said, You pretty buzzed?

She nodded and smiled some more.

Then it was quiet and dark again, the way we liked it. Just the two of us. Just Ivy and All, these two dumb kids. At midnight or one in the morning. Neither one of us with a parent at home.

Then Ivy began to talk, and I'm not sure why. Why talk, and why that particular night. There had been plenty of other nights.

Ivy got another beer from the fridge, and I asked her if she wanted another pill. Maybe a benzo, because they weren't as strong as pain pills. She said sure, so I went into the bedroom, and went through the dresser drawer. There were still twenty, thirty, maybe forty bottles of pills. And there was a ton of money, rolled up and held with rubber bands.

I didn't even know how much money. Maybe ten thousand, or fifty thousand dollars. Peg never spent money if she could help it. She just put it in the drawer with an elastic around it. Then she forgot about it.

We had bottles of diazepam, clonazepam, and lorazepam. I took two diazepam, which was also Valium, five m.g. each, and gave one to Ivy. This was more than we had ever done before.

We only ever shared a single beer, and we only ever took a single pill each. But here we were, on our second beer, and second pill. And we had started with Dilaudid, which was real strong, only a level or two below morphine.

We took the Valium with little sips of beer, then Ivy started.

She said she had lied to me about her mother, two or three years ago, and she was sorry for that. You don't lie to your friends, no matter what, she said. That was just wrong.

I said, What do you mean? And she said she hadn't been truthful.

She hadn't meant any harm. She hadn't meant to trick or deceive me.

I told her I could hardly remember. I said it was a long time ago.

She said she had read a book, a kid's book with pictures, and there was a kid, and a monster, and as you read you realized that the monster was really cancer, she thought, and the kid's mother or father had cancer and was dying, and the boy or girl, she couldn't remember which, was trying to face the monster, the disaster of disease and death.

She didn't read many books when she was a little kid, and she had no idea how the book got into her hands. But as the monster got closer, and bigger and darker, she said, the boy—

she thought he was a boy—got more terrified, and the dying mother—she thought it was a mother—got smaller and weaker. She cried at the end. God, she cried. She thought the world was over, and that life would have to end.

I mean, she said, the world would eventually be over, and life had to end for everybody. She knew that. This wasn't magic, this was life.

So she started to imagine that the boy in the book was her, was Ivy, and the mother in the book was her mother. This was ten or twelve years ago. She was maybe five or six. Maybe seven, but she couldn't remember very well.

There were so many veils and clouds and shadows in time. You never knew, never really could tell, what was black or white, up or down, near or far.

Sometimes the whole world was haze and mists. And you did your best with not being able to see very well.

She read that book, the book about the monster and cancer and death, three or four or five times. Ivy slept with the book under her pillow. She could touch it, even hold it, in the middle of the night, when she woke up for a moment or two. The breeze might make the curtains billow out into the room like a sail, and sometimes, through the open window, she heard a truck moving up a long steep hill, way in the distance.

Around then, when she was maybe seven, her mother and father were both around. They were young and tall and lean, and they both had beautiful hair. Hair that was young and curly, hair that shined, that smelled like an apple, like grass that was cut in summer, like citrus.

Ivy's mom sang sometimes. Ivy couldn't remember what the songs were about. She guessed they told about birds and clouds and the blue sky. Maybe about a boy with a pilgrim soul. About roving.

Henry, her dad, was driving a truck already, even though she didn't think he stayed away very long in those days. And a very small Ivy stayed home in the apartment with her mother. She didn't know then how the time passed.

But Ivy was five or six, and by then she could remember chunks of time without interruption. Except for certain words, or the day of the week or time of year. Winter, summer. Spring, fall.

Her dad was on the road for three or four days, and he was coming home Sunday.

Saturday night, her mom went out. Her name was Jane or Jean, Joan or Julie. It was a short J. name. Later, her dad asked her to never say the name. After a while, after years, she could no longer remember her mother's name. Just the initial. Just the letter, and just that the name was short.

Her mother had a suitcase, and a car pulled up out front. There was a man driving, and another man, wearing glasses, in the passenger seat. There was a woman in the back seat with a white headband holding her dark hair in place.

Ivy, at five or seven, watched from the front window on the second floor. The car was small. A Toyota or Honda. Maybe gray, and not new.

Ivy's mother said she wouldn't be home for a while. She squatted down. She hugged Ivy, and kissed her on the lips, which was new and strange. Her mom had always kissed Ivy on the neck or cheeks, or sometimes on the top of her head.

Be good, honey, her mom said. I love you.

Then her mother added, Your father will be home tomorrow. Keep the doors locked until he comes home.

She looked at Ivy and said, You understand?

Ivy nodded. As though she understood about locks and doors and windows. She nodded again, as if she really did understand. But she didn't understand at all. She didn't have any idea what was happening.

Something big and important was going on, she thought. Something that would matter for a long time.

The suitcase, and her mother going away for a while. The kiss on the lips, the car out front. Ivy could feel her mother's excitement. Nervous as a cat, her father sometimes said.

Then her mom picked up her suitcase, kissed Ivy on top of

her head, said, I love you so, so, so much, went out the front
door, her suitcase bumping the doorframe, and closed the door.
The lock clicked into place.

Ivy watched from the window as her mom put the suitcase
in the trunk of the car. Then she got into the back seat with the
hairband woman.

The car door closed, and the car was gone, leaving a dark
blank space.

This was how Ivy remembered. The hairband, the gray car,
the guy with glasses in the passenger seat.

Me and Ivy, Ivy and I, were pretty well buzzed by then. Like
everything was sweet and warm. Everything was good and in-
terconnected. Every small piece of light, every drop of water
and stone and grain of sand.

That was how she left me, Ivy said. That was how she left
my dad.

And almost all the time, Ivy thought her mom left her and
Henry, especially her, because she didn't love Henry, and especially, her mom didn't love Ivy. Ivy wasn't lovable, she wasn't
worth the time and effort.

And that was why Ivy replaced one story, the real story, with
the story about cancer and the monster. Because the story was
the same. Her mom was gone. She had run away, or she had
died of cancer. It was the same, she said again.

With cancer, it was nobody's fault. With running away, it was
almost completely Ivy's fault.

42

At first it got cold in November. For a week or so the temps were in the forties, with a lot of rain and wind. The kind of winds that made the trees bend and the branches sway, and smaller branches fell to the lawns and streets and sidewalks.

At night the temperatures went down to the thirties, down to the upper twenties one night, and when people walked past many of them were wearing puffy winter coats, the kind you'd see in January or February, along with hats and scarves and gloves.

The wind and rain kept on. They blew and fell and blew and fell, and you could feel how raw and chilly they were. Down to the bone. Down to way deeper than jeans and socks, T-shirts and sweaters.

I'd put on a T-shirt, a shirt with a collar, a sweater, and then after a half hour, I'd put on a hat and a hoodie. And I was still pretty chilly. There was something penetrating in the cold. Like we were already in high winter. We'd gone from early fall to winter in a week or two.

I kept thinking, Oh, shit, we're in winter. The long months, the cold months, the gray months. They usually stretched from December to March. I didn't think I was ready for it, but when had I ever been ready for anything? I didn't know squat.

When I went to sleep, I could feel the rain patter the windows, patter the shingles of the house, patter the driveway and lawn, if that was possible. I could feel the wind press the windows and sides of the house, move through branches, stripping them of their last leaves.

When I woke up, the wind and rain were still there. I'd pull back the curtain on the window, expecting to see snow, but there was no snow yet. Just the shine of rain on everything. Just the bare branches against the dark sky. Then I don't know how or why, but one night around midnight or one, all of it changed. In a few blinks of an eye, I could hear and feel the whole world out there go quiet and still. After a full week of rain and wind and storm, something else had come to us, right here, in the middle of the dark and night.

I looked out the front window at the street, and there were still no people out there, as there had been none for a week. But there was no frantic wind whipping the branches and bushes, and the cars didn't have small puddles of rain on them. I opened the window at the bottom, and the air was almost warm. It was dry.

I swear that I could feel a warm front sifting up from the southwest, and it was at least thirty degrees warmer than it had been. How could it change like this? And change so fast? It had gone from December to September in an hour.

Nothing ever waited for anything.

Ivy seemed to have gone away, and I didn't know where. Maybe she had gone to find her lost mother, somewhere in the country, or somewhere in the world. Maybe she went with her father on the road, from here to Baton Rouge, then to Houston and Bakersfield and Edmonton. They were gone for a week or a month.

Ivy might have been bored at home. Ivy was bored with me, and I could see how that might be.

I was fifteen and really, really tall. I was ugly as a canker sore, and skinny as a broom handle. I barely knew how to talk to people I saw on the street, or saw behind the counter at a store, when I bought cigarettes or a Gatorade. It was like my tongue was strapped down, and there was glue in my mouth.

So the night after the warmth came in, I took a lorazepam and an oxycodone, smoked a cigarette, and drank a beer. I dressed all in black or in navy blue, put a black watch cap on, and waited for the buzz to grow and fill me. All that warmth and serenity, from the strands of hair on my head to the nail beds on my toes.

I waited for the anxiety and fear to fall away like the leaves on the trees. I sat in the dark, on a stool near the front window, and I thought, I'll be out there. I'll be darting from shadow to shadow.

I don't know how, really, but the black clothes made me bigger and smaller at the same time. The black clothes made me stronger. As though nobody could see me, as though black clothes made me bulletproof. You couldn't kill what you couldn't see.

And nobody saw me. I knew that. Nobody had seen me in a long time. I liked it that way, at least most of the time.

The air had become warm, as warm almost as a summer night. But it was as though nobody knew it was warm except me. It had to be one a.m. by then. There were no cars moving, there were no people or dogs. There was just the air, and the wet leaves on the ground, the rain-soaked lawns. Everything was drying off, but it was taking some time.

I went toward the Belle Sherman neighborhood, where I nearly always went. On Harvard and Irving and Monroe, there was nothing. Just houses and parked cars, bushes, fences, and soaked lawns. There were play structures on a few back lawns. On Linden Street the houses seemed even quieter and sleepier than the other houses of the other streets in Belle Sherman.

There were a few low lights, here and there, on the inside of some places. Probably night lights, in a bedroom or bathroom or hallway. So when you stumbled awake for the bathroom at two a.m., you didn't have to blast your eyes with light.

I avoided houses with play structures in the yard, and I avoided houses where I was pretty sure I'd seen kids during my daytime reconnaissance missions. I never ever wanted to hurt or scare a kid. That was my only rule. Never in all my life.

I didn't especially like kids. I knew that. Once in a while, just for a moment, I'd imagine grabbing a kid from a lawn or backyard, and strangling the little shit. But I knew why. I had figured it out.

They had nice lives. They had two parents who loved them. There was plenty of money in their world. If they needed help, any kind of help, they got it. They had a brother or sister, they had grandparents and cousins.

That made me real angry sometimes. So angry that the rage could build and build like a fire. It wanted to consume everything in its path.

Once I knew why they made me angry, the anger lost some of its power. I would tell myself that it wasn't their fault. They were innocent. They had never done anything to hurt me. They were just kids. Perfectly good and decent kids, for God's sake.

I said to myself, I even whispered it out loud, Don't ever, ever even think that.

And though I might think of it, of hurting a kid, I would do anything to not hurt a kid. I just had to be really careful.

On Linden Street, there was no movement anywhere, except for the silent, warming breeze. Already, the street and sidewalks were dry, but I knew it would take a while for the dead leaves and lawns to dry.

Then I saw it. A big orange cat, a big ginger. He must have weighed fifteen pounds, maybe more. He could have weighed twenty. He was sitting on the sidewalk, looking at me. Only looking and looking. He was very still. He didn't seem to blink or even breathe. Just sitting and watching me like a witch or ghost.

He was probably named Jack or Rufus. Maybe Nico. Nico would be a good name for a big orange cat. Nico sounded noble.

I looked at the houses, and there in the middle of the block were two places, across the street from each other, that had no toys or play structures in the yard or on the porch. There were no cars in the driveway either. One of the houses, a really big bungalow house, had no low lights on at all.

Across the street, there was a big Victorian house, at least that's what I think it was called. There was the big porch that wrapped around the front, and on the second floor there was a round part, with small windows all the way around at the top.

From the side yard there was a single low light on in a room at the back of the house. Maybe a study or laundry room or TV room. Some people even had rooms for their TV.

I'm not sure why, but I'd bet anything that this was an old person's house. No toys or cars that I could see, and even a few bushes near the house were wrapped in canvas for the winter.

I checked on the back and sides of the house, but all the windows were locked. Then I went to the porch in front, and there was nothing, and nothing and nothing.

Then bing. At the far left-hand side of the porch, a window was unlocked. I took out the screen and pushed the window up. Warm inside air flowed out at me.

There was this dark square, and I could see a Chinese or Arab carpet, and the edge of a dining room table that was shiny in the dark. There were old wood chairs around the table. I swear, I could smell furniture polish.

I stepped in, very quietly, and it was the dining room, as I'd thought. I moved so soft through the room, and was in a really big living room with heavy beams in the ceiling. There were two or three couches, a fireplace, easy chairs, small tables.

There was a thick carpet on the floor, and the boards under the floor didn't squeak.

Then I heard a few slow, creaky footsteps upstairs. One, then two, then three. They were very slow and very short steps. A voice, probably at the top of the stairs, said, Who?

The voice said, What is it?

Then the voice was quiet a little while.

I sat in the middle of a big couch.

The voice was thick with sleep, and was kind of gravelly. I wasn't sure if it was a woman or man. But this person was old.

I sat, silent, on the couch.

43

Ten more days and it's Thanksgiving. We're in the middle of November and it's cold as snow already. Put a bowl of water in the yard overnight and you have solid ice in the morning. In the days, you've got the forties. Nothing more than that.

Inside, the steel and concrete stay cold, or deep cool, almost all the time. That's what we have in here. Cold and hot, wet and dry, dark or light. That's what we share with people in the rest of the world.

The guys are thinking about Thanksgiving out in the world, I know. Turkey and string beans, mashed potatoes, gravy. Cranberry sauce with the ridges imprinted from the can. Wine and beer, bourbon on the rocks, ice clinking on the sides of the glass.

And those people. Parents and children. Grandparents, uncles and aunts, boyfriends or girlfriends. The little kids dressed up like church, with bow ties and hair ribbons. Tights, shiny black shoes.

Two or three women, maybe a man or two, are running the kitchen, which is very warm from the stove. A man, someone's husband, has oversight of the dining room. The regular dining room table has two card tables added to it, and two white tablecloths cover the tables.

Something like this happens in most, if not all, homes in our country, I think. Some adults are in the living room or den, drinking, telling jokes, laughing. The little kids, or nearly all of them, have gone to the bedrooms on the second floor. They play hide and seek, they crawl under the beds, they tell ghost stories.

A small boy, maybe two years old, goes into the living room, and stands by his father's knees. His father is sitting in a big chair and sipping bourbon. The boy has black hair that's a little curly, and he's wearing black sweatpants, a white shirt, and a red bow tie that's lopsided.

The father talks and laughs, over the head of his son. Then the boy puts his hands on his father's knees. The father looks at his son, smiles, and lifts him onto his lap.

But in here, for real, none of us went to Thanksgiving dinners like this. With family and friends, with mashed potatoes and cranberry sauce. With wine and bourbon to drink. At houses with shutters or screens or storm windows.

There might be a few who did, but very few. And none, not even one, ever wore a bow tie as a small child.

There were no fathers for any of the guys in here. Just about none. The few who were ever around, even for an afternoon, or a few days, or months or a year, they were drinkers, and they were bullies, and they were violent.

They had lots of tattoos, on their arms and chests, on their necks, a few even had tats on their faces. They never had jobs, or if they had a job, it only lasted a few days or weeks, a few months at most. Then they hurt their back, on the job, and they collected disability or unemployment or something. The hurt back, the terrible pain—that lasted forever. So did the government checks, the pain pills, and the father or the boyfriend of the mother sitting on the couch. Watching TV no matter what was on. Sipping a beer, the pill bottle sitting on the table at the end of the couch.

So we're more quiet in here. Someone, I don't know who, has taped cardboard cutouts of turkeys and pilgrims to the concrete pillars in the mess hall. There are four or five of them. Two turkeys, two pilgrims, and a picture of a big white family sitting down to a feast.

There's no yelling, no big laughter, just guys sitting and eating the chipped beef on a piece of toast.

We're all in our dark green work pants and shirts, and the guards are in their gray uniforms with the patches on the sleeve and chest. New York State Department of Corrections. They have keys and batons and walkie-talkies on their belts.

This is Wednesday, and according to the two TVs sheltered by small roofs in the yard, bolted into the cellblock wall, this is the heaviest travel day of the year. The news on TV shows airports full of rushing clusters of people, long lines at train stations, packed highways, all three lanes on each side, crammed with cars.

On TV, they say that the Christmas season is almost upon us.

Maybe a third of the guys in here are wearing coats as they eat. I'd guess it's fifty, fifty-five. I'm wearing long underwear tops and bottoms, then the green shirt and pants, and a heavy sweatshirt with a waffle lining over that.

Even with all that, I'm still thinking that I should have worn my coat. You get older and you get much colder, much more easily. They don't put the heat on in here, not really, until December, sometimes, it seems, until January. Aside from that, this place has got to be very hard to heat. Giant buildings, bigger than cathedrals, surrounding stacks of cells. All the stone and steel, the concrete and shatterproof glass. They hold the cold.

Mellor's eating by himself, two tables over, and I'm eating by myself. We look at each other, we nod and smile. But neither of us moves to sit with the other. We'd never do that, not in this place.

In here we stick with our tribe. Blacks with Blacks, whites with whites, Latinos with Latinos. There's not many Asians. Maybe a dozen. I guess they roll with each other, same as everyone else.

You don't stick with your tribe, you get trouble. Someone'll put a lock in a sock, and beat you. Maybe they kill you.

And that's weird because Mellor is the closest thing I have to a friend. Mellor listens, and he doesn't talk too much. Just like me. All that time in the cell, and Mellor's the only thing that's remotely like comfort. Like human.

I think that Mellor's the only person who's almost a friend

since I was a kid, and that girl, Ivy. She was a friend. The girl
with all that frizzy dirty blond hair.

That was thirty years ago. That was more than thirty years
ago.

Mellor gets up, dumps his tray, and a minute later I get up
too.

I catch up with him in the halls. It's okay for a white guy to
walk with a Black guy in the halls. I don't know why that's okay,
but sitting together in the mess hall is not.

All I know is that I obey the rules, the regular rules and the
unspoken rules. I'm like Mellor. I'm trying to do my time, without getting beat up, or crippled or killed. I'm trying to be aware
and alert, and at the same time I keep my eyes on the floor.

Mellor tells me that Gates, the old guy in the cell next to me,
on the other side, has been taken to the medical unit. Gates
has asthma, pretty bad asthma. You can hear him, especially at
night. The loud breaths, the old man trying to get air into his
lungs. And the air sacs in his lungs. They're all closed up.

He's wheezing and choking and almost drowning. Plus all
the mold in here, all over the place. That can't help.

Mellor can't breathe too good either.

It's a terrible thing, not to be able to breathe. It's awful to
hear someone fight for each breath. You can feel how close
they are to dying. How little separates life from death.

I don't know what to say to Mellor about Gates. That's too
bad, I think. But Gates has been almost dead for a long time.
So I don't say anything.

Gates has got to be in his late seventies, even early eighties.
He's been in over half a century. Fifty-three years, I'm pretty
sure. Arson and murder. Triple murder. Torched his former
girlfriend's house. Killed her. Killed Sharon, and killed her two
little kids. All fucked up on booze and dope.

Gates was twenty-two or twenty-three. Gates was almost
just starting out his life. So were Sharon and the little kids. Two
or three in the morning, and the smoke, and then the flames.

Jesus.

Then in here forever. Never getting out. Never seeing trees, never seeing the world again. No lakes or ponds, no flowers, no real sky, no hills in the distance. Now Gates is up there in the medical unit. Barely able to breathe. Can hardly open or close his eyes. Can hardly lick his lips. And the weight in his chest, like a big guy sitting on him. The tightness. Air. Basic air. He can't really get air anymore. Just tiny sips. And it will be over for Gates this time. Maybe this time. Probably this time. This will be the end of everything for him.

Mellor and me, we get to D-block, and I say, Too bad for Gates.

Mellor shrugs. His face is neutral.

All, Mellor says. I asked around.

I look at him.

About that dude, about DeMarco, he says.

I keep looking at Mellor.

We've both stopped, and we're standing at the bottom of the block, the tiers of cells and the caged windows of the block itself.

He's part-time, Mellor says. Two days here, three days at Attica.

DeMarco? I say.

Mellor nods. He smiles a little.

He's real, All, Mellor says. You're short-time.

44

I didn't know about Margaret anymore. It had been a long time since I'd seen her. Many months. Maybe a year or two. I just didn't know for sure.

Mabel still came around, at least once a week, usually late in the afternoon. In the first months or year that Maggie was gone, Mabel was in touch with her. They'd talk on the phone. Peg was in the rehab, then she was in the sober living house. Then she had moved from sober living, and was in an apartment near Rochester, with a few friends from the program.

There was a guy called Donnie or Ronnie. He had been sober almost a year. Before that, he cooked and did meth.

Peggy never said it directly, but Mabel had the impression that maybe the two of them were a thing.

Then Mabel stopped hearing from Marge, and when she tried to call Mom, she never got an answer.

So Mabel came by with beer and groceries every week, and I'd give her a fifty or a hundred from the rolls in the drawer. Then she brought me pills every two weeks or so, and I'd give her a fifty for each bottle. A few times she looked disappointed at the fifty, so I began giving her a hundred for each bottle.

The pills always came from a pharmacy, and each bottle had a different name on the RX label. Richard Jenkins or Rose Carter, Darius Rolfe or Jason Segal. I didn't know who any of these people were, and I guess I didn't know if any of them even existed. But the pills were good. Xanax, clonazepam, Dilaudid, oxycodone, Percocet. Diazepam, which was another name for Valium. I don't think I ever had fewer than a thousand pills. I used to dream about being alone in a drugstore, and being behind the counter, looking through the shelves. Reading the labels on jumbo bottles of pills.

I had no idea how Mabel got them. She knew a lot of people, I guessed.

Welfare paid the rent, and they put money in my bank every month. Once or twice, someone from welfare came to the apartment, and she asked me questions, mostly about Mother, and then told me to call her if I needed anything.

I knew I was good with the welfare until I turned eighteen. I think I was almost seventeen around that time. I had reached my full height by then. I was six-foot-three. I weighed a hundred and forty pounds. I was a big skinny boy. I had a real big nose, and my eyes were set close together like a possum. I'd see myself in the bathroom mirror, and think, You could hang from a tree branch, still as stone. You're a possum.

Probably I had a little over a year more of this life. Thirteen or fourteen more months of free rent and the welfare checks, and then something else. Maybe get a job, washing dishes or greeting customers at Wal-Mart. Cook burgers and fries at Five Guys or Mickey D's or Burger King. Work the cash register at CVS or Walgreen's. Clean the bathrooms. Wipe up the pee from the floor, the brown stains from the white porcelain of the toilet. Wear rubber gloves. Try not to puke.

I started to carry a pill or two in the watch pocket of my jeans, just to have them on me. All the time. As though I wasn't fully dressed without the pills. A Valium or clonazepam, an oxycodone or perc.

Anywhere, anytime, I'd fish one of the pills out of the pocket with my index finger, and I'd swallow it without water. No problem. I knew the size and shape of each pill, the way a hunter knows the woods. Oxycodone were tiny and white, Valium were flat and round. Valium were blue or yellow, depending if they were brand name or generic, five m.g. or ten.

I walked during the day, and maybe twice a week I walked late at night. I didn't know where Ivy was anymore. She had been gone a long time. Gone a month, gone three months. She was no longer here, and she had never said goodbye. I didn't think she was ever coming back.

And Mommy? She might have been in Lincoln, Nebraska, or Hibbing, Minnesota. She might have been on a coroner's table, or in the furnace of a crematorium. Maybe she was alive, and had a rich boyfriend. The men used to love Margie, and maybe they still did.

Peggy drove a Benz now. She lived in a house with a view of the hills. With a view of the water. A pond, a lake, an ocean. I didn't know. I didn't know much at all. Just that people needed to do things, and those things had pretty much nothing to do with anything else. With other things or other people. It was like the pull of gravity.

On the radio, the young woman named Vanessa, on the Jimmy Summers show, was more and more scared. Someone had slashed her tires and broken her windshield. She had the creepy feeling that during the day, when she was at work, someone had come into her apartment. He had gone through her drawers, and left underwear under her pillow.

She didn't know how he got in. Maybe he had a key.

The houses on my walks, day or night, in darkness or in the full light of day, they were always there. The big bungalows, the Victorian piles, the oversized Cape Cod houses, the wood frame houses with the beautiful additions, the new porches and decks, the skylights.

There was so much life in every house. Young families, old couples, a few couples who were not even married, a lesbian couple.

I needed to know about them. How they slept and what they ate for dinner. If they had kids named Dakota and Chloe and Zoe. What the kitchen smelled like, and if there was whole milk in the refrigerator. Were they baking brownies or roasting a chicken. Had they just baked bread. If there was a note on the kitchen counter; if there were photographs magneted to the fridge. If sneakers or sandals or shoes were lined up in the front or back hall, and if coats hung on hooks in those same halls. If fresh-ground coffee in a plastic container stood on the counter near the sink. If car keys sat in a bowl near the back door. Keys for a Subaru and a Honda. Keys for cars that were reliable, that wouldn't leave you stranded by the side of the road.

I always wondered what the fathers were like. Tall or short, fat or skinny. Long hair or bald. Somewhere in between. Just normal looking, whatever that was. One father drank, and was mean as a snake. Or he drank, and he became more and more sad and quiet, the more he drank.

He wore a suit and tie almost all the time, except when he was sleeping. He wore a light-blue or white button-down shirt, tan chinos, sensible brown shoes. He wore glasses with dark brown plastic frames, or he wore glasses with small metal frames. His eyes were gray. His eyes were brown. His eyes were blue.

He was nice. He was scary.

I wanted to ask Ivy about some of these things. I wanted to ask if she wondered about her mother. Where she was, and if she was alive. Ivy, I think, had been gone a month or two or three. I didn't see or hear her go. I didn't see Henry leave either.

Ivy used to say that if something left your life without saying goodbye, then you'd have to wonder about it forever.

I wished that I had taken her more through the neighborhoods at two or three in the morning. I wanted to see what she would see and what she would think. If she would feel this great need to know what life was like inside those houses. And what the houses would say about the people who lived there.

The pictures on the walls, the rugs on the floor, how polished the floors would be, so you would see the grains of the wood. The big dining room table, made of oak or cherry, and the wooden chairs lined up, three on each side, and one at each end. And the grandfather clock ticking, tall as a man, its hands thin and gold as an old man's fingers.

How did these people get to have such lives? Lives of comfort, lives with full bookcases, lives where they had a cello or a baby grand piano in the living room.

Did they even know how good their lives were?

I went out in the afternoon, around three-thirty, to look at houses. I went on Linden and Irving and Mitchell and Harvard.

This was the end of an overcast day, and this was in the week just after Thanksgiving. Many of the houses seemed empty, the people gone to see parents or children. The sky was deep gray, the sky seemed ready to rain. There didn't seem much light at all, and the streetlights had not come on. It was half-night already.

I went up and down the streets. I paused at some curbs, and looked around. I could see six or eight houses, and only three of them had lights on. Lights on the first and second floors. Lights that did not seem like they were on a timer.

There were toys in the backyards of two houses. A few Big Wheels, a tiny seesaw, a sandbox, bright red and yellow balls. The houses had porches, and two of the houses had porch swings and Adirondack chairs. One house had a small balcony on the third floor in front, and only two houses had cars in the driveway.

By then it was almost completely dark, and the trees on the tree lawn, the trees in the back and side yards, were dark and looming.

I went to the backyard of one house I was sure was empty. There was a single car in the garage, and no toys in the yard. Everything was neat and clean and squared away. This had to be an old person's house.

There was a big window in back. Three windows, really, that were so close together that they were one window, and there was a dim light on. This was a kitchen, because I could see the top of a refrigerator.

I thought, Oh, they left the kitchen light on.

Then I saw an old lady, gray hair, glasses, a little stooped, leaning over what must have been a stove. Baking brownies, baking cookies, making a cake.

I watched her, and she suddenly turned. She looked out the window.

Her face, her long thin nose, her glittery glasses, were very close to the window.

She was there. She was looking right at me.

45

By then, it had come around to summer again. I only opened the windows a little, maybe an inch or two, but just when I was awake and moving around in the apartment. It got real hot inside, but I kept the fan going, and I usually sat around in my shorts and a thin T-shirt. I liked the T-shirts with the V at the neck. I don't know why really, but I sort of liked the way they looked.

I really liked ice, too, and I drank ice water almost all the time. I loved how the ice melted in the glass, and how incredibly cold it made the water. Even if I was drinking a beer, I'd have an ice water next to it on the table.

There were usually six full ice trays in the freezer. There was always plenty of ice.

I slept till around noon most days, and I even took a nap in the late afternoon. The rooms were really, really hot around four or five or six. That's when it was getting less hot outside, but inside was hours behind the outside.

Sometimes I went out for a walk around eight-thirty or nine, just to be outside, just to feel if there was even a slight breeze. I could feel the breeze on my arms and legs and neck. I could feel it moving through my hair, cooling down my brain. The world was turning to night, and almost all the students had gone. There were a few older students, and they were graduate students, I thought.

They were studying something molecular or chemical, something I would never understand.

So in July, in early July, I was seventeen, and I knew I had less than a year to go. I had about a half year until I turned eighteen, and my way of life would end. I would no longer be a kid.

I took a pill, usually a clonazepam or diazepam, as soon as I woke up. I knew I was taking more of them than I had in the past, but it didn't seem to affect me. I wouldn't take a pain pill until later in the day or night. So it was okay, I thought.

I didn't know any more how long Mother had been gone. Now, I no longer knew how long Ivy had been gone. It was me. Only me. This grotesquely tall creature with a nose as big as Ohio. Somebody people left.

By then, I guess, I was up to a hundred and fifty pounds. Maybe a hundred and sixty.

I remembered Mommy from much earlier, when she was younger and I was young. How I was pretty innocent, at least for six years old. I just wanted Peg to love me, to hug me, to tuck me into bed and read me a story. Squirrel Nutkin or Harold who had his purple crayon. There was *Goodnight, Moon*, and *Frog and Toad*. There was Pooh and Piglet and Tigger and Eeyore. Eeyore was always sad. Eeyore loved his popped balloons.

If I had mac 'n' cheese, if I had a piece of pizza, and if Marge was smiling and humming, then the world was good. The world had given me everything I wanted.

When Maggie's johns came over, and they came over all the time, every day and late into the night, they were nice men. They were nice to me.

From real early, from when I was five and six, I saw Margaret put money and pill bottles into the top drawer. I don't know why, but I thought the pill bottles were food, in case there was some kind of emergency out in the world. If there was a flood or fire, if there was a blizzard and nobody could go to the grocery store.

One night, I think—and I'm almost certain this happened—I was asleep in the big bed with Mom, and it was two or three in the morning. We lived on the third floor of a house on the side of a steep hill, and we heard—I heard—a low tapping, a low knocking on the door.

Peg went to the door, and I heard some whispers. There was quiet for a few seconds, then more whispers, then the chain on the door rattled. Then Maggie came in to me. She opened the drawer, fumbled around, and she said, All.

She put half a pill in my hand, handed me a little water glass from the table next to the bed.

She said, Take this, All.

I tried to swallow, but the pill got stuck in my dry mouth.

I sipped a little water, tried again, and this time the pill went down.

She took my hand, and led me to the couch in the living room. She put a pillow under my head, a blanket over me, and then she brushed the hair off my forehead.

She said, Go to sleep, All. She said, Sweet dreams.

Then it was only a few minutes later, and I was floating at the ceiling. The rest of the room, the couch, a chair, the windows, a few boxes, the great darkness, was way down below.

That had never happened before, and I didn't know how it happened then. Like my head was funny. Like something was in my brain or breath or blood. Like I was deep in a dream, even though it didn't feel like a dream. Because there was air on my arms and face, and there were cars going by on the street down below.

There could have been voices too. Students laughing and yelling, grown-ups saying things to people on the far side of the street. A man's voice loud as thunder, just talking, talking, talking, until he moved farther away, and then you couldn't hear him anymore. But you knew that he knew everything there was to know in the world.

There was noise coming from Mommy's room, but I tried not to listen to that noise. I tried not to think about that noise.

Instead, I felt that sweet, sweet feeling in my bones and brain. Like every tiny piece of me was cool and warm, tingling and peaceful. I could and did float on the air. I could hear voices singing. The high pure voices of small children. Sounding and moving so beautifully, that it was almost painful to hear.

Like how much could you feel, could you hear. Like too much of the sound would vibrate and almost shatter you.

The voices lifted and went sideways, went up slightly, then down and up, then sideways, and it was so beautiful but painful too. Like you could stand the pain, as long as it kept being so unbearably and bearably lovely.

Somewhere in there I thought that maybe this had almost everything to do with the pill that Mother had given me. But how could such a tiny pill, such a tiny half-pill, do all these things. Like cause the world to grow deeper and wider, and make sounds, the music of children's voices, so achingly beautiful.

And June, late June and early July, arrived and the heat was the same early summer heat as it had always been. It felt the same and smelled the same. Like something I knew well, but had not felt or smelled in many months. Just as, in four or five months, I would turn eighteen, and everything would be different.

Ivy was still gone. The apartment across the hall stayed empty, and that gave me a slice of hope that Ivy and Henry might come back.

Once in a while, usually late at night, I would think that they had come back. I would hear a sound or two, out in the hall, across the hall, and it made me think that sometime when I was sleeping, maybe in late morning, they had arrived and carried their bags inside.

But I was wrong about that, just as I was wrong about so many things. I went out to the hall, and pressed my ear against their door, but there was nothing, there was nobody, there.

She was gone at least six months by then. Maybe more. All that gorgeous frizzy hair. Her hat. The leggings. Her long pale skin. Like warm silk.

When she said, All. All. And nobody had ever said my name like that.

Not even Maggie. And I was pretty sure that she used to love me, before I got so tall, and my nose so big. Before acne, before I was strange. Before I no longer talked, hardly at all.

Ivy was my friend. Me and Ivy, we walked the dark. We looked at the trees and bushes, at the houses and at the buildings on campus. We usually didn't talk so much. We walked and looked, and we were always aware of each other. At least I was always aware of Ivy, and I thought she was aware of me.

Except one night, we were walking at the far east side of campus. We were past the veterinary college, and then there were acres and acres of fields. There were rows and rows of greenhouses, there was a huge water tower, there were thin paved roads snaking though the botanical gardens. Formal gardens of flowers and herbs, and a little farther on, a road into fields of trees. So many trees, but not like a forest. Trees like an arbor, with silver metal tags on each one, that said the name in regular language, WHITE OAK, then QUERCUS ALBA, in Latin.

I think Ivy had once told me that. I wasn't sure and I had no clue how Ivy knew that.

Then I was deeper into the arbor, and it was at least two or three in the morning, and it was a dark and moonless night. I had been walking for three or four minutes, among trees, and along paths, and then I didn't know where Ivy was, and had not been aware of her for a while.

I said, Ivy, but not very loud, because I was worried someone else might hear. I said her name again and again, in a loud whisper. I moved around among the trees, along several paths, then along the paved road.

There were trees all over and around me. There were bushes, and ground, and there was a dark, lightless sky over everything. But Ivy, she was as gone as two nights or two weeks of nights ago. She'd been disappeared, she'd been sipped into the ground.

46

It is the first week or so of December, with Thanksgiving behind us. The guys are pretty subdued in here, and I can feel that slight spring in the step of the staff, even the COs. Like they're walking on their toes, sort of. They're a little happy, or at least less miserable.

We've had a few dustings of snow, in the yard, and on low roofs and gates that we can see. At most, it's an inch, possibly two, and it doesn't stay around long. Just a patch of white, another patch, then a thin line of snow at the edge of the high fences, or along the side of one of the buildings.

In the windows, the windows of administration buildings, at the front of the joint, you can see Christmas things. Ornaments, and Santa Clauses, tiny sleighs, reindeer, hanging in some of the office windows. If those are office windows. I guess I don't know. Not really. Maybe DeMarco's up there. Maybe he's the window with Santa Claus and candy canes, and a few colored blinking lights. Red, blue, green, yellow. Winking and winking.

Some of the guys, they have jobs in the offices out front. Trusty guys, guys who have been in a long time. Drug guys, and armed robbery guys, and simple battery guys. But no killers, no domestic abuse guys, no rapists or pedo guys.

The baby fuckers, they're the lowest. Everyone hates them. Everyone knows who they are. A guy named Marvin, another guy named Inky for his tats, another one named Donald.

They look kind of normal. They don't have horns or a tail, they don't have small piggy eyes or wet lips.

They keep them in protective custody, although I don't think the COs would much care if they got stabbed or killed. The guys and the staff are of one mind about the pedos.

They'd never let me work out front on account of what I

did. Even though I'm a model prisoner. At least I'm not a pedo. But the blinking lights, Santa and candy canes and the snowman, these are not for us. These are for the staff. The administrators, the office staff, the COs. They leave here every day at the end of their shift. They go home. They have husbands and wives, they have kids, they have neighbors and friends. Maybe they have Christmas trees at home, with all the lights and the tinsel. The candy canes and angels. They have pork chops and mashed potatoes and asparagus. They have cake with lemon icing; they have a cold beer. The kids come in while he or she is watching something on television. A movie, a football game, a sitcom about two roommates.

The youngest kid is a boy and only four years old. He smells sweaty, all day and night, and his hands are usually sticky. With jelly, with the remnants of a peanut butter sandwich, with a piece of hard candy. The boy climbs onto his mother or father's lap, and then the oldest, a daughter, comes in. She sits in the middle of the couch, and eats a piece of red licorice.

She holds the licorice out to her father or mother, and says, Wanna bite?

Maybe it happens something like that. A mother and father, two or three or four kids, a house with furniture, dinner, television, a little kid sitting on his mother or father's lap.

This has been a long time since I was out there. This has been thirty years, well over half my life. Do they even have takeout anymore? Regular phones, I hear, are gone.

Everybody uses what are called cell phones, and everybody uses these small portable computers. They go on this thing called the internet. Everything in the world is on the internet. Shopping, dating, travel, drugs, sex, friendship. The whole of everything.

Life is on the internet. Life is not where it used to be.

So if I get out of here, as DeMarco said, what do I do and where do I go? Will it be like science fiction out there? With cars that drive themselves, and these powerful phones—smart phones, they call them—and these computers you can carry around. These little computers you can hold on your lap and that contain every last thing in the universe.

I still haven't heard anything more from DeMarco or anybody from the administration or A-building. Only that Mellor had asked his people, and they had heard of DeMarco. DeMarco did exist. He wasn't a dream, a delusion, a hallucination.

A long time ago, when I first came inside, none of this seemed real. It was like a film or scrim had come down between the world and me. Everything was at least one remove, maybe two or three removes because I couldn't take any of this in. It was too big and too awful and too overwhelming. And it was going to last for most of my life. It was going to last until I was pretty old. Till most of my life was already gone.

Now the look from inside was switched around. Down was up and up down. The world out there had kept going. Time passed, and it kept passing. Time went by in the day and in the night. It went by on weekdays and on weekends. Time passed in the city where I grew up, and it passed down there in New York City. In Barrow, Alaska, in Ventura, California, in Great Falls, Montana.

There was nowhere in the world it didn't go by, every morning and afternoon and night. The highest mountain in Nepal, the deepest trench in the Pacific Ocean.

At first it had all seemed impossible—that I would spend most of my life in here, behind these walls and in these cages. With these guys, who were not the best people in the world. These loud, crude, violent men. Being ordered around by COs. It was so impossible that for over a year, in the beginning, I couldn't take it in. I couldn't process any of it.

Then after a year, after two years, first at Dannemora, then here at Auburn, I started to get used to it. I don't know how. Just that we can get used to anything. Just that every person in here, who was not on staff, was in the same position I was in.

And now, Jesus, the whole of it is about to be turned upside down again.

Everything I am, everything I know, is going back to the way it was thirty, forty years ago.

Though the world thirty years ago doesn't exist anymore. Half the people who were around back then are no longer alive. Half the people who didn't exist back then are now here. Now they have DNA to catch criminals. Now they have computers in every home and office. Smart phones in every pocket and purse.

And the person I was thirty years ago, he doesn't exist anymore either.

So it gets dark early these days. It gets dark around four, four-thirty. By five it's totally black, dark enough to go out and prowl the streets. But that doesn't happen for me anymore. Not since the beginning of forever.

The yard has really bright lights, bright as a football field at night. They come on at four, and they're called halogen lights. They're crazy bright, and they flood the yard. They don't make shadows.

The big windows on the cell blocks are covered with bars, and someone has taped those white snowflake cutouts to the window, high up. Every other window has one, and they must be fifteen or twenty feet above the ground. As though someone's kid came and hung their grade school project up for the rest of us to admire. Just as in the regular world.

This could be my last Christmas inside. I could be out by February or March, if that's possible. If Mellor's right, if De-Marco's real.

But I haven't heard a thing from anybody else on the staff. A few guys—Lacy, Smothers, Semple—they've come to ask me if it's true.

Even Tommie Lee Wales, the A.B. guy, he comes up to me in the yard. He says, Oliver, I hear.

I nod. I say, I think so.

You don't know?

This guy DeMarco, administration guy, he called me out a while ago. Said I'm out the beginning of next year.

Tommie Lee Wales has small eyes, very bright blue. Flat eyes. Hard to read anything there.

What'd you say the guy's name was? Tommie Lee asks.

I tell him, and he says he'll ask around.

I start to walk slow, around the perimeter of the yard. You always feel the lights, and the fences, the razor wire, the tall outside walls. The glass in the guard towers, the COs with rifles in the towers.

But as I'm walking, guys here and there nod at me, a few reach out to bump fists. Black guys, white guys, one guy with so much crazy hair I don't know if he's white or Black. A few guys say, Hey; someone else says, All.

It's strange. Like I've done something good.

47

Everything got more weird and lonely by then. Everything got deeper. Down to dark and strange places that I had never even imagined were there. Spider webs, mold, centipedes, snakes. You just couldn't tell because the light was so dim.

Probably, there were three or four months until I turned eighteen, and then all this life I had known, all this life I had lived, was over. And I didn't have a remote idea what I would do, or where I would go.

Mabel still brought groceries, usually once a week, but she left them by the front door, and I left cash in an envelope, taped to the front door. I hadn't seen Mabel in many, many weeks. I made sure to leave her plenty of dough in the envelope. At least a few hundred bucks a week.

There were only three thick rolls of bills in the drawer, and maybe ten or twelve bottles of pills. Plus there was always at least a case of beer in the kitchen, and an icy six-pack in the fridge.

There were usually apples and oranges, there was some chocolate, there were cans of Progresso soup—split pea with ham, Manhattan clam chowder, chicken noodle, beef barley. A can of Progresso with a sleeve of Saltines—that was all a boy could ask for.

I think Maggie had been gone a year or two or three. I really didn't know any more. I guess it could have been six months, or it could have been four years. Mabel hadn't heard from her in a long, long time.

Ivy had been gone a long time too. Not as long as Peg, but still many, many months or even years.

The thing that happened was that people showed up, they hung around for a little while, you learned to love or like them a little or a lot, and then at night, almost always in darkness, when you couldn't see or know, they went away somewhere. For a little while or forever, to Great Falls, Montana, to Independence, Missouri. To pretty much anywhere. For pretty much always.

I think by then I never went outside in the daylight, and I only went out in the evening to buy cigarettes at a convenience store in Collegetown. Even though I was seventeen and underage, I was almost freakishly tall for my age, and nobody asked to see an ID.

And then, of course, I went out at one or two or three in the morning. When almost no people were alive and moving in the world. Where a car passed every five or ten minutes.

I carried a screwdriver and a small, wide pry bar by then. They fit nicely in the inside pocket of my black jean jacket. And they were more or less the only tools I would ever need.

The apartment was less and less clean and more and more cluttered. Every few weeks I put a big black trash bag of beer cans and bottles out at the curb, and it would usually be gone within a day. I also took the trash out once a month or so, when the white and black trash bags were filling up and collecting along one wall of the kitchen. The trash started to smell after a week or two, and I'd take the bags to the curb when the smell got real bad. The stink, the stench, was worse in the hot weather.

More than anything, the pills and beer got to be kind of central to my life. Instead of one or two pills each day, I was now taking five or six. Instead of one or two beers in the evening, I was now sipping beer very slowly, almost all the time I was awake. I was up to four or five beers a day.

A few times I worried about the booze and pills. I started to think that I was an alcoholic and addict, and that bothered me, even though I didn't know why it bothered me. You always heard that alcohol and drugs could ruin your life.

But then I'd think, So what. My life was already pretty ruined for good.

Now and then I'd swear off the beer and drugs, and within

a half day, everything got really nasty. This intense anxiety, this feeling of near panic. My brain racing like a monkey in a tree, these awful feelings that something terrible was about to happen. Every sound from the street, from other parts of the house, was a gunshot. I was some kind of freakish criminal. I had wet lips; I had darting eyes; I had trembling fingers. They would walk me into the death chamber, they would strap me to the gurney. They would find a vein, snake the needle in.

I had done ghastly, horrible things. Things I couldn't remember, things I didn't even know about anymore. Maybe they didn't happen, maybe they did. Maybe they only happened in my brain.

The lines that used to tether me to the earth, to the regular world, were no longer there. I slept at all hours, almost always in the daylight. I also had this patchy facial hair, because I didn't know how to shave. Not really. I had patches of hair on my chin, on one cheek, and a wispy line above my upper lip that looked like dirt. But I did take showers, often twice a day. I was a clean, freaky boy. I had hair down to my shoulders.

I'd wake up in the late afternoon, usually around four or five. It was between Christmas and New Year's by then, so it was dark or near dark when I woke up. I'd crack open an icy-cold beer, and I'd sip slowly, and each small swallow was a comfort to me. It was solace.

I'd think, Well, here I am again. I'm not dead at least.

I had no idea what I was gonna do with my waking hours, with the time when I wasn't asleep. Sometime later, after the first beer, around seven or eight, I'd take my first clonazepam or lorazepam, to boost the beer. I'd smoke cigarettes, I'd blow smoke at the ceiling and windows and doors, then I'd watch the smoke curl and eddy. I could watch smoke, I think, for hours.

Maybe an hour or two later, I'd take the first pain pill of the night. An oxy, a vike, a codeine. Then I'd wash it down with another beer. I had a buzz on. I definitely had a good buzz.

For a while, maybe for an hour or two, I sat on the couch

and smoked my Kools, and felt warm all over. I felt pretty pain-less, and I thought that life was good. No worries. Everything was gonna be fine with me and my life.

This one night, two or three nights before New Year's, I sat on the couch a long time. I felt so good, sitting there. This deep calm, this feeling that people and the world were good, were kind, were really decent underneath everything.

Thanksgiving and Christmas had gone by, and we were al-most at the new year. I'd been at home in the apartment for the holidays, and I'd been by myself, of course. I was pretty much always by myself, and I didn't think I minded that. I had my beer, my cigs, my pills. I had everything.

So this one night, this night right before the end of the year, I stayed on the couch a long time. I had another beer, a third beer, then I took an oxy and a diazepam. I was real high, real jacked, but not in a sleepy way. More like calm and focused. More like a hunter. In the woods of the world, still as a stone, watching everything carefully and closely.

At midnight, according to the clock on the stove, I got into my stalking clothes. Black jeans, black socks and sneakers, black turtleneck and sweater, black beanie cap, black jacket with the screwdriver and pry bar. I was almost invisible, except for my gigantic nose.

Outside was pretty cold. Not totally freezing, like mid-Jan-uary, but maybe twenty degrees and heading down into the teens. Snow had fallen three or four days earlier, but most of it had melted. There were still small heaps of snow from where people had shoveled their driveways, or at the edge of the road from snowplows.

I felt so strong, so tall, and I felt as though I could walk any-where in the world. I was almost eighteen. Three more months, and I'd be a grown-up.

All the streets were still there, in this neighborhood of beau-tiful houses. Oxford Place, Elmwood, Fairmount, and Bryant Avenues, Delaware, Harvard, and Irving Place.

The streets and houses were as quiet as they ever got. I heard a truck or car go by a mile away, on one of the big roads. But it seemed as though the whole town, almost, had cleared out. There was nothing, nothing, nothing. Just houses and trees, streets and sidewalks. Bushes, some fallen leaves.

On Elmwood Avenue, I saw a house that I don't think I had ever noticed before. There were big, tall bushes covering most of the front of the house. There were two stories, and despite the big bushes, it looked well-kept. Freshly painted in the last year or two, with two Adirondack chairs on the front porch.

It wasn't the biggest house in the neighborhood, but it looked plenty nice. Lace curtains, I think, as far as I could tell, in most of the windows of the first floor.

I went down the driveway on the left side of the house, and there were more bushes between the driveway and the house. There was one of those doors that went in, probably, between the basement and the first floors. Stairs going up, stairs going down.

There was no car in the driveway, and I thought, there's nobody home.

Then I went to the backyard, where there were a couple of big trees. The branches were all bare, and when I looked up through the spider legs of branches, I could see the moon, which was almost full. It was pale and cold, and I stared for a little while.

I thought, I hadn't even noticed it was there. I thought, That moon, like me, is a long way away.

48

I took two pain pills, both oxycodone, from the watch pocket of my jeans. I swallowed them without water, and thought that I'd feel the boost fairly quickly. I already had booze and drugs in my body, so the extra pills would just support the buzz. Push it up a notch or two.

I walked slowly around the house, on the frozen lawn, and there were no lights on inside. No car, no lights. There couldn't have been any people there. No humans.

The moon was still up there in the sky, still faithfully doing its old work. So I sat on the cold lawn in the backyard, and I saw shadows from the moonlight, shadows of the house, the big bushes, the trees.

Then the pills were kicking in, and it was beautiful, the way they made you feel. Just lovely and warm, like you were floating, and nothing could touch you. Like everything was numb, but your brain, the center of everything, was shot through with sweetness, and was linked to every large and small thing in the universe.

I thought, I could die now. I could sink away into death and darkness and oblivion, and I would be happy. Perfectly happy.

I could go away forever, or almost forever, and that would be fine. That would be better than fine. That would be perfect.

Nobody would know that I was dead. No one could possibly care. Not Peggy, not Ivy, not even Mabel. Maybe I wouldn't care either, even though I wouldn't be there to care.

That was the strange thing about thinking you were dead. By the time you were finally dead, you wouldn't be there to realize it or think about it anymore. None of it would matter. It all came down to nothing.

The pills kept building up in my breath and bones and

blood. I was nervous and a little scared, but I was also happier and warmer and more numb.

I stood up from the grass, and looked at the moon for half a second, and it was very pale and still, and hung by an invisible string. There was a screened porch on the side of the house, hidden by more big bushes. All the bushes, all around the house, made me feel protected. Maybe they made the people who usually lived in the house feel protected too. Now, whoever they were, they were somewhere else. In St. Thomas, on a beach, or visiting family in Omaha or San Diego or Joplin.

There were two or three steps going up to the porch door, and the door was latched but loose. I think it was latched with an old hook and eye device. I slid my screwdriver in and unlatched the door. It made a slight, metallic tinkling sound.

Then I stood just inside the door. I listened, and listened, and listened some more. There was no sound. Just a car, way far off in the distance, moving, I think, on North Tioga Street or Route 13. There was a faint rumbling sound of the furnace or the refrigerator. I could feel the vibrations of the motors, much more than I could hear anything.

The porch had screens all around it, and the tall bushes just outside the screens. The screens and bushes enclosed everything, made everything feel like a small safe place. A place to sleep, to feel secure, where nothing would threaten me.

There were two chairs, and a chaise lounge, but they were covered in plastic. There was a small table between the chairs, and there was a candle in the glass.

My eyes were used to the dark. Maybe because I spent so much time in the dark, even at home, I was kind of like a cat. A house cat, or a cat on a savannah, hunting. Lurking in the dark, watching everything. Missing nothing.

Maybe on summer nights, the owners of the house sat out here. They lit the candle, and they sat in the chairs or the chaise lounge. They sipped a beer, maybe they listened to the radio. They heard music. Maybe classical music or opera. A bunch of people in these neighborhoods, I bet, listened to that kind of music.

Maybe instead of beer, instead of a cold one, they sipped from one of those glasses with the long stem. A wine glass, to sip wine. Or a tall glass with gin and tonic, or vodka and tonic. With ice and a slice of lemon or lime.

Probably they didn't sip whisky or rum or cognac, whatever that was.

Sounds from the neighborhood would come in through the bushes and screens. Snatches of music, pieces of dialogue coming from televisions, kids in yards or on sidewalks, laughing and yelling, calling to each other. A father, say, calling to his playing kids to come home.

Time for a late dinner, time for bed.

Day is done, a mother called. Gone the sun.

The pills kept kicking in, kept building. I think it was one or two in the morning. I felt safe, and I guess I almost felt something like happy.

There was a very slight breeze, and it made some of the leaves on the bushes scrape the screen, making a kind of whispering raspy sound that was almost hypnotic. I was total high alert, and my eyes and ears, my skin, my sense of smell were so sharp and excited that it was almost painful. But the pills, the beer I had sipped earlier, were pushing against my nerves.

This was such a peak of something. The booze and pills, the being out so deep in the night, standing outside, on a porch, of an empty house. A double, a triple, a quadruple buzz, all banging around in my brain.

The porch was almost completely dark, much darker than out in the yard. My eyes were good in the dark, but it took a few minutes to get used to this deeper dark. To this coffin space inside the bushes.

Then I could see a door into the house, and a window on

each side of the door. I looked at them a little while, and I sat down on one of the chairs, on top of the plastic covering. I got a cig from the chest pocket of my jean jacket, and lit it with a match. I dropped the dead match into the candle holder, and sat back, puffing and blowing smoke at the ceiling. Cigs always tasted pure wonderful when you were taking pain pills. Like you couldn't suck them in deep enough or often enough. You could sit down and smoke a pack, one after another, and every cig would taste great. Booze boosted the pills, and pills boosted the booze. Cigs boosted all of them, and they boosted the cigs.

Go outside, in dark clothes, at one or two in the morning, and you were in heaven. You'd gone to Eden, and you could stay there as long as the drugs held out. You could float between the moon and the stars, pretty much forever.

You got to be God.

I sat there a long time. I smoked one cigarette, dumped the butt in the candle jar, and lit a second one. I kept thinking about the people who lived here.

There were no toys anywhere, no play structures in the back yard, and simple white curtains on the windows, and on the window part of the door. But everything was neat, and looked clean, as far as I could tell.

Probably an old couple lived here. Maybe a retired professor of something. Of chemistry or history or computers. Maybe the husband was professor of one thing, and the wife was professor of something else.

A siren started to wail, way off somewhere, a mile or two in the distance. An ambulance or fire truck or a police car. Possibly taking a sick person to the hospital. Somebody with a bad heart, or with trouble breathing. With serious pain in the belly or legs.

A person who would have been scared, who might have been worried that he or she was dying. Very late on a Monday or Thursday night. An old person who often thought, who wondered, when and where and how he or she would die. In the back of an ambulance. In the cubicle of an emergency room. Attended by doctors and nurses who were impossibly young. Younger than the old person's grandchildren.

Maybe he wondered if there were ghosts. Maybe she wondered if there were invisible spirits, hovering in the corners of rooms.

Then I wondered where Maggie and Ivy were, and what they were doing. It had been forever since they had gone. I didn't know if Maggie was alive or dead. If she was doing drugs and drinking, if she had boyfriends who would pay her for sex or would bring her drugs. I wondered if they ever thought of me, even half so often as I thought of them.

I dropped my cig into the candle jar, and stood up.

I went to the door, tried the knob, and God. This was crazy. The door was unlocked.

49

Now we're past the holidays. Now we're in the very dead of winter in upstate New York, about halfway through January, about halfway through winter. Maybe thirty, forty miles north of here is Lake Ontario, and about halfway across Lake Ontario is Canada. So the winters are cold. Worse than the cold, though, is the gray, is the darkness. Probably we get ten sunny days all winter, if that.

The gray sky just lurks and crouches and hovers over everything, pretty much always. For days and weeks and months.

When we get that rare sunny day, or even an hour or two of sunshine, it's startling, almost blinding. Like we don't know what to do with it. We get confused.

What's that blue up there?

Huh?

I got called up front to the A., or administration building, a few days ago, for the second time in several months. The CO who brought me up didn't even cuff me. That was strange.

The CO was a little guy with a shaved head, and a ton of muscles. As I walked behind him I could see that he didn't have much of a neck. He had slabs of muscle that sloped down from his head, directly to his shoulders.

This time I didn't see DeMarco, who didn't seem to be in his office anymore, but a tall strong woman with black hair, a long face like a deer, and big glasses that covered half her face. She smiled and shook my hand. She asked me to sit down.

She said, How you doing, and that was unusual. The staff hardly ever asked that.

She said her name was Karen DeVos, and she was a social worker.

She said she understood that DeMarco had met with me, and that I understood that I was going home.

Was that correct? she asked.

I think so, I said. I mean, that's what I thought I heard. But I also thought I was dreaming.

She smiled, and I thought, She has a beautiful smile. Her eyes, behind the lenses of her glasses, were shiny and warm.

She hasn't been here long, I thought. She looked like she was nineteen or twenty, but she had to be older than that. Twenty-four or twenty-five.

The CO who had escorted me, was in the hall, just standing.

I heard clicking keyboards and quiet conversations from down the hall. I heard beeps and rings. There were no howls, no screeches, no heavy metal doors slamming. Heavy metal on heavy metal. You could feel the ground shake.

Karen DeVos said, You'll have a board March third, and assuming it goes well, you'll be leaving March fifth. Barring anything really strange. You haven't had a ticket, an infraction, in over sixteen years.

The state will give you two hundred dollars in cash. And a bus ticket from Auburn to your home city. You'll be staying at a group home, and reporting to a parole officer once a week. Any violation of your parole, it goes without saying, and you're back here.

She said she was sorry to even mention that, because she had every reason to believe that I would succeed. She said she knew that I would do well.

Then she smiled that smile of hers, and it was still beautiful. It was lovely and warm. There was a hint of humor in her smile, as though she and I were both amused by the same thing, and for the same reason.

Karen DeVos had very dark hair and very pale skin. She asked me to sign some papers. First one, then a second and third paper, and finally a fourth one.

In two months, I was gone. In two months I was on the streets again. In two months, I was on the sidewalks of neighborhoods again.

In less than two months, really.

The CO had to cuff me on the way back to my cell. He cuffed me in front instead of in back, and that was a relief. He said there had been a stabbing outside the chow hall, and that we were in lockdown. Every inmate was confined to his cell.

On D-block, Gates was next door as usual, but Mellor was not in his house. Gates said that maybe he was at a medical appointment. Mellor had something wrong with his lungs. Mellor might have tuberculosis, or something like that. He coughed something fierce sometimes. Especially at night.

Then it was later and they were passing dinner into the cells between the bars. This was a serious lockdown. The guy who got stabbed was dead. The knife got his carotid artery, and he was dead on the table at the Emergency Room.

His body was lying on a big steel drawer in the basement of the city hospital. Who knows where it would go from there. Maybe wrapped in a sheet or two and dumped in some unmarked hole in the ground.

I was finishing my baloney sandwich on white bread, and the peas and carrots, when I heard jangling keys and the big steel door just next to me.

Mellor was back.

When I heard the CO walking away, I went to the vent, and said, Hey, to Mellor.

All, Mellor said.

Everything okay? I asked.

He said that things were fine. They took a chest X-ray, and the nurse said his lungs looked clear. She kept saying that she wasn't a radiologist, that she wasn't even a doctor or an X-ray tech, but he didn't look like he had TB or lung cancer, or anything like that.

He coughed all the time, she thought, because of mold or dust, or maybe a fungus that grew somewhere in the buildings. She said the specks of blood from coughing were probably from his lungs or throat being irritated.

She said that she thought his lungs were the same as anyone's lungs.

Then she said again, I'm not a radiologist or a doctor. But she thought he was good to go.

What do you think, Mellor? I said.

He paused, and I could hear his mouth moving around, trying to make a sound.

He said, Motherfuckers.

He said, That nurse didn't know shit, and she knew she didn't know shit. They were too fucking cheap to hire a doctor. There was blood in his spit. He had a little bit of a fever all the time, and he felt tired, like he never slept, even though he slept day and night.

The fuck, he said.

You tell them that—about the blood and the fever?

'Course I did, All.

We were both quiet a little. There was just the usual noise. Televisions and radios, hoots, talk, bangs on the bars and walls.

All, he said, and I didn't say anything at first.

All, he said again. Then he said, I don't wanna fucking die in here, All.

I can't die in here, All, he said. That's a fucking nightmare. In this dumpster. This broken toilet.

Mellor, I said.

No, All, I'm fucking serious. I got kids. I got the mother of my kids.

But, Mellor— I began.

There was a crash somewhere. Probably only a cell door.

I could hear him breathing deep and kind of labored, even through the vent. It sounded like dead leaves scraping the sidewalk in November. Rasp and scrape, rasp and scrape.

Not loud, not obvious, but kind of like with every breath. Like every breath was a struggle.

I couldn't see Mellor, but I guessed that his face was at least a little sweaty, and his eyes a little yellow or red, surrounding the iris. I bet he had a temperature too. A point or two above normal.

This had been going on as long as I'd known him. But in the last months it had gotten worse. It was way worse.

And some nurse, some medical technician or assistant, looked at the X-ray and told him he was fine. No tests, no doctor, nobody who knew about reading X-rays or symptoms. Just, You're fine. Everything's okay. Because why would they care? If Mellor died, so what? As long as he did it quietly, in some corner, lying on the thin mattress in his cell, it didn't much affect anything else.

They left the prison at the end of each day. They got in their cars, drove home, and changed clothes, just to get the stink of inside, the sweat and rage and piss and shit off them. Imagine a cell block with five hundred cells, and imagine a toilet in every one of those cells. And all these guys doing their business, two or three feet from where they slept.

Maybe a quarter of the toilets broke down every month. So the smell. God, the stink was everywhere and on everything. So you got used to it. You no longer knew what it was like to breathe regular clean air. Like you were out in the woods on an October morning, the world a thousand miles away. In here, the world was so, so far away. A million miles away. Light years.

Mellor stayed on the other side of the grate. His breathing was still not great. It was still dead leaves on cement.

I said, Mellor, you want me to get a guard?

He didn't say anything for ten, fifteen, twenty seconds.

No, All, he finally said. I be all right.

Then it was only quiet on the other side of the vent. Quiet like three in the morning. Quiet like a small space on the ground, on the side of a hill, deep in the country.

50

I couldn't believe the heat inside, and the silence. Like someone had forgotten to turn off the heat before they left town, and the heat, the dry heat, built and built inside. And everything was dark as a tomb in there. Not just because it was night but because all around the house on the first floor were these tall, thick bushes that covered all the windows.

I'd been out in the dark for an hour or two, and my eyes were used to darkness. But in the house, I had to get used to a whole other level and depth of dark.

It took five or ten minutes. I found my way to the living room, to the couch, and I lay down. Bit by bit, I began to hear ticking, from what might have been the kitchen. A clock, I thought. An old-time clock. A tick every second.

Then I got up, and I could make out pictures on the walls, a mirror, and chairs and small tables. The dining room had a table with a shiny surface like a mirror, and beyond the dining room was the kitchen.

I stood between the dining room table and the doorway to the kitchen. The clock was loud from there. It went tick and tick and tick.

I listened, and there was nothing else.

Then there was.

At least at first I thought there was.

Something rustled. A mattress spring. A sheet rubbed against a blanket.

I waited, still as a chair.

Waited some more.

But there was only silence. Deep silence. Only ticks and silence.

I felt myself breathe again. One, two, three, four. Each breath a little slower and deeper.

Then I was pretty sure I was imagining it, but someone small and old was walking toward me from a bedroom in the back. Slow, short steps.

Someone who had been sleeping. Someone who had woken up.

A she, I thought.

Then she was there. In the doorway across the room. An old lady with crazy gray hair, I was pretty sure. A long pale nightgown.

She didn't stop at the doorway. And she didn't turn a light on, and that surprised me.

Maybe she thought that this would be pretty much a dream if it happened in the dark.

She didn't scream, she didn't say a word.

I didn't say anything either.

She came across the kitchen with her small slow steps, then she stood in front of me.

My God, she was tiny as a nine-year-old. The top of her head didn't even reach my shoulder. And her hair—it was gray and white, I think, and stuck up and went sideways, in every direction. Like a mad scientist or a bag lady raving on a subway.

She smelled like sleep, but she smelled like Peggy too. Lavender, rose water, lady things.

She wasn't wearing glasses, and I didn't think she could see very well. It was still dark as a grave in the house, even after your eyes got used to it.

But she didn't turn and go back to bed. She didn't go and lock herself in the bathroom. She didn't scream, and she didn't say a word.

And she was really, really old. Sixty or seventy or even eighty. Maybe she was even ninety or a hundred. I didn't know. I couldn't tell. I had no experience with old people. I guess I had no experience with people.

There was no sound from anywhere outside. There was a faint buzz or rumble from the refrigerator, and maybe from a furnace in the cellar.

I could hear her breath. A little whispery, a little quick, as though she was scared, even though she was brave.

The drugs and booze were still going strong in my blood and brain. I was so calm I almost wasn't there. I knew where I was—in some old lady's house, not even a half mile from where I lived. I had broken in, and it was two or three in the morning. It was a dark and winter night.

The house was still hot. It had to have been eighty degrees in there. Outside was maybe twenty.

I have no idea how long any of this took. Five minutes or an hour.

I know I was really jacked on beer and pills.

Then she did something that shocked me. She reached out, fast as the tongue of a snake, and grabbed my wrist, my right wrist. It's like that broke through the idea that none of this was happening.

And it was shocking too how strong, how powerful, her grip was. Like she was a twenty-year-old weightlifter or stone mason or farmer.

I tried to pull away from her, but she was clamped on to me. That old hand, hanging on for life.

There was still that whispery breath, and the smell of lavender or rose water. Still the deep darkness, still the dry heat.

So I pushed at her hard, and pulled my wrist free.

There was a crash, and maybe she hit the edge of a counter or the edge of the refrigerator.

I was out of the kitchen in a second, and then I was near the door to the porch. Maybe I stood there a minute, maybe I stood for ten minutes. Somebody somewhere must have heard something.

Such a burst of noise in all that silence.

I waited for sirens, I waited for cruisers to come rushing to the house, I waited for beefy cops to grab me and slam me against a wall to put the cuffs on. But there was nothing. Nothing anywhere.

Just a very slight breeze, moving through bushes and

branches, moving against the sides of houses. The breeze was so gentle it would hardly have lifted a leaf. A stray dead leaf clinging to a tree. Then I stepped on to the porch, and stood there a little while. I almost sat down to have a smoke. The drugs were strong in me, and I was weirdly relaxed by then. The bushes still surrounded the porch. Nobody could see out, nobody could see in. Then I thought, You idiot. Get out of here.

I figured the old lady must be knocked out, or that she must have broken something. An arm or leg or hip. Maybe a collarbone. Her grip was so strong that I figured she must be much younger than I thought at first. She must be fifty or sixty, not seventy or eighty.

Maybe I could go in the kitchen before leaving and check on her. Put a pillow under her head, cover her with a blanket.

It had to have been past three by then, and the world started waking up by five. The old lady would wake up and maybe call the cops. Maybe her broken arm or leg would be throbbing with pain, or maybe it would all be numb. Maybe she'd be in shock. She'd feel no more pain than I felt.

Finally I went out the porch door. It felt cold after the house, and the moon was still up there, hanging in the sky by an invisible thread, doing its job.

Nothing was moving except for the slight breeze. There were no cars, even in the far distance. None of the houses had lights on. Not really. Two or three had nightlights on in bedrooms or bathrooms, maybe the dim light of a clock on a microwave or stove. There were a few lights on in driveways or the back of houses, on porches and garages.

I went down the driveway, and then left along the sidewalk. The world stayed pretty cold and pretty silent.

Something ran fast across the street and into bushes. It went so quickly that it was gone before I even knew it had been there. Gray with black stripes, I thought. A cat. A cat left out all night.

When I got to my street, everything was still dead quiet. It was the same place, of course, but it didn't quite look the same. All of it looked and felt and seemed different somehow. I didn't know why or how. I just wanted to get inside as quickly and quietly as I could.

There was a dim light in the front hallway that stayed on all night, and two doors—one to Ivy's old apartment, and one to mine. Then the stairs to the second floor. When I got inside, everything was dark, and everything was just the way I had left it. A sheet and blanket bunched up on the bed, dirty dishes in the sink and on the counters in the kitchen.

There were two big bags of trash and empties under the kitchen window. They smelled sour and rotting like something dead, like something left out in the woods or in a basement.

My heart was going pretty fast, I guess from when the old lady had grabbed me, and my breath was quick too. Even after five minutes inside, the heart and breath were still racing along.

So I did something I almost never did. I cracked a beer and swallowed more pills, two clonazepam and two oxycodone, at this late hour. And they kicked in fast, maybe because my insides were already oiled up from the earlier booze and pills.

But within ten or fifteen minutes I felt the next bump, the next boost. I got a blanket and pillow from the bed, and half lay down on the couch. More and more, the beer and pills kicked in. There was a straight clear line that went from deep in my brain to deep in the sky, to the space between stars. The line was icy cold and warm at the same time. It put me millions of miles away.

I was just right there, way far away, and I was right there too on the couch.

I kept thinking about the house with the bushes, and the tiny old lady with crazy hair. I kept thinking and wondering what she was doing there. In that house, at that hour.

Then I wondered who she was. If her name was Myrtle or Alma. If she lived alone because her husband died, or if she had always lived alone. If she had a job, or if she used to have a job. If she had kids who had grown up and moved away. If she had grandchildren.

Was the lady sixty years old or eighty-five? I thought of how shocked I was when her hand shot out and grabbed my wrist. I was amazed by the power of her grip. She was fast as a cat. Then I got another beer. I got back under the blanket, and felt the line between my brain and the stars. I heard a car go by out front, and the light at the edges of the blinds became deep gray. Not long after that, I went to sleep. I slept a long time. So long that when I finally woke up late the next afternoon, the light at the edges of the blinds was nearly dark.

51

I stayed under the blanket a long time. It took a little while, but all at once I remembered the house with the bushes and the old lady. At first I thought that that had been a dream, a bad dream that had never happened to me.

Maybe I could have a beer, a pill or two, because it was more or less the evening, and that's when people would start to relax after a day of work. Maybe I could take the trash bags in the kitchen outside. Then I could wash dishes and clean the kitchen. Maybe clean the bathroom too. I could use an old rag, and I had a bottle of Clorox. I could wipe things down.

So I got up, grabbed a beer, and took some pills to put in the watch pocket of my jeans. I cracked the beer open, fished three pills from the watch pocket, and washed them down with a slug of beer.

It was weird because I could still feel the pills from the night before. But then I thought that it wasn't the night before. It was early this morning, and then I remembered the bushes surrounding the house, and the screened-in porch. I thought of sitting in the chair on the porch, and the small table, and the glass or jar that held the candle.

I smoked two or three cigarettes and dumped the butts in the candle jar. Then I tried the door into the house, and God, it was open.

Then I thought, All this is from a dream. This didn't happen.

Then I remembered the dry heat hitting me when I opened the door, and I remembered how absolutely silent and still everything was, inside and outside the house.

This did happen, I thought. This wasn't a dream.

And even with the beer and the pills coming on, rising from my toes to my brain, I thought again, There's no way this was a dream.

Going inside, standing in the doorway to the kitchen. The tiny old lady, who was at least a foot shorter than me. Who appeared like a ghost or something, with wild white hair, and some pale nightgown.

I sipped beer, and took another pill. I picked up one of the big black trash bags from the kitchen, and took it outside, around back, to the little trash shed. I went back to the kitchen, got another bag, brought it out, then got the last black bag and brought it out.

Then I sat on the couch and drank my beer, and I don't know what else. I sat some more, and then I sat some more. I don't know what I did. There was no television, because you had to pay cable for even basic reception in this town, and I was too cheap.

I finished the first beer and got another, then I got two more pills from my watch pocket. I found the little radio on the table in front of the couch, and turned it on. I scanned through stations, through brief bursts of music and voices, and then I found one of the local stations.

The radio was magic to me. How it brought the world in to my world. It brought music and talk radio, news and weather. I loved the talk shows late at night, and how stray people called in to voice their opinions about pretty much everything. To tell stories. Vanessa and Jimmy Summers. UFOs, life after death, snow, pizza, a television show. One woman called often to talk about her cats, and a man called in to talk about hunting.

You know me, Carl, he said to the host. I'm never happier than when I'm outside in the woods with my gun.

Then the man said, Right there. He said, Right there, after every third sentence.

Some people said, You know. Others said, To be honest.

The cat woman said she had seven cats, and her favorites were named Crispin, Pinky, and Nico.

What about the others? Carl asked. The other four? You don't like them so much?

Oh, I love them all, she said. They're all my babies.

The cat lady's name was Irene. Her husband had been dead seventeen years. They never had kids.

Then the news came on at the top of the hour. There were ads for a hair color kit, for meals in a box, delivered straight to your home. For how to get a nursing degree, for a radio show of Golden Oldies. From the Miracles to the Supremes to the Pips, we've got it all, to give to you.

An eighty-four-year-old woman had been found dead on the floor of the kitchen in her Belle Sherman home. She was found by a cleaning woman. Edna Perloff, a former chemistry researcher, had lived in her Belle Sherman neighborhood for forty-six years.

Police said the manner and means of her death was unknown. Pending an autopsy, investigators couldn't say whether there was foul play.

I thought, No. This was impossible.

I was cold, freezing cold, all over. I could hear the radiators hissing and clanking. I took another pill, then I drank off the rest of my beer.

Then I thought of something. I went to look but I couldn't find it. My pry bar, which had been in the inside pocket of my jean jacket, was nowhere. Absolutely nowhere.

I had to have dropped it. And I hadn't worn gloves.

Then a day, two days, three days went by, and I stayed pretty buzzed the whole time. I slept a ton, always during the day, when it was light outside. I kept the heat down low, so it was pretty cold. I wore sweatpants under my jeans, and two or three sweatshirts, two pair of socks, and a black watch cap. I took a pill or two every few hours.

And I almost always had a beer open. I didn't swig it down. I sipped slowly, then after a few minutes I sipped again.

A few times I fell down. I had been walking slowly, my vision kind of blurred. I reached for the wall, to steady myself, but my hand slid on the wall, and boom, down. It took a little while to get back on my feet.

Another time I went down outside the door to the bathroom. I hit the door and floor hard. My head bounced, and one knee hurt like anything. But my buzz kept me cushioned for the most part.

I tried to slow myself down. To wait two hours between another beer or pill. Then I could walk and see a little better.

Sometime later, on the third or fourth day, in the middle of the afternoon, there was a loud banging on the apartment door. It went boom, boom, boom. Then it paused, and went boom, boom, boom, again. They were powerful knocks, and a voice said, Oliver, Oliver, open up.

It could have been the landlord, who I had only ever seen once, years ago. But why would he show up?

Then there were more booms, and another voice, a loud voice, said, Oliver, police. We need to talk to you.

Maybe they'd smash down the door.

But I turned over in bed, and sipped from a half-empty can of beer on the night table. They did go away, and I managed to sleep a little longer.

When I woke up, I was still slightly drunk and buzzed from pills. I thought, That was cops. I'm almost positive. That was definitely cops. And they had come about the old lady.

They knew.

So they came back the next morning, and they had a warrant. They banged on the door, and they must have kicked it, and the door came blasting open. There were two cops and two detectives.

Neighbors had seen me, a real tall, skinny guy with a big nose, walking the neighborhood numerous times.

They did have a warrant, and they wanted my fingerprints and DNA. They were all pretty big, and some of them had guns and handcuffs. None of them were as tall as me, but they were all thick and strong. They wanted to talk.

They had DNA from cigarette butts at the scene, they had a pry bar with fingerprints, they had a door frame and doorknob with more fingerprints.

One of the uniform cops had a black name tag on his coat

that said Lauricella. One of the detectives wore a long gray overcoat. He said his name was Dressler.

I said almost nothing this whole time.

They said a woman, an old woman, had been murdered near here. They said they were questioning everybody.

They wanted me to come down to the station.

Even though they didn't arrest me right there, even though they didn't put the handcuffs on me, I knew that that world, that life, was over.

Now I was walking into the rest of forever.

52

I t's cold as hell on the cell block, and it's even colder outside, as far as I can guess. This is my last full day in here, and I'm giving stuff away. I give my TV to Mellor, and I give a couple of books to Gates. I only have two shirts, a sweatshirt, and two pair of pants. I have a few more books, and some paperwork about parole. I have boots, and a pair of cheap sneakers. My official release date is February 28. They'll give me an envelope with 200 dollars in cash, plus a bus ticket to my hometown. It's only an hour away. The bus station is a half mile or so from the front gates of this place.

Breakfast's at five, I leave between five-thirty and six.

I don't know what to think or feel. Mostly I'm nervous as a cat, and pretty damn scared. Almost as scared as when I first came inside. I didn't know what anything would be like, and I was only eighteen. I had about nine months in county jail, and I pled guilty to avoid a life without parole sentence.

So now I'm almost fifty, and let's face it, I've never really been out in the bigger world.

I've never driven a car, or shopped for groceries. I don't know how to use a bank, or a computer. I don't even know how to walk down a street in the daytime. How do you go to a restaurant? How do you get a driver's license?

I have a room in a halfway house, near downtown in my small city. Down the big hill from the university, and from where I used to live. Down from where Edna Perloff used to live, from where she died.

I didn't mean to kill her. I didn't even mean to steal anything. I never stole anything or hurt anyone before that.

But I did break in, I entered illegally, and I did kill her. And she was just an old lady who happened to live alone. I don't think she had ever been married. Or maybe she had. I didn't know if she ever had kids. I used to think I knew, but then I couldn't remember anymore. It was so long ago. It was more than thirty years ago.

And over the years, I've thought of that time, before prison, when I was a boy, really. When I was a skinny, homely, gawky kid. Who almost never went to school. There was Maggie. There was Mabel. Then there was Ivy. My first and only friend. They all left, except, I guess, for Mabel. Mabel stuck around, and she bought me groceries. I paid her, of course, but it was still a stand-up thing for her to do.

Ivy just left. Probably because her father, Henry, wanted to go or had to go. And they went to an apartment in Maine or Florida or southern California. And Henry drove his truck all over the country, and Ivy stayed behind and listened to music or read a book.

Ivy might have dropped me a postcard or a letter. She might have said, Hey All, or Dear All, and she might have ended it, Love, Ivy, or, All my love, Ivy. Or, Sincerely, Ivy. But she didn't. Maybe she forgot the address.

Maggie too. Maggie went to rehab, I think. Maggie went to live with a friend. A guy named Ralph or Tony or Glenn. Somewhere near Rochester here in upstate New York. She didn't call because I didn't have a phone. She didn't send a postcard because I somehow remember that she hated to write.

But Peg left me a boatload of drugs and money. Enough to last for at least a few years.

There's a boom and some yells way down at one end of the cell block.

Motherfucker, somebody yells over and over. Someone else, someone with a real deep voice, yells, Wall, Wall, Wall.

Mellor is not feeling so good. He's tired as three a.m. He's been tired like this for weeks, and he's spitting blood. He won't be going to dinner at three-thirty.

Gates, on the other side, is real quiet too. He's always pretty quiet, but he says through the vent that he's not going to dinner either.

Eat that swill, he says. Ain't fit for a pig.

The long halls have floors worn smooth and shiny by years and decades of trudging feet. Steel plates on the walls are bolted together in some places, and the bolts have been covered with dozens of coats of paint over the years. They look as though they're original to the building, and have been there since the 1820s.

Some days and nights, it seems as though I can feel the ghosts of dead prisoners, moving without steps. They hover and float, and they can't rest easy in their graves. So they move in the yard and the halls, and along the catwalks of the cellblocks. We only see them as flickers and tricks of light and shadow.

Kemmler, from the first electric chair, and Chester Gillette, who killed Grace Brown, his pregnant girlfriend on an Adirondack lake. Chester's story became a famous novel, and then a famous movie with Elizabeth Taylor.

I think that maybe I should stay here, like Gates and some of the really old people. Sleep in the cell, work in the laundry, get older and older, and then die.

If I go out, I could end up sleeping under a bridge, eating at a soup kitchen, getting robbed by people young enough to be my sons. Predators. Feral teenagers.

Like me. Like what I was.

Mellor's been asleep a long time, since five or six in the evening. I can hear his breaths, can hear his coughs. I can hear him shift in sleep. Back to side, back to back. Then to his side again.

Gates has been out, snoring lightly, since nine or ten.

Then it's later, and I can hear church bells, somewhere off there. Dong and dong and dong.

In the apartment, decades ago, I don't think I ever heard church bells. Maybe the university chimes, a dong here, a dong there, and on a Saturday or Sunday, sometimes a song. "Jingle Bells" or something. "Greensleeves." Things like that.

From this really high tower, next to the libraries on campus.

It's like I can picture things, in my small city, over thirty years ago, when I was a kid. The look of the tower from close up, at some ungodly hour. A half-moon in a sea of thin clouds, stars on a clear, dark and cold January night. Just winking, just sparkling.

Or trees and flowers in the botanical gardens at night in July. Acres and acres of trees and flowers. Even after a brutally hot and humid day, the gardens were cool at one in the morning. Because of the green fields, the thousands of trees. And almost every tree had a silver tag wired to a low branch that said the name of the tree in Latin and English.

Pinus resinosa was a red pine. *Platanus accidentalis* was an American sycamore.

There were oaks and maples, beeches and ashes. All kinds of them. There were more kinds of trees than people. I swear.

On the night of a terrible hot and humid day, when the temperature had to have been in the nineties, at least, I was in the gardens very late, at two or three in the morning. There were parts that were all trees, and other parts that were fields. Some of the fields had long grass, but other parts were mown. There were hills throughout the gardens, and small paved roads.

I went out to the middle of a mown field, and lay down on the grass. There was almost no moon in the sky, just a thin sickle. But the smell of cut grass, the smell of the earth, the sight of so many stars up there, the coolness of the ground on my back and legs, the sound of bugs cheeping and clicking and droning. God.

For a minute, for five minutes, it seemed as though so many things were possible. Lying there.

Ivy was still across the hall, and Marge hadn't gone to rehab yet. Maybe I was twelve or thirteen. I had a few more years.

Nobody anywhere in the world knew I was out, knew I was lying in the grass at two in the morning at the botanical gardens.

The sky was huge, the sky was immense. The sky was bigger than a thousand oceans, than ten thousand oceans. And all the insects, they were making their small noises, they were letting the world know they were alive.

And I was part of it. The world was in me and I was in it. This enormous web, this gigantic net.

Then Gates was asleep, and Mellor kept coughing and breathing in his sleep.

I had this sudden feeling, this thing in my mind, that Mellor wasn't going to make it out of here. He wasn't going to see his kids again. Not with the cough, and not with the blood in his spit.

Then breakfast, which I can hardly eat. Just a bite or two of a biscuit, and half a cup of coffee.

All my stuff, what there is of it, is in a black trash bag. I meet the CO in the yard, and we're it. Just us two in the yard. He doesn't put cuffs on me.

The CO is an old guy. Kind of pudgy, not much hair. Glasses with heavy black rims.

He says we walk out the back way. Through a doorway in the southwest corner of the yard, down long corridors, left, right, left.

Then we're outside in a little courtyard with a picnic table. There's an inch of snow on everything, and it's cold. It's really cold.

We go along a walkway, and we're real close to the outer wall. It's gotta be at least thirty feet tall, maybe more.

There's a building like a large garage, and it's all lit up. Two COs are inside. There's a big metal door in the wall, big enough for trucks to drive in and out. Then a small door for people in the big truck door.

We go inside and one CO says, Rupe, to the old CO with me.

They pat me down, and look through the black trash bag.

Then two of them take me to the small door. A younger guy unlocks the door. First one lock, then another lock.

He opens the door, and I'm afraid I'll faint. I'm afraid I'll fall down and die. This is why I thought I might just as well stay.

I go through and I'm on a sidewalk, and the wall looms over me. But there are houses and parked cars out here.

This is maybe six in the morning, and it's still dark out. I'm afraid I'm gonna throw up, my guts are so tight. But I don't. I walk, and the wall is above me. And then beyond that, the stars. Hanging there. Doing what they do.

In the deep cold and great darkness. Each star hung by a thread. And the huge black spaces between the stars.

Winking and winking and winking.